CW00765606

Vengeance

Book Three of the Bryce Chapman
Medical Thriller Series

Brian Hartman

Doodle Media, LLC

Contents

"There is nothing on this earth more to be prized more than true friendship."

-Thomas Aquinas

Chapter One

"Go ahead Medic 93, we copy loud and clear."

"We are five minutes out with a medical alert. Fifty-year-old female dialysis patient with massive hemorrhage from her leg. She has lost a lot of blood. We don't have an IV, but we'll be there in two minutes."

"Copy that, see you in Trauma Room One," replied the nurse in charge of ambulance triage.

A few moments later, Jackie Sirico acting as charge nurse today, tracked down Dr. Bryce Chapman as he was coming out of a patient room. "Chapman, there's a bleeder two minutes out. Probably a ruptured dialysis fistula. They're going to be in trauma."

"Okay, I'll be right there. Get the rapid infuser ready and have some gowns ready. This could get messy," said Bryce, the Emergency Medicine physician in charge of the trauma rooms for this shift.

He glanced down at his watch. Eleven forty-five. *Tom gets here in fifteen minutes, not exactly the case I wanted to start right before my shift ends.*

He walked back to the trauma room and put on a fluid-resistant gown and gloves. "Can someone get me a suture kit and some 2-0 silk thread? I need a bottle of lidocaine with epinephrine as well." He looked around the room at the assembled team. Several nurses, a tech, and a registration worker. "Anyone who is going to be close to the bed should wear eye protection. This is likely an arterial bleed, and if you're close enough to hear me, then you're in the splash zone."

A few moments later, the requested supplies were placed on a table and pushed next to him at the bedside. "Oh, I'm going to need some Betadine and gauze as well." The tech turned around to grab a bottle and a few more packs of gauze. Bryce drew up a syringe of lidocaine and placed it on the table, preparing ahead of time to act as quickly as possible to stop the bleeding.

"They're here!" called a nurse as she opened the doors to the ambulance bay.

The medics rushed through with a pale appearing woman, groaning and holding a hand on top of a firefighter's hands that were pressed firmly into her groin.

"This is Shelly. She's fifty-three and a dialysis patient. She woke up to pain in her leg and saw blood spurting out. When we got there, she was lying in a pool of blood. Bobby's been holding pressure since he walked in and found her," said the paramedic. "The bleed is too close to her hip to get a tourniquet on there."

Bryce looked at the patient and the monitor. She was pale and weak with a heart rate in the mid-one-forties. *She's in hemorrhagic shock and needs blood. And we need to get control of that bleeder. Now!*

The team moved her over to the cot and started working on two peripheral IVs. When a patient is sick, the standard protocol is to have two IVs. If one should fail, there is another one ready to use.

"Ma'am, I'm Dr. Chapman, I'm going to inject medicine into your leg to numb it up and then I'm going to take a look and see what's going on. When is the last time you had dialysis?"

"Please hurry; it hurts so badly. I missed my last appointment two days ago. I was planning to go to today, but I was too tired."

Wonderful. Why do people decide to skip their life saving treatment and then come in here critically ill?

Bryce made eye contact with the firefighter and explained what he wanted. "I'm going to trade positions with you, but I want to do it stepwise. I'll put my hand up top and then you put both of yours on the bottom of this wound. If you feel something pulsing, push down hard."

Bryce put his left hand on the patient's hip and then slid it down until he felt the femoral artery pulsating. "Okay, move your hand down below the wound," he said. When the firefighter complied, a large spurt of blood rose from the wound and went over Bryce's shoulder. He quickly readjusted his fingers a few centimeters, and the blood stopped. "Okay, now we know where it's bleeding from. It's this wound on her leg."

He was the only one who laughed at the joke. He picked up the Betadine-soaked gauze and cleaned the wound around the three hands holding pressure. Next, he grabbed the syringe and removed the cap from the needle.

"I won't poke you with the needle, I promise," he said, looking at the firefighter.

He quickly injected lidocaine in a large rectangle around the wound, creating a field block to anesthetize the entire area. He managed to avoid all fifteen fingers in the process. Once the epinephrine started working, he could examine the wound better. The patient's dialysis fistula had become swollen and red. There was a three-centimeter rupture in the skin over it, with some pus oozing out as he applied pressure.

"Ma'am, has this fistula been hurting you recently?"

"Yes, I think that's why I felt so bad this week."

"It looks like it got infected and then the skin broke down and ruptured completely open. I can try to close the skin, but you need a surgeon to repair the blood vessel."

"Someone call vascular surgery and tell them we need them to repair a ruptured dialysis fistula. And I need that suture kit open now. Go ahead and dump two 2-0 silk sutures on the field as well. Let's also give her two units of uncrossmatched blood."

"I got an 18-gauge IV in her left arm. What labs do you want, doc?" asked Jackie.

"Just the usual, and a type and screen," he answered.

Bryce grabbed the needle driver and used it to pick up the first suture needle. He pulled it through the skin outside the wound tied a one-handed knot to anchor the suture. He then made several passes through the skin, bringing the suture underneath the last one to create a locking stitch capable of holding firm pressure along the wound. With each suture, he marched closer to the hand of the firefighter.

"When you feel my fingers on yours, go ahead and pull your hands back. I'll hold the vessel closed. I'd rather risk poking myself with the needle than you."

"Thanks doc, I appreciate it," said the fireman. He pulled his hands away once Bryce was in position and went to wash his hands. "Clay would have loved this type of run. It's different not having him around the firehouse."

"I can believe it. He would be so disappointed if an interesting run came in when he was off," said Bryce. He then spread his thumb and index finger wide to hold pressure on both sides of the wound while he finished closing the wound. Bryce then tied the suture off and slowly lifted his hands off, watching the wound for breakthrough bleeding.

"Her heart rate is down to one twenty," said Jackie. "First unit of blood nearly in."

"Excellent. The wound is holding; I think she's out of the woods." He pulled his glove off and put his hand on the patient's shoulder. "Ma'am, how are you feeling?"

"A lot better. What happened?" she said.

"You tried to die tonight. Your dialysis fistula ruptured, and you nearly bled to death. Next time, don't skip dialysis and mention it to the nurses or doc if you think there's an issue with your access, okay?"

She closed her eyes and rested her head back on the bed, nodding her agreement.

"You okay Bryce? What do you have?"

He turned around and pretended to not see who asked that. Then he looked lower and jumped back, feigning surprise. "Oh, I wondered who said that. There you are."

"Hilarious, jackass," said Dr. Elisa Morales. She was small but feisty. Her competence in the operating room allowed her personality to come through with little concern for reprimand. "I was just finishing a bowel obstruction case from an incarcerated hernia and heard they were preparing the OR for a vascular case. I figured I'd see if you needed any help down here."

She looked at the fresh suture line on the patient's leg and the blood soaking the bed sheets. "Did you go a bit deep on your abscess drainage attempt? Hit the femoral artery? Rookie move, ER."

Bryce laughed at the good-natured ribbing. "No, she's a dialysis patient whose fistula ruptured in her sleep."

"Wow, and she lived?"

"So far, yes."

The patient's eyes snapped open. "What? Do you think there's a chance I might die?"

Bryce turned around and apologized. "No, I'm sorry. I was just joking with my surgical colleague. You're going to be fine. They will probably put in a temporary dialysis catheter while you're in the operating room and you'll get dialyzed later today."

When Bryce turned back around, he saw Elisa walking backward through the doorway and out of the ER. She raised her right hand with the index and middle fingers spread apart.

He waved goodbye and then headed back to the physician's work area. *Tom, I hope you're on time. I actually have my patients completely taken care of at the end of my shift for once.*

The firefighter pulled Bryce aside before he could leave the trauma room. "Hey Doc, is there anything else we could have done back there? I thought she was going to die on us."

"No, you guys did great. You controlled the source of bleeding and got her the hell out of there. Nice work." He extended his hand, and the firefighter shook it with a smile. Everyone loves to be told they did a good job, no matter how old you are. "You keep saving people like that and you'll give Clay's legacy a run for its money."

"Not a chance, doc. It's sad not having him around the house, but I'm glad he's doing better. He's dating that redhead lawyer chick now. Doing some private investigating for her too, I guess."

Bryce smiled. Clay had nearly ruined his life several months ago, but they had gotten past it through intense conversations and a physical altercation. The resulting large pressure washer wound on Clay's back had healed, but Bryce still hadn't touched a pressure washer since. *I need to reach out to him. It's been too long.*

He slapped the fireman on the shoulder and headed back to his workstation to dictate the chart of his recent patient. He was describing the procedure he performed when he felt someone lean over his shoulder.

His friend and partner, Dr. Tom Sharpe, leaned toward the microphone. "At this point, the patient was circling the drain. She direly needed saving, and no one knew what to do. Then I, Bryce, grabbed a gown and stepped into the supply closet, pulling the door closed behind me. I quickly put on the gown and tied it in place. I then added a protective hat and gloves before re-opening the door and emerging as Dr. Bryce Chapman, savior to all!"

Bryce reached over his shoulder with his left hand and punched his friend in the chest. "You don't need to dictate all of that. It's part of my note template. It's automatically loaded into each chart when I create it."

Tom laughed. "Why am I not surprised? It seems pretty slow. Are you ready to get out of here?"

"First, never say the S-word in the ER, you know that. Second, yes. The only active patient I have is the lady in the trauma room. Her dialysis fistula exploded while she was asleep. I closed the skin and stopped the bleeding, but vascular needs to come in and take her to the operating room for definitive management. We paged them, but they haven't called back yet."

"I don't mind saying it's slow. I'm not superstitious. Want me to prove it's nonsense?"

Bryce nodded.

"Okay. Do you know how long it's been since the Swedish Bikini Team came in for the annual physicals?" asked Tom with his palms up and elbows flexed.

"No, how long?" said Bryce.

"That's my point. It's never happened, but I ask that question several times a month. For over fifteen years. If superstitions meant anything, they would show up soon after I asked it."

"That wouldn't be too bad, actually. Maybe I'll start asking that as well. We can team up to tempt fate."

"Sounds good. You should get out of here; get home to that wife of yours. Say hi to your kids for me," said Tom.

Bryce agreed and grabbed his bag, then headed for the door. He ran into Jackie before leaving the department.

"Remember, we leave in one week. You ready?" he asked.

"Are you kidding me? I've been looking forward to it for a month. A week on a private island with no patients to care for? I'm ready any time. Sharpe has asked me the same question daily for a few weeks."

"This is going to be epic. Have a great night, Jackie."

Chapter Two

The next morning, Bryce came downstairs in the middle of a conversation between Val and their children.

"Kids, take a look at the new swimsuits I got you," said Valerie Chapman to her two young children.

"Wow, mine has a shark on it!" said Noah. "Is that like the nurse sharks we're gonna swim with?"

"I don't know, it may be a nurse shark. Hannah, what do you think of yours?" asked Valerie, looking at the younger sibling.

"I like it, but I don't have an animal." Her gaze went to the floor and she let her arm sag at the side, lowering the suit to the carpet.

"Sweetie, yours doesn't have an animal because mine doesn't either." Val pulled a third suit out of the bag and held it next to Hannah's.

"We have the same one!" said Hannah, her face suddenly transformed from sadness to joy.

"Yep, and I bought us matching cover-ups as well. Kids, this trip is going to be so much fun. I'm glad we're taking you with us this time. The last trip down there was a bit too much action."

Val's words were an understatement. The last time she went to the Bahamas with Bryce, they were involved in an altercation that led to someone drowning. They both performed CPR on him and saved his life. Unfortunately, that set off a series of events that led to assault charges in the Bahamas and Bryce's job at risk. The person who drowned turned out to be Tony, the son of Niles Proffit, the man whose company owns Washington Memorial Hospital where Bryce works.

Valerie snapped a picture of the kids holding their suits and opened the Facebook app on her phone. She posted the pic and tagged Bryce with the text 'See you next week, Swan Cay!'

"Did we get new suits?" asked Bryce from the front hallway.

"Well, good morning Bryce, and yes, the kids and I got new suits today. You have plenty, I think."

Bryce grinned. "Yes I do, and I'll be bringing Screaming Eagle along. It's been a while since he's gotten to fly."

Val rolled her eyes at her husband. "Did they have to make the beak centered on the front and give it a 3D effect?"

"Probably just how they cut the fabric. Whatcha gonna do? Kids, we're going to have such a great time. I'll teach you how to snorkel and we'll catch some fish, too. Who's ready to go?"

Both kids jumped up and down with their hands in the air.

"Excellent. Just a few more days. Why don't you guys run upstairs and get out your favorite pajamas? We will bring them down with us."

Chapter Three

"Hey, look at this!" yelled Emily Baldwin from the cockpit of the Cantius 60 motor yacht. Her boyfriend Tony Proffit continued swimming along the reef without acknowledging her.

That idiot. He can't even hear me when there's no one else around. She stood and collected her mask, fins and snorkel and walked down to the swim platform on the transom. She pulled the equipment on and fell backwards into the crystal-clear water of Shoal Bay.

She swam quickly toward him; he was floating at the surface with a six-foot-long pole spear in his right hand. As she approached his fins, he lifted his head out of the water, bent at the hips, and kicked his legs over his head. In a few seconds, he was twenty feet underwater and searching the rock ledges for lobster.

Damn it. Get your butt up here. We need to talk.

Tony surfaced nearly two minutes later, holding two large spiny lobsters. He spit his snorkel out and smiled at Emily. "Dinner's on me!"

"Yeah, great," she said. "But there's something I need to show you back on the boat."

Tony rolled onto his back and followed her while holding the lobster out of the water. "I was under at least two minutes on that dive. It felt amazing!"

When they reached the boat, he placed the lobster in a plastic bucket on the transom and then removed his snorkel equipment. He glanced up at Emily drying off in the cockpit.

"Would you please put a swimsuit on? Nudity is not legal here in Anguilla, and we don't need any reason for the police to come over here and check us out."

Emily turned to face him and then spread her arms wide, spinning in a circle. "Look around us. There is literally no one here. Besides, I'm getting sick of always trying to hide from people. I think we've changed our appearance enough that we can start going into town more often."

"Maybe. But if you're wrong, then we're going to prison. I'd rather keep eating lobster and mahi mahi than take a risk of being recognized. What did you want to show me?"

She pulled out her phone and opened the Facebook app. After scrolling for a few seconds, she handed the phone to Tony.

He shielded the screen from the sun and looked at what she had pulled up. "Already? I thought it was going to take months to get an opportunity like this. Bryce Chapman stole my future from me. Now my dad won't let me take over his business because of my head injury."

"You're also a fugitive from justice, remember? We're both wanted for kidnapping Peter. Honestly, that's kinda hot."

Emily dropped her towel and sauntered toward him, her hips swaying more than the rocking of the boat required to maintain balance.

Tony continued, "When I kill his favorite little employee, maybe then he'll realize exactly how capable I am."

"That's right, you are very capable. And once Bryce is out of the way, we can finally move forward with our lives." She wrapped her arms around his neck and leaned in close. "Why don't you follow me up to the bow lounge? There's one more thing I want to do before we leave this place." She climbed the stairs leading to the front of the boat and paused, looking back over her shoulder. "Unless you're still concerned about people seeing us..."

Tony answered by jumping up and chasing her to the front of the boat.

Chapter Four

"Lunch was great, thanks Val," said Bryce. "I'm going to head to work a bit early to finish my charts from yesterday. I want to be completely caught up when it's time to leave. Not planning to think about work at all down there."

"Then why did you only invite people you work with?" asked Val.

Bryce cocked his head. "Fair point, but this is a thank you gift to the people who have had to put up with me at work over the last year. Jackie has saved my bacon more than once, and she works harder than anyone else there. They kidnapped Peter as a ruse to get to me."

"I think that deserves more than a week on an island, but this is a good start," said Val.

"Tom helped me get the memory card back from our first trip to the Bahamas. Remember the one that had outstanding footage of us saving Tony?"

"Of course I do. That was also the one that had outstanding footage of us that no one else was supposed to see. Till that little twerp from Duke found it."

"Stetson. I still can't get over that name. I think I bought someone that perfume thirty years ago," he said with a laugh.

"And Graham?"

"Well, that's an easy one. He's my best friend, not that I get to see them very often. He helped me climb out of my depression and procure the semen sample."

"I like Graham and his wife. It will be good to catch up with them again. Plus, their kids will help keep ours entertained. You know what that means?" she asked.

"I think I do, but why don't you show me when we're down there?" He glanced at his watch and stiffened. "Hey, I gotta run. I'm off at midnight again, so don't wait up." Bryce gave her a hug and then jogged upstairs to say goodbye to the kids before heading into the hospital.

The first person he saw when he walked in was Dr. Ashford Tate, the senior most member of his group and administrative leader.

"Hey Ash, good to see you. I saw your name on the schedule next week. Getting your hands dirty at the bedside again?"

"You guys didn't really give me a choice. Three of my docs all gone on vacation at the same time? Someone needs to stay home and keep the grim reaper at bay."

"Look at it this way. Since we're all going together, we won't be needing off for a while. The rest of you can take it easy two weeks from now."

"I'm glad you put up with the administrative burden of this place and still pull shifts. The rest of us don't really want anything to do with it," said Bryce.

"Yeah, I've noticed. I'm happy to do it though. It keeps you youngsters free to kick ass at the bedside. I'm out of here;

have a good shift." Ash walked past Bryce and out into the warm summer air.

Bryce continued to the ER workstation, but stopped near the secretary desk when he heard familiar music. *Christmas songs? In the summer? Is she back already?*

He turned the corner and saw Paula sitting at her desk. She was informing another caller that she cannot give medical advice on the phone, and yes, the Emergency Department is open right now.

"Paula, how are you?" asked Bryce.

"Dr. Chapman, I'm good. I was hoping I'd see you today. How is your family?"

"We're all healthy, which is unusual for us, honestly. I'm glad you're able to come back to work. That blood clot was nasty business. Are you breathing okay?"

"Yes, I am. I actually feel better than I have in years. That was a wake-up call. I'm eating better, my husband and I go on walks every evening, and I'm down ten pounds. I feel like I'm twenty years younger."

Bryce smiled at his friend. "That's amazing. Who knew you had to die in order to start living?"

"Pretty sure I learned that in Sunday school, Dr. Chapman. But I sure got a reminder that day. Thank you again for being there and getting me back. I owe you one."

"No, you don't. It's literally my job to do that. Besides, I'd been indebted to you for all the help you've given me and my patients over the years. Let's call it even."

"Very well then." She glanced down at the phone and its three blinking lights. "I need to pick up these calls. The hospital grades me on how long it takes to answer them."

"Ah, metrics. The bane of my existence. We'll catch up later." Bryce turned around and sat in front of an open workstation to finish his charts.

"Oh, good, my relief is here," said a loud voice from behind Bryce. "And an hour early, too. This is my lucky day."

"Hi Peter, I'm just here doing charts. The department is still yours for the next hour."

"Heck bro, I'll cover it for the next two, since you're taking me to the Bahamas for a week."

"That's unnecessary, but thanks for the offer. How does it feel doing your own charts now that Emily is gone?"

"Man, it sucks. I spend at least an hour every night finishing them up at home. How do you handle it with a wife and kids? I just drink beer and watch sports while I do them."

"That's exactly what I do, but I wait for everyone else to fall asleep first. Remember the good old days when charting took two minutes, and you didn't have an in basket full of charts at the end of the shift?"

"Exactly. We spend more time charting than we do treating patients. And the only people who care about the chart are the lawyers, the government, and the insurance company. I could chart a single paragraph and cover all the pertinent medical information. It's not like anyone reads ninety-nine percent of our chart, anyway."

"New topic," said Bryce. "I don't want to start my shift off mad. Are you ready for the trip?"

Peter leaned back in his chair and stretched his hands behind his head, the sleeves of his shirt pulled tight by his flexing biceps. "Man, I have been ready for this since I climbed out of Emily's bed for the last time."

"You're talking about the time she handcuffed you to it with a pair of underwear shoved in your mouth, right?"

"Of course. You think I've seen her since then?"

"You have a weakness, my friend. Just checking," said Bryce. He punched Peter in the shoulder for emphasis.

"I know I do. But I'm not dating anyone now and not bringing anyone on the trip. Finally, some alone time for Peter."

"There's a joke in there somewhere, but I don't want to ruin the moment."

"Thanks Bryce, that's kind of you," said Peter, as he chuckled to himself.

Bryce worked efficiently and finished most of the outstanding charts from the day before, until his phone interrupted his workflow. The screen showed an incoming call from Graham Kelly.

"Hey Graham, what's up?"

"Bryce, I have bad news. We are going to have to back out of the trip."

"What? Why?"

"It's my wife, Stacey. She's been having abdominal pain for a few weeks and it's gotten worse. She can barely eat. Turns out her gallbladder has been chronically inflamed and needs to come out. She's scheduled for surgery soon."

"Oh no, that's terrible. I'm sorry she's facing that. I was really looking forward to hanging with you guys next week. And our kids will be sad that yours won't be there to play with."

"I know, man, I'm sorry. I offered to take her gallbladder out myself but I looked into it and come to find out there were no bones in it. We thought about postponing the surgery until after the vacation, but what if it got infected down there? I can't imagine having surgery on a small island in the Bahamas."

"No kidding. Well, again, sorry to hear your family won't be joining us. We do need to get together sometime soon. Maybe you can come down and look at all the pictures we are going to take."

"That doesn't sound like as much fun," said Graham.

"Just messing with you. I'm actually at work, I need to let you go. We'll find a time to catch up."

"Sounds good Bryce. I'll let you go. Have a great time on the trip."

"Will do. Tell Stacey we're thinking about her."

Bryce put his phone down and sighed.

"Who was that? Someone back out?" asked Peter.

"Yeah, my friend Graham Kelly and his family. He's an orthopedist up north whose wife decided to lose her gallbladder at an inopportune time."

"Well, that sucks. Are you going to find someone to replace them?"

"We probably should. We have room on the plane and the villas. Who would you invite?"

"If you're looking for someone from the hospital and wanted to earn some brownie points, what about Elisa?"

"Seriously? Huh. I hadn't considered her."

"She was pretty pissed about the thoracotomy on the police officer. It was the right thing to do, but I think she's still upset about it."

"She sure acts like it. Elisa is actually on call today, so I'm sure I'll have to talk to her at some point. Thanks for the idea."

"It doesn't hurt to bribe the surgeons once in a while," said Peter.

"Who bribes us to do stuff? We just call it doing our jobs. What has medicine come to?"

Chapter Five

Tony kissed Emily one more time and leaned back onto the cushion. "I think I'm starting to like the yachting life. Frequent sex, lobster whenever we want and sunsets that don't disappoint. Why did I ever live on land?"

"At least one of us is enjoying the frequent sex," said Emily, rubbing the low right side of her abdomen. "What did you do to me?"

"What do you mean? Same thing I always do. You've never complained before," said Tony.

"Well, something was different. It hurts a bit on the right here. No sex for a day or two."

"Okay, sorry. I didn't mean to hurt you," said Tony, rubbing her back.

"Whatever, I'll be okay. It's hard to believe we need to leave this place," said Emily, reaching for a sheet and covering herself. "How long do you think we'll need to grab Bryce? A day or two?"

"Well, if you want it to look like an accident or just a random disappearance, it'll take some time to plan. If you just want to smash and grab, that can probably be done quicker. I mean, we're already wanted for kidnapping and assault. Maybe we just do it the easy way. No way they'll have guns on Swan Cay."

"How far is it from where we're at now?"

Tony consulted a navigation app on his phone before replying. "Swan Cay is eight hundred nautical miles from here. If we do a nice steady cruising speed of twelve knots it's just under three days. We can get there with one fuel stop and then fill up in Georgetown, so we're prepped for the escape. It's a mile deep pretty close to shore. They'll never find him."

Emily laid back on the lounger and watched the clouds go by. *So close. In less than a week Tony will have dealt with Bryce and then it's time to work on getting access to the hundred million in cryptocurrency. And then Tony can challenge Bryce to see who can hold their breath longer.*

"Hey, bring me a beer, would you?" Tony complied and Emily leaned back in the sun, enjoying the feel of the cold bottle against her skin.

Chapter Six

Bryce spent his shift trying to find a reason to call for a surgery consult and was failing miserably. Every possibility was either depression manifesting as chronic abdominal pain or an injury that wasn't bad enough to involve the trauma team.

That is, until a nurse came up to his workstation and grabbed his attention. "Dr. Chapman, can you come see this new patient? He's been vomiting at home and looks miserable."

"Sure, lead the way," said Bryce, hopping up from his chair and following her toward the patient room.

He walked into the room and saw a middle-aged man sitting up in bed and clutching an emesis basin. Loud retching preceded the sound of water splashing into the bucket as yellow-green vomit poured out of his mouth. Bryce grabbed a pair of gloves and introduced himself.

"Hi sir, I'm Dr. Chapman. How long have you been doing this?"

The patient looked up but didn't answer. He leaned back toward the bucket and began another round of vomiting. A woman sitting in the corner with a concerned expression answered for him.

"He had some abdominal pain for the last few days but dealt with it until tonight when the vomiting started. Since he's been vomiting, the pain is much worse, and he's been miserable."

"Can you show me where it hurts?" asked Bryce.

The patient placed his right hand on his abdomen and rubbed it around a bit before wincing and holding a spot just above his belly button. "Right there. It even seems swollen a bit."

"Have you ever had abdominal surgery before?"

"I had my gallbladder taken out ten years ago. They did it with the camera and a bunch of small holes."

"I'm going to lay you flat. Do you think you can do that for a minute or so while I examine you?"

"Yeah, but not too long."

Bryce reached behind the patient for the bed adjustment level and laid the bed flat. He placed his right hand on the area the patient described and felt a firm mass below the skin. *Gotcha!*

"It looks like you have an incarcerated hernia. When they took out your gallbladder, the surgeon had to make a few holes in the peritoneum, the membrane that holds your abdominal contents. Over time, the repair came apart on the inside and now there is some bowel that is caught in that defect in your abdominal wall. It's causing an obstruction of your intestines and that's why you're in pain and vomiting so much. The pressure on the bowel is reducing blood flow and if we don't get that back inside properly, your intestine could die."

"How do you fix it? Does he need surgery?" asked the patient's wife.

"He will definitely need surgery, but maybe not as an emergency at eleven at night. I am going to try to push the hernia back in. Usually there is at least a small pinhole connection that's still open. If I can get enough of the liquid stool to squeeze through that and back into the rest of the intestine, it can shrink the portion that is stuck and make it small enough to fit back through the hole."

"Okay, what do I need to do?" asked the patient.

"Once your nurse gives you a large dose of pain medication, we're going to have you bend your knees all the way up and relax your abdominal muscles. I'm going to tilt the bed back so far that you think you're going to fall out, and then I'm going to hold firm pressure until it goes back in."

"Oh my. Henry, I'll be here if you need me, but I won't be watching," said the patient's wife. She adjusted her chair, so she was facing the wall, but held her arm out behind her to grasp his hand.

Bryce looked at the nurse who had just established IV access. "Can you give him a milligram of Dilaudid and a liter of fluid? Let's get this fixed quickly if we can."

She nodded and returned quickly to administer the pain medication and start the fluids. Bryce pushed the lever to lower the head of the bed and kept it depressed until the patient slid upward in the bed.

"You ready? I need you to keep your abdominal muscles as relaxed as possible. If you're pushing back at me, that will make it much harder to get this fixed."

"Whatever you gave me is working. I feel really strange right now."

"Perfect. Time to push, then."

Bryce cupped the hernia in his right hand and placed the left one on top. He leaned forward and pressed firmly on the hernia, rotating his shoulders a bit to change the direction of force. Slowly, he felt the hernia shrink in size until everyone in the room heard an audible squishing sound and the hernia sac slithered back inside the patient's abdomen.

"Oh, that felt weird," said the patient. "But I think it feels better now."

Bryce leveled the bed out and then raised his head up to a sitting position. "You still feeling okay?"

"It aches a bit, but nothing like before. And I think my nausea is gone. Thanks, doc."

"You're welcome. But we're not done yet. You still have a hernia and it could come back out at any time. Let me order a CT scan, and then I'll talk to the surgeon about getting you repaired. This should probably be done later tomorrow rather than as an outpatient. I don't want you to come back in with dead intestines if this happens again and you don't come in right away."

Fortunately, there was no logjam of patients in line for the CT scanner tonight, and the results came back in under thirty minutes. The report confirmed the hernia defect and appearance of a partial small bowel obstruction.

Bryce asked the secretary to page the on-call surgeon, Dr. Morales, who returned the page promptly.

"Elisa, hey it's Bryce. Sorry to bug you, but I have a patient who presented with an incarcerated hernia and small bowel obstruction."

He could hear the groan through the phone. "Are you serious? I just got home. Can't you just push it back in for me?"

"Oh, I did, and he's feeling much better now. The CT scan only shows fat in the hernia and they're reading a partial small bowel obstruction. He was puking bile when he arrived but hasn't had any nausea since I reduced it. I think this can wait until tomorrow, but I was thinking it would be better to admit him and fix it this hospital stay."

"Yeah, that's fine. Admit it to medicine and don't call me any more tonight."

"There is one more thing, actually," said Bryce.

"Nope, no more things. I've had enough of your things, Bryce. I'm at home, my husband is home for a month and I want to spend time with him. Call someone else."

"I would, Elisa, but a doc specifically recommended you for this."

Elisa groaned into the phone. "That's what sucks about being good. Everyone wants you to operate on their disaster of a patient. What is it?"

"Actually, it's not a patient. Remember the guy I saved down in the Bahamas? The one who drowned?"

"You mean the son of the guy who owns our hospital? Yeah, I remember that. Why? Does he need surgery?"

"No, hear me out. His dad felt bad about what happened and promised me and my friends a week on a private island in the Bahamas as an apology. The trip is next week and one of my friends had to back out because of his wife needing surgery. Peter Thrasher suggested we invite you to take their place."

"Really? Why me?"

"You were part of the team that helped me with Kent Carpenter. You've been a solid part of the hospital team and always care for my patients well. Plus, I still feel bad about asking you to do the thoracotomy on the police officer. I thought maybe this would help patch things up between us."

"You don't need to patch anything up, but thanks for thinking of me. When are you leaving?"

"We leave this Saturday."

"Bryce, that's five days from now. I'd have to clear my schedule and book airfare. My husband is home on leave though, and we haven't taken a trip in a long time. Can you send me a link to where we'd be staying?"

"Sure, I'll text it to you. Don't worry about airfare. Niles Proffit is providing his private jet to take us down there. Let me know as soon as possible. I'd really like to bring as many people as we can."

Bryce hung up and sent her a text containing the website for Swan Cay.

The secretary let him know the medicine team was on the phone, and he quickly staffed the hernia patient with them. Once he hung up, he glanced at the clock. *Tom should be here any moment.*

His phone screen lit up, showing a new text arrived.

> Elisa: The island looks incredible. I talked to Julio. We'd love to go, but I need to get a few shifts covered. I'll let you know in 24 hours

"Bryce, you look happy. What's wrong?"

He spun the chair around and saw Tom standing next to him. "How much do you like Elisa?" he asked.

"She's okay. Great surgeon, but a bit ornery if you ask me. Why?"

"How would you feel about spending a week on a private island with her?"

Tom leaned back and stared at the ceiling. "What? How did this happen?"

"My buddy Graham can't make it. His wife needs her gallbladder taken out in a few days. I wanted to bless as many people as I could with this trip, and Peter suggested Elisa. She has had to deal with a lot of the stress along with us lately. Plus, it's never a bad thing to have a surgeon owe you something."

"True, and I bet she doesn't look half bad in a bikini," said Tom.

"You're probably right. And neither do I for that matter."

Tom dropped his bag on the counter and sat next to Bryce. "I told you I didn't want to think about that ever again. Have you noticed I haven't been back to your pool since?"

Bryce laughed loudly. "Oh, come on, quit being so uptight. This is our only life. Gotta enjoy it when we can. And remember, I don't drink alcohol anymore. And you know what? Clay hasn't been back to my pool either, come to think of it."

It was Tom's turn to laugh. "Well, can you blame him? You about sliced him in half last time he was there. Hey, what about Clay? Shouldn't you invite him?"

"I actually did. Said he was busy and couldn't make it."

"Oh well, you tried. Guess it's Elisa, then. Why don't you tell me what you have left and get out of here."

"Thanks, I have to get up early tomorrow and put on my coroner's hat. I need to make an appearance and check on things before we leave for the trip."

Chapter Seven

Bryce drove to the county administration building and parked his black Yukon Denali in a spot reserved for the coroner. It was several months in and he still wasn't entirely comfortable with the job.

The previous coroner had been a political appointment because of a vacancy, and the mayor nominated a close friend to fill the role. Like most political offices, the incumbent usually wins re-election, and the same was true for the coroner. Unfortunately, crony politics often leads to incompetent office holders, who compound the problem by appointing staff through nepotism rather than accomplishment.

Bryce had not sought out the office of coroner. He had long complained about their superficial investigations and even had a lawsuit filed by a patient's family because of an improper conclusion. When the police officer who was struck and killed by a prominent businessman's daughter, the coroner investigator ran someone else's blood sample and falsely accused the officer of being intoxicated while on duty. Bryce and his colleagues figured out what had happened and cleared the name of the officer, much to the relief of his fellow officers.

Prior to that, Bryce and his friend Graham had broken into a sperm bank to obtain a DNA sample of his patient Kent Carpenter, the one who the coroner's office made a wrong conclusion on the cause of death. An Indianapolis Metropolitan Police Officer suspected Bryce committed the crime but did not yet have enough proof to seek a warrant. They interacted several times during the investigation of the slain officer and formed a relationship built on mutual respect. When it was determined the coroner's office had mistakenly concluded the officer had been intoxicated, the police chief held a press conference announcing Bryce was running for coroner in the upcoming election. The detective implied that defeating the current coroner was his get out of jail free pass for the crime of breaking and entering along with semen theft.

Once Bryce had won the election in the primary, the incumbent resigned and the mayor appointed Bryce to fill the position.

Fast forward several months to today and the city has a less experienced, yet more qualified coroner. This has slowed down the process of certifying deaths, but improved the conclusions. Several deaths that were initially assumed because of natural causes had turned into successful murder prosecutions.

Bryce exited his vehicle and walked through the front door. He submitted to the security screening and metal detector search of his body. As if *a criminal, intending mayhem, wouldn't just shoot the security guard and continue inside, but whatever makes people feel safe, I guess.*

The city administrative building is a large granite structure on the near east side of the city. The planners wanted the government offices close enough to the city center to be fashionable, but not too close to reduce the potential for private businesses to pay property taxes. Once past the metal detectors, he proceeded through the lobby with high ceilings and numerous balconies overlooking the tiled floor. A large marble tile mosaic of the state flag adorned the floor.

"Good morning Bryce. Ready to check up on the grim reaper?"

"Just trying to make sure he's not trying to pull anything over on us, Monique. In the ER I try to stop him, here I just make sure he's not cheating. Does my top medical examiner have any news I need to know about?" The pair walked together down the stairs to their department.

"Your top examiner? Did you hire someone to help me out, or am I still the only one?"

"You're still it for now, but we're getting close. I have two people I'm interviewing. How much experience do you want them to have?"

"At this point, I don't care. I'll take any warm body down there to help deal with all the cold ones."

"I'm trying. This administrative stuff is a lot harder than I imagined. As an ER doc, I don't have the patience that politics requires. I just want to lower my head and bust through the barriers to make something happen."

"Well, we appreciate what you're trying to do. Everyone I talk to says how much better it is with you in charge."

"I appreciate that feedback. Let me know if you hear anything otherwise. Still have some changes to make, and I'm planning to tackle those once I get back from vacation."

"Yeah, a week in the Bahamas. Poor guy. I would love a week with no dead bodies in my life."

"That's the part I'm looking forward to most," said Bryce. He broke away from Monique and stepped into his office, leaving the door open behind him. After sitting down, he grabbed all the manila folders from a wire rack on the right side of the desk marked 'Incoming'. He counted six fresh cases since the last time he was in the office two days ago. The oldest one was thirty-two.

"Damn gangs and drug dealers. Why can't it snow in the summer? Warm summer nights are a risk factor for death if you're young and live in the city," said Bryce for no one's ears but his own.

He skimmed the files and saw nothing that appeared unusual. Gunshot victims struck with less than ten percent of the rounds fired. Typical gang marksmanship. The overdoses were young, with a history of numerous ER visits for drug related complaints. He signed the report and moved them to the 'Completed' rack.

He opened his email and saw one from Officer Gregory Stephenson, a detective with the Indianapolis Police Department with whom he had developed a relationship with over the last year. The detective had Bryce nailed for the sperm theft and breaking and entering, but rather than push for prosecution of an essentially victimless crime, he used that information to persuade Bryce to run for coroner. Later, they both decided that persuade was a more agreeable term than blackmail.

```
To: Chapman, Bryce
From: Stephenson, Gregory
Re: Something to look into
```

```
I have reason to believe a death that
was certified a few years ago may have
a criminal component to it. Decedent's
name is Larry Nelson, DOB 4/13/1964.
Can your office examine the records
again and let me know what you think?



Thanks,
Greg
```

Bryce clicked over to the records database and searched for the chart of Larry Nelson. The initial date of the file stated July 17th, 2017. It was closed on July 20th, 2017. *Wow, quick case. Open and shut. Government efficiency at its finest.*

He read a bit further and sighed audibly when he read the brief biography content.

Employer: Hearst Automotive
Occupation: Chief mechanic

Bryce picked up the phone and dialed the number for the detective.

"Stephenson," said the detective.

"Hey, it's Bryce Chapman, I got your email. What's got you interested in this case again?"

"Ah, thanks for calling back. Last night we pulled over a semi hauling auto parts down from Chicago. The paperwork showed a final destination of a Hearst dealership on the west side."

"Okay, don't they get shipments of auto parts in all the time?"

"Probably, but not packed with meth and fentanyl."

Bryce whistled quietly. "How much did you find?"

"Enough meth to host a hell of a party for fifty thousand people, and enough fentanyl to kill every one of their family members."

"Bastards," said Bryce.

"Exactly."

"How does this relate to Larry Nelson?"

"I assume that you saw he was the chief mechanic for Hearst Automotive. Turns out our semi driver was supposed to meet the current chief mechanic, Kevin Mitchell, at the store after hours, to unload the products."

"Are you saying Larry was the drug contact when he was chief mechanic?" asked Bryce.

"No, back then, the current chief was only second in command. He took over once Larry died. Co-workers have told us that Kevin often stayed late and unloaded the parts trucks himself. Said he wanted them to be with the families and he liked the overtime."

"I see. That is a bit sketchy. I didn't read much of the report yet, but it said Larry died of blunt force trauma from a single-car accident while driving home late one night."

"I'd like you to take another look at the records and see what you can find. Guess who else was at the dealership the night Larry was killed?"

"Kevin?"

"Yep, and the parts truck from Chicago. I don't like coincidences when they involve drugs and felons. It's amazing how many coincidences turn into intentional acts once we discover more facts," said the detective.

"Right. I'll look into it on my end, but I'm going on vacation in a few days. I'll ask my medical examiner to look at it and we'll have a report for you when I get back from vacation."

"Just keep me in the loop if you find anything sooner. I'm going to keep looking into it on my end."

Bryce ended the call with a promise to do just that and then continued reading the file.

> They found the decedent in the driver's seat of his truck. Air bags had deployed.
>
> No other vehicles were involved in the accident. Tox screen negative. Injuries are consistent with severe blunt force trauma to the head. Pronounced dead at the scene.
>
> No autopsy performed.

Bryce printed the file and placed it inside a manila folder, which he then placed on the wire rack marked 'Incoming'. He then printed a second copy and walked out of his office, looking for his medical examiner.

He found her in the morgue cooler, pulling a body from the cold storage system.

"Monique, can I add something to your list?" He held up the folder and extended it toward her.

She turned around and tilted her head forward, looking at Bryce over her glasses. "Another case? I'm behind as it is."

"Yes, another case, but it's one that's already been certified."

"Oh great, we're slammed with recent cases and you want me to revisit one we already closed?"

"It's a request from Detective Stephenson. He has new information that makes him concerned this was not a simple vehicular death."

"Ah, well, that is a bit more intriguing. Are you saying this is the type of case that takes high-level critical thinking and problem-solving skills? Not just 'how drunk was he before falling off the bridge'"?

"No, this could have some broader ramifications involving a prominent local family, so we'll need to get it right."

Monique took the folder and flipped it open. She read the first few lines and nodded. "I see what you mean. I'll get started this afternoon."

"Don't feel like you need to rush it. I'm leaving town in a few days, so if you find anything suspicious, can you let Detective Stephenson or the deputy coroner know?"

"It's a good thing I like you, Chapman. Because dumping work on people before you leave on vacation can look bad."

"I know, and I'm sorry. I just found out about this half an hour ago. Email will be the best way to reach me if you need anything. Remember, the dead sometimes do tell tales."

"So it's okay that I hear them talking to me?" asked Monique with a straight face. She looked back and forth quickly and then whispered, "because they do that once in a while." She held the blank expression for a few more seconds before busting out in a loud fit of laughter. Her knees buckled and her head leaned back, filling the cold room with life.

Bryce shook his head and smiled. "You need help."

"You're damn right I do. If you'd hurry up and hire someone, that would be a great start." She turned around and continued her task of preparing the body for transfer.

Chapter Eight

Emily stood in the cockpit, staring through binoculars off the port side. "What island is that?"

"The one you are looking at? Or the closest one that you can't even see?"

"The one with the big mountain."

"That's Virgin Gorda, part of the British Virgin Islands. About ten miles closer is Anegada, but it's low-lying so you may not be able to even see it."

"Do we have time to stop? The cruising guide said it's so beautiful and has a great reef to snorkel."

Tony shook his head. "We probably have a little time, but the customs enforcement in the BVI is next level. If we stop without checking in, they'll flag us and send someone out to inspect us. I don't want that kind of scrutiny."

"You said our fake passports are actually valid. What's the problem?"

"They are, but do you want to risk someone recognizing us? The yachting community isn't huge, and stories of fugitives running around on a yacht get shared all over the place. It's fun gossip at the bars and the bodegas."

Emily dropped the binoculars and her shoulders followed along. "Is that what it's going to be like from now on? Hiding from everyone? That won't be much fun."

"I have been thinking about that. Once we get rid of Bryce, how do you feel about faking our deaths and then changing our appearance even more? We could re-emerge as a power couple in the Caribbean, Europe, wherever."

She smiled and walked over to the helm, leaning on Tony's muscular forearm. "Now that sounds intriguing. What did you have in mind?"

"I have been keeping a generic diary of sorts for the last few weeks, writing about how bad I feel about my injury and how much I hate Bryce. I wrote about how depressed you have been being away from everyone you know. How you won't be able to be a doctor anymore."

"Well, that's not exactly a lie."

"Sure, but that's what makes it believable. I put in there how we can't get you help because we're on the run and I don't know what to do. I said I bought some depression medication from a pharmacy in St Maarten, but it's not helping."

"Where is this going? Am I going to die in your book?"

"Yes, we both are. After I kill Bryce, I'll start appearing more erratic in my writing, suggesting I'm losing it. One morning I'll wake up and find you gone and a suicide note on the table. Our dinghy anchor will be missing along with the rope we used to attach it."

"Oh, that's nice. I'm going to the bottom of the ocean?" Emily leaned away from Tony and sat down at the table. "You suck at writing fiction."

"Hear me out. It has to be believable, right? Once I see that note, I'm going to lose it as well. I'll write about how distraught I am and it will turn into a suicide note. I'll apologize to my dad and everyone I hurt. Then I'll make it look like I shot myself and then fell overboard."

"How are you going to do that?" asked Emily, appearing more interested in the story than she was a few minutes ago.

"Here's what I was thinking," said Tony. He engaged the autopilot, scanned the horizon and radar screen for any boats they may encounter, and then joined Emily at the table.

"We pull into some island and buy another boat. One that's not as nice and not as noticeable. Probably a sailboat. We learn how to sail and run a boat like that, then we stage our disappearance. I head out in the sailboat first and then a few days later, you take the yacht out. We find some deserted area of the ocean to meet and then we move all the important things onto the sailboat, but leave enough on the yacht that it looks like we intended to continue living on it. I splatter blood across the back of the boat, set the gun on the swim platform, and then we leave in the sailboat. The yacht can drift until someone finds it."

"And when they find it, they'll see the gun, the blood, and read your journal."

"Yep."

"And think we're both dead while we sail away to live new lives?"

"What do you think? Do I still suck at fiction writing?" asked Tony with a grin, widened beyond normal by his inflated self-esteem.

"How are they going to know it was you, though? We'd have to use your blood. How are we going to do that?"

"You can draw blood, right? You worked in a hospital for years. And I plan to leave out genuine passports in a drawer for them to find."

"I have seen it done thousands of times. It doesn't look hard. I'd just need a few supplies, but we can probably get that from a clinic or pharmacy." She leaned over and rested her head in his lap, looking up at him. "You know, I think your plan may actually work."

"Of course it will." He rubbed her hair slowly until she drifted off to sleep.

Chapter Nine

Bryce walked into the hospital and met Tom as he walked out of the trauma area.

"Something strange is going on today, Bryce."

"What's that?"

"Nothing. Nothing is going on, and it's weird."

"You just came out of the trauma rooms. That had to have been something," said Bryce.

"No, it was a one-year-old who the grandparents think may have sucked on a Tylenol tablet."

"Sucked on one tablet? Goodbye. Enjoy the rest of your day."

"Exactly. Nothing is happening today."

A high-pitched tone signaled the arrival of an elevator, and the doors opened shortly thereafter.

"Of course you guys are just standing here," said Elisa. "Shouldn't you be pulling something out of someone? I just finished my last case of the day and I'm not on call, so don't bother me."

Bryce gave Tom an exaggerated look of surprise. "What? We never bother you. We simply ask you to use your surgical skills to help our patients."

"But you always wait until ten minutes after I leave the hospital to let me know about it."

"The age-old problem with surgery consults. Do you want to be called too early before the workup is complete, or too late when you've already left, or when the disease process has progressed further? Some docs call us to see if anything may head their way before they leave. Or you could walk through the department and ask us in person."

"No way. I'm like that Dr. Glaucomflecken video about sneaking through the Emergency Department. I take off my heels and go into ninja mode. Any time you guys see me, it magically leads to a consult."

Bryce and Tom shared a mutual laugh. "That guy's videos are hilarious. They make me want to rock climb my way to work," said Bryce.

"I do have good news, though. I cleared my schedule and you guys will be stuck with my husband and I for a week." She raised her hands above her head to prepare for a double high-five. "We're going with you to the Bahamas!"

"Hey, that is good news! It's going to be amazing. And the best part? No operating rooms and no patients," said Tom.

"The island is all-inclusive, so really all you need to bring is clothing and a passport. Niles Proffit is lending us his private plane and we'll leave from the private terminal on the east side of the airport. You can find it on Google Maps. We need to be there at six-thirty to get checked in."

"I am so down like six-thirty," said Elisa, dropping into a squat and pressing her hands to the floor.

"You're what? What did you just do?" asked Bryce.

"I thought ER doctors were supposed to be cool. I have to spend a week on an island with a bunch of lame-os? Six-thirty means let's get down. Let's party. Both hands of the clock are getting down, so why not join them?"

"Ah, because the hands both point down at six-thirty. I get it," said Bryce.

Elisa laughed and walked down the hallway. "You can say you get it, but you don't got it, know what I mean? See you guys in thirty-six hours."

"Hey, I'm cool," said Bryce, frowning at Tom.

"I know man, I know. But just in case you're not, it doesn't matter because you're already married and have an awesome family. Once you're a dad, you don't have to be cool anymore. It's like a get-out-of-vogue-free card."

"The Vogue. I was definitely cool back in med school when we went there. One of Indy's best nightclubs. Anyway, let's get you out of here. This is my last shift to finish and then it's Bahama time."

"Not what I meant, but I hear you. If it's the last shift before vacation, did you wear the lucky underwear?" asked Tom.

"It's slow today, isn't it? The flamingos are doing their thing!" said Bryce.

The shift never picked up, which made it seem like it was three times longer than usual.

Bryce picked up his phone and sent a text to Val.

```
Bryce: Hey babe, you up?
Val: No, I am sleep texting
Bryce: This shift is taking forever.

I want to be home with you guys.
Val: I want you here. I hate these

late-night shifts
Bryce: Be home in 2 hours. Stay awake

for me.
Val: ZZzzzz…
```

```
Bryce: Suit yourself, but we're still
making love.
Val: That's fine, you're like a white
noise machine, anyway. I'll sleep
right through it.
Bryce: Wow, ZING! Good night, see in
the morning.
```

Bryce dropped his phone back on the counter and scanned the tracking board for a new patient to see. None. He shook his head and glanced at his watch. Two more hours.

He opened his list of incomplete charts and began catching up, hoping to have his administrative work complete by the time his shift ended.

"New patient, room thirty-two." The announcement came over the digital communication system and prompted Bryce to head there immediately.

Chapter Ten

He walked in to find the EMS crew still in the room, preparing to slide the elderly male patient over to the hospital bed. The nurse looked up and was able to voice her frustration through a smile. "Dr. Chapman, you're not even going to let us get the patient off the board before you interrupt us?"

"Interrupt? No. I'm just here to help you move him into bed. Figured I'd help out a bit."

"Well good; happy to have your help, then. I'll call you in a bit when we need to roll the patient in thirty-three and change her."

Busted! Bryce shook his head and thought quickly. "Sorry, I'll be wrist deep in charting in a few minutes."

The nurse frowned at Bryce. "Of course you will."

The medic began a quick report. "This is Ralph. He's seventy-nine years old and called us for severe abdominal pain. It's been intermittent for a few days but much worse tonight. He started vomiting and having a bit of fecal incontinence. Vitals were stable. We put in a line and gave him 4mg Zofran and hung a bag of fluid."

The team moved him over to their bed and the nurses began their assessment. Bryce snuck in a quick physical exam and a few questions while they did the required charting. "Sir, I'm concerned about your pain. This could be several bad things. I'm going to get my ultrasound machine and look for an abdominal aneurysm, bad gallbladder, urinary retention and kidney stones."

He returned two minutes later and quickly assessed the patient with the ultrasound probe. *Gallbladder looked fine. Aorta normal. Kidneys normal. Bladder appeared normal. Wait, what was is that mass behind the bladder? Is that an abscess? Cancer? The colon looks distended above it.*

Bryce repositioned the probe and looked from a different angle. *Whatever it is, it is certainly not small. Damn.*

"Sir, can you tell me what else has been going on recently? Anything unusual? Weight loss? Bloody stools?" *Let's just skip to the part where I'm going to tell you we found a cancer that is causing a bowel obstruction. What a way to end my shift before vacation.*

"I have been doing fine. Only thing is I haven't pooped in almost two weeks," said Ralph, frowning as he said it. "I have no problem puttin' stuff in, just can't get nothin' out."

Now it was Bryce's turn to frown. "Now your ultrasound images make more sense. I suspect you have a fecal impaction. Basically your rectum and colon are packed with solid stool that you can't pass. I need to do a quick rectal exam."

The nurse helped roll the patient and Bryce inserted a lubricated finger into the patient's rectum. This is a very emotionally charged situation for both the patient and the doctor. The patient is nervous, uncomfortable and embarrassed. The doctor hopes to not find a large ball of stool that needs to be manually removed by the one who touched it last.

Bryce leaned toward the patient during the exam, eliciting a groan from Ralph and an apology. "Well there is definitely a lot of stool there, but it's too high for me to reach it." *Thank goodness for short fingers. And it's probably not cancer, just constipation.*

The nurse glared at Bryce, knowing what was coming.

"Sir, let me get some labs and a CT scan to make sure nothing else is going on. If not, we'll do some things to get you cleaned out," said Bryce.

"What kind of things?" asked Ralph.

"I have my own technique I developed a few years ago."

"Not the Cleanout..." said the nurse, shaking her head.

"Oh yes, the Cleveland Cleanout," said Bryce.

"What about Cleveland?" asked Ralph.

Bryce leaned down onto the bed rail and explained. "It's my award-winning treatment for constipation. The problem is you have a firm ball of stool in your rectum and there is a lot more backed up on top of it. Your body is trying to push it through but meeting resistance so it causes cramping pain and nausea every so often."

"You're right, that's exactly what I'm feeling."

"So what I do, is ask our wonderful nurse here to give you an enema using warm soapy water. This helps hydrate and lubricate the stool so your body can pass it easier. That's step one."

"There are multiple steps?"

"Ralph, have you ever known a successful strategy that only has one step? Now, after the enema has been administered, you need to hold it as long as you can. It takes time for the soapy water to do its thing."

"How long do I need to hold it?"

"Have you ever had horrible diarrhea and knew that you might not make it to the bathroom in time? You get this uneasy feeling like you're about to make a dramatic social faux pas, and your forehead breaks out in a sweat?"

Ralph laughed. "You look young, doc, but you're describing the life of an old man rather well right now."

"That's how long you need to hold the enema. Until you have beads of sweat running down your forehead. Ready for step two?" Ralph nodded and Bryce continued. "Have you ever seen the military or SWAT teams breach a door?"

"Son, I was in the Army. I've breached my share of doors."

"Okay great, and thank you for your service, sir. And that means you know what I'm talking about. Do you just gently lean in with your shoulder to open it?"

"No, you get a running start and bring hellfire down upon that door."

"Exactly. Step two is we give you a double dose of psyllium dissolved in water. This is an organic fiber that your body can't digest or absorb. It's going to be the battering ram."

The nurse sighed and leaned her head down to her chest.

"I've used those too. But we usually had four men on them. Who is going to handle the ram inside me?"

"Our friend Miralax. Polyethylene glycol. It's a laxative. You're going to drink five capfulls of that powder mixed in a sugary drink like Gatorade."

"And then what?" asked Ralph.

"And then we wait. I can't ask you to walk down the hallway with all this primed and ready to go. That's like asking a man to drive a wagon load of nitroglycerin over a bumpy mountain road. The slightest jolt could spell disaster."

The nurse excused herself and left the room, trying to suppress a laugh while maintaining her frown.

"She is going to get a bedside commode. We're going to let you take care of business in your room here."

"The Cleveland Cleanout, huh? That sure sounds like what I need. Thanks, doc."

"No problem. I need to get your CT back first and then we'll get it started if there's nothing else going on. Good luck, sir. Remember, we're counting on you." Bryce saluted Ralph and then stepped out of the room. *I sure love my job sometimes. I'll take Ralphs all day long.*

Bryce spent the rest of his shift finishing charts and had his in basket empty of deficiencies when his partner showed up to relieve him.

"Deion, welcome to the slow department, courtesy of the flamingos," said Bryce.

"Are you still wearing those? I thought you weren't superstitious?"

"I'm not. But, I am a little stitious."

Deion laughed at his colleague. "I love The Office. At least while Steve Carrell was on it. If the flamingos are on it must mean this is your last trip before you leave. What do you have for me?"

"Actually only one patient. The rest are either admitted and waiting on an inpatient bed to open up or waiting to be discharged. The patient is Ralph, and he is in room thirty-two. I think he's constipated. His labs were fine and I'm just waiting on an official read on the CT scan. I didn't see anything unusual on it but I wanted to wait for the official read before I get him cleaned out."

"The Cleveland Cleanout?" asked Deion with a single raised eyebrow.

"Why offer anything less than the best to my patients? And how do you do that single eyebrow raise? Did you get botox on the other side?"

"Chapman, I've spent years conditioning my body to perform at its peak. Controlling isolated muscles is only one thing I've been able to accomplish. You should join me in the gym some day."

"I leave tomorrow. Do you have tips on what I can do by then so Val can walk the beach with a sexy hunk?"

"Sure. Give me your plane ticket," said Deion, bursting out in laughter.

"Very funny," said Bryce. "Drop me a text and let me know how the Cleanout worked. I'll be up for a bit. Too excited to sleep."

"I will man. Be safe heading home. And any chance we can name your method something else? I grew up in Cleveland. It's not what I want to associate fecal impactions with."

"Rename it? To what? Tijuana Torcher? Birmingham Blowout? Raleigh Rammer?"

"Okay, okay. Cleveland Cleanout it is. Just get out of here," said Deion as he logged into his computer. "Never hang around the ER longer than you need to; you know that."

Bryce agreed and signed out of his workstation for the last time before the trip. He wanted to jog to his car but resisted the urge.

Chapter Eleven

"Six-thirty sharp." Bryce pumped his hands downward and said, "We are down like six-thirty."

Val looked at him sideways. "What was that you just did?"

"It's a thing cool people say when they're excited to do something. They're down like both hands of the clock at six-thirty. It happens to be six-thirty now, and I'm cool, so I did the move."

"Kids, don't listen to your father. Try to get your style advice from me, okay?"

Bryce tried to slap Val on the knee, but she moved out of the way in time. "Not cool and not fast, either," she said before rubbing his thigh. "Just messing with you. You're the coolest guy around."

Bryce pulled into the private aviation entrance of the airport and followed signs to passenger parking. His Yukon fit in well against the Cadillac Escalades, Mercedes G wagons, and the other high-end vehicles in the lot. He saw a few people from their group standing near their vehicles and parked in a spot next to them.

"Okay kids, stick close to Mom and me until we figure out where we're going."

The Chapman family exited the car and joined the others waiting in the parking lot.

"We've never flown private before. Where are we supposed to go?" asked Jackie. She was standing next to her husband, who was leaning on a forearm crutch held in his right hand.

"The flight is being handled by Hamilton Air Services, which is that building over there," said Bryce, pointing to a large steel building a hundred yards away. "Let's go see what they have to say."

Bryce looked around and saw Tom Sharpe and his wife Rebecca, Peter Thrasher, Jackie Sirico, and her husband. *Where's Elisa? She was supposed to be here.* "Has anyone seen Elisa and her husband?" he asked.

"No, we got here an hour ago and have seen no one besides this group," said Tom.

"Okay, we'll let's go inside and I'll send her a text." The group moved toward the enormous structure as Bryce sent an urgent text to Elisa.

```
Hey, just checking. Our flight leaves
in 90 mins. Are you close?
```

Bryce dropped his phone in his pocket and hurried to catch up to the group, who was now entering the building. He pulled his suitcase through the door, turning around to make sure the wheels cleared the bump at the threshold. When he turned around, Elisa Morales was holding her phone and shaking her head at him.

"Come on ER, I'm a general surgeon. I get up at four in the morning every day of my life. You think I'd sleep in and miss a free VIP trip to the Bahamas?" she said.

Bryce smiled and apologized. "Sorry Elisa, Tom said he'd been in the parking lot for an hour and hadn't seen anyone. Just checking. Is this your husband?" asked Bryce, looking at the clean-cut man wearing a golf shirt.

"Yes, this is my husband, Julio. He's active duty with the Marines. Fortunately, he's on leave and could join."

Julio stepped forward and offered Bryce a firm handshake, staring him in the eyes as he introduced himself. "Hi doc, I'm Julio. Thank you so much for inviting Elisa and me on this trip. We don't get out much. I heard a rumor there might be some fishing competitions?"

"Good to meet you, Julio. I'd love to have some friendly competition down there. Biggest fish. Most fish. Most lobsters. Best tan. You name it, I'll compete for it."

"That's great. I used to fish all the time in Puerto Rico but don't get the chance much now that we're in Indiana. I love saltwater fishing. Just knowing that there could be an enormous fish waiting to take my bait is so exhilarating."

Jackie put her arm around her husband and addressed the group. "Guys, this is my husband Salvatore. He usually goes by Sal."

He smiled and made a deliberate motion to form his lips into the proper position before slowly speaking. "Hello, nice to meet you."

Jackie smiled at him and rubbed his back. "Sal had a stroke when we were on our honeymoon a few years ago." Her face held a thin smile, one that had the potential for joy but looked more like ironic disappointment. "Not exactly how we saw the trip to Cancun going."

Bryce noted the atrophy on Sal's right side and reached his left hand out for a greeting. "Hi Sal, glad to have you along. You're going to love this place."

Sal returned the handshake and offered Bryce an uneven smile, the right side of his face not quite coming up to where it should.

"Each villa comes with its own all terrain golf cart. You should be able to zip right around the island and even down onto the beach," said Bryce.

"I can't wait," said Sal.

"Ladies and gentlemen, if I could have your attention, please." The words came from a well-dressed woman who had just stepped out of an office door. The group turned to listen to her.

"Is everyone here for the private charter to Georgetown, Exuma?"

The group nodded, and a few vocalized their agreement.

"Wonderful. Your flight crew is ready. If there are no questions, I'll take you out to the plane." She paused for a moment and when no concerns were raised, she waved the group forward and walked toward a door in the building's rear.

"Bryce, dude, I can't believe this is happening. Thanks for saving that dude's life and earning this trip. Shame I don't have any lady friends with me though," said Peter as he carried a small suitcase toward the plane.

"Who knows, you may meet an island beauty down there and decide to stay permanently." Bryce looked down at the small suitcase. "Is that really the only luggage you are bringing?"

"Sure. Three swimsuits and a few shirts. What else do I need? There are no restaurants on the island and I have no one to impress. I plan on floating and fishing all day long."

"Woah, is that our plane?" asked Noah, pulling on Bryce's arm and pointing. "That whole thing is just for us?"

"I think so, buddy. It's a Gulfstream 550. It holds sixteen people plus the crew. Pretty cool, huh?"

"Yes!" he said, letting go of Bryce's arm and walking faster toward the plane.

"What do you think this would cost to charter if we wanted to rent it ourselves?" asked Tom.

"I looked into that. They charge a base rate per hour and then additional crew fees along with taxes. Easily $11,000 per hour for a plane like this. It's about eleven hundred miles to Georgetown, and it cruises at 500 knots, so figure two-and-a-half hours."

"Thirty grand just for the flights?" asked Jackie, her face locked in a surprised stare.

"Each way," said Bryce. "So sixty grand minimum, and there may be some fees for the plane sitting on the runway, or moving to its next location too."

The woman from the charter company stopped next to the plane and held her arm out, pointing at the stairs.

"Leave your luggage here and we'll load it onto the plane. You can make your way into the cabin and take a seat wherever you'd like. There is a bathroom up front and one in the rear."

"Sal, there's no railing on the first part of the stairs. Be careful," said Jackie.

"I know," said Sal, his words came out slow and measured. Most of the party quickly entered the plane and walked backward to claim a spot in the luxurious cabin. Peter and Bryce hung back to help Sal up the stairs.

"We got this Jackie. You're on vacation," said Peter, holding out an arm for Sal to grab onto.

Jackie thanked them and carried Sal's crutch onto the plane, along with their carry-on baggage.

Sal leaned on Peter and lifted his left leg onto the first step, then leaned toward Bryce and lifted his right leg up onto the step. He repeated the process until he reached the halfway point where the railings began. When he could reach them, he grabbed on and let his helpers know he could manage the rest on his own. Peter stayed close behind on the stairs, his arms in a ready position as if he were spotting someone on bench press.

Once everyone was aboard, the pilots stepped out of the cockpit and introduced themselves.

"Welcome aboard, everyone. This is a G550 jet, owned by Optimus Equity. Mr. Proffit let us know you are VIP passengers and you'll be treated as such. The weather looks just about perfect, so we expect a smooth flight all the way into Georgetown, Exuma. When we land, we will clear customs and then get you on board your transport to the island. If you'd please take your seats, we will get underway. There is complimentary wifi available for the duration of the flight."

Julio watched the pilots as they turned and stepped back into the cockpit, crawling over the center instrument panel to take their seats.

Bryce sat down in a custom upholstered leather seat with the Optimus Equity logo sewn into the cushion. "Ooh, this is nice," he said, wiggling himself back and forth in the chair. His kids sat across from each other with a small table between them. They had already found the fridge and were each drinking a bottle of water.

A stewardess walked down the aisle, taking orders for mimosas before takeoff. She needed a second trip to deliver them all.

The takeoff was smooth, and the plane quickly rose to its cruising altitude. Large round windows provided excellent natural light in the cabin and incredible views of the scenery below.

Bryce turned around and looked back at his friends. Every one of them had a smile on their face and were eagerly chatting with someone else. He touched Val's shoulder and pointed for her to turn around and look. She glanced back and then smiled at her husband. "This is a good thing, Bryce. We deserve it." She leaned in closer. "But it's going to be tough for you to cook some of your signature Bahamian bacon with other people in our villa."

"I guess you'll just have to use your imagination. But remember what happened a few hours after that? Maybe cooking bacon while naked was a bad omen that brought on the disaster."

"If I'm using my imagination, it'll probably be some celebrity chef with an accent and abs doing the cooking. And you know I don't believe in fate or omens. There is no mysterious power sitting around waiting to strike someone dead because you cooked breakfast in the nude. That's ridiculous. Things usually happen because of choices we make, like getting drunk and raging against strangers. That event is all on Tony."

"You're right, of course. Let's focus on the good parts of this trip to come, not the bad parts of our last trip." *Mental note, work on my accent. And abs.*

"What do you want to get out of the trip, Bryce? At the end of it, what would make you say the trip was a success?"

"I want us to come together as a family, to put each other ahead of ourselves. For the adults to develop deeper friendships that extend beyond casual interactions in the hallways. I want genuine relationships with them." He lowered his voice and leaned toward Val. "Like Jackie and Sal. I have known her for years and did not know that her husband had a stroke and was living with that amount of disability. If you had asked me yesterday if I was good friends with Jackie, I would have said absolutely. But now I realize I don't know her at all."

Valerie nodded in agreement. "I know what you mean. It's so easy to smile, wave and send a text anymore. But to sit down and actually get to know someone takes effort. I'm willing to sit on the beach and have you bring me drinks until I feel I know everyone this week." She leaned back in her chair and looked down at the buttons next to her knee. She pushed one and slowly a leg support elevated out of the bottom of the chair as the entire seat leaned back. She held it down until she was nearly flat.

"Comfy now?" asked Bryce.

Val smiled and snuggled into her chair before closing her eyes.

Bryce looked at a monitor hung on a wall behind the cockpit. It displayed a map of their current position along with current speed, altitude and time to destination. Two hours left.

Chapter Twelve

The speakers crackled, and then the captain's voice projected through the cabin.

"Folks, we're almost to our destination and have begun our descent. If you look out the windows, we are flying over Great Abaco, a large beautiful island in the Bahamas. To your right is Grand Bahama Island. The next island up ahead is Eluthera. If you own a sailboat, spend some time here. You won't regret it. At this time I'd like you to prepare for landing. We should have you on the ground in about twenty minutes. The weather is eighty-five degrees, partly cloudy, and winds out of the east at thirteen knots."

Bryce snapped awake at the first words spoken by the captain. He looked up and saw Hannah and Noah each sleeping in their fully reclined seats. Val had a line of drool dripping down the side of her face.

Behind him, there was an intense game of euchre between Tom, Jackie, Sal, and Julio. Bryce walked back to join them before waking his family up for landing.

"How was your flight? Those chairs are the most comfortable I've ever sat in on a plane."

"The views are incredible. I never knew how beautiful the Bahamas were," said Rebecca. "He has never taken me here before."

"We've really never been to the Bahamas? We've hit most of the other Caribbean islands. Now you can check this off your list," said Tom.

"It doesn't count unless I get a geocache, you know that. Don't worry, I looked and there's one at the airport."

"Good, we can knock that out quickly and then get to the island."

"The flight's been great, but these four have played euchre the whole time. I've never even heard of it before," said Peter. "I just watched them throw cards around while I threw down some champagne. Bryce, have you seen the bathroom on this plane?"

"No, but I think it's time. Be right back." He walked to the back of the plane and pulled open the bathroom door. He let out a low whistle and shut the door behind him.

Elisa stood and stretched. "Julio, last hand. We need to get ready to land. I want to take some pictures before we get off the plane. My partners need to see how I roll now."

"What, now that you're hanging with the ER crowd?" asked Peter.

"I will take every surgical patient you have if you take me to the islands once a year on a private jet," said Elisa.

"Talk to Bryce. He just needs to get assaulted by rich kids every so often and then save their lives. We could really live it up if we hang out with him."

Bryce exited the bathroom as Peter was finishing his comment. "Are you guys offering my body up as bait to get free trips?"

"Absolutely. But we'd be with you to make sure you're okay. It's mutually beneficial," said Tom.

Bryce slapped him on the shoulder as he walked back to the front of the plane. "Thanks buddy, I appreciate it." He shook gently Val's leg, waking her up. She looked around, eyes wide, and glancing in several directions.

"What? Where are we?"

"Almost there. We're about to land so I thought you'd want to get up before then. The kids would love this view as well."

Val opened the sunscreen on her window and gasped. "It is so beautiful. Can we just fly around and look before we land?"

"We have been. You just slept the whole time," said Bryce. He then leaned forward and tapped his kids to wake them up.

"Oh wow, look at that yacht down there. Wouldn't you love to be on that? Actually, they're probably saying the same thing since they're checking us out with binoculars."

The pilot battled the strong cross breeze and brought the plane down expertly in the center of the only runway at the airport. In ninety seconds, he had it parked by the small terminal and the ground crew prepared to unload the plane.

The group snapped a few more pictures of each other on the plane before stepping out into the warm tropical sun. Then moved toward the terminal building to clear customs.

"Ah, Mr. Chapman. Welcome back," said the friendly customs agent from behind the plexiglass screen. Her Bahamian accent adding warmth to the greeting.

"You remember me?" asked Bryce in surprise.

"Not directly, but I saw the video of you saving that guy who drowned. The entire island chain was talking about it. Is this pretty lady here your wife who helped also?"

"That's me," said Val, waving.

"Did you know you caused a twenty percent increase in tourists after they released your video? We had so many people come down here to see what it was all about. It was the busiest we have seen the island in years."

"I did not. That's incredible. That video certainly had enough views."

"My brother runs a grocery store, and you made him a lot of money. My cousin runs an aquatic tour company, and he was also quite happy. Welcome back."

She stamped their passports and passed them through the window.

Bryce tried to take them from her, but she kept her thumb pinched hard into her index finger and wouldn't let them go.

"But promise me no more funny business, okay?" She added a wink at the end of her comment before releasing the passports.

"We're here on vacation. Not planning anything too exciting."

She cleared the rest of the party through customs, and they gathered their luggage for inspection.

"Don't worry about these people. They are very important guests whom we pre-screened. I have transportation waiting outside."

"I'm sorry, who are you?" said Elisa.

"Oh, please forgive me. My name is Edward Ferguson. I am the local manager for Swan Cay, and will escort you to the island. Is everyone here?"

The group looked around to assess their numbers and then nodded.

"Wonderful. Let's step outside and into the vans. It's about a thirty-minute trip to the dock and then just over an hour to the resort. The weather is perfect today, and the sea is calm. Should be a beautiful trip. I must warn you; it looks like we're in for a bit of a tropical storm in two days. The prediction is simply a storm, not a hurricane and it is fast moving, so it should be through in a day."

"So we could have some good wave action? That works for me," said Bryce.

They followed Edward outside, loaded into the vans and were quickly underway.

Chapter Thirteen

"How much longer?" asked Emily. "We've been sitting here for over a day."

"The tracker app says they should be here in about five minutes. FlightAware is so cool. You can track any plane. Not the best for security, but it's handy for us."

"I suppose they'll be coming in from the north?" said Emily, pointing off the port side.

"Yeah. That's how we always land here. I guess if you were coming in from the south, you could land on that end, though. Can you toss me a beer?"

Emily opened the fridge and removed two cans of Carib. "Let's drink these up front on the loungers."

Tony followed her up front and brought the binoculars with him. He popped the can open and filled his mouth with the cold local beer.

"Is that them? I didn't see any other planes on the app," said Emily.

"It's got to be. G550, the same plane my dad owns. When it gets closer, I'll check out the logo on the tail."

"Hand me the binoculars," said Emily, putting her beer down and reaching her arm out toward Tony. He handed them over and leaned back to finish his drink.

"It's got your dad's logo on it, a large golden O, right?"

"Yeah, that's it. Looks like phase two of our plan is in motion," said Tony.

"What's phase two?"

"Reconnaissance. We'll let them get comfortable for a day or two while we learn their routine. Then one night we slip ashore and grab Bryce, dump him over the continental shelf and get our lives started."

"How long are we going to wait?"

"There's a tropical storm rolling through in a few days. That sounds like the perfect time. Everyone will be hunkered down inside and won't be paying attention to the shore. We can use the jet ski to get back and forth."

Emily held her lower abdomen and breathed in quickly. "There is that pain again. I wonder if I have an ovarian cyst bothering me. Or maybe appendicitis."

"Are you going to be okay? We need a few days and then we can get out of here."

"I think so. I hate being out here isolated. If I was in a hospital, I could look with the ultrasound."

"You know how to do that?"

"I saw it done enough. How hard is it? Put the probe on and then it's image recognition. Those ER docs think they're such badasses with their ultrasounds. I could train a child to do them in a few days."

Tony smiled at her. "You would make a great doc. Why did the schools not accept you?"

"I don't know. My scores are fine. I get interviews and then rejection letters. I guess the people doing the interviews are morons. But that dream is over now. Who is going to take someone who kidnapped two doctors and helped kill one of them?"

"It doesn't matter. You've got all the money you need now. And you have me."

"Awe, thanks," she said, raising her beer toward him. "But I want to feel like I accomplished something. Did something that no one else in my family has ever accomplished."

"How many of your family have spent months on a luxury yacht in the Caribbean?"

"Probably none. I haven't had time to ask since we've been on the run. I didn't want anyone to track us." She leaned back on the cushion and stared up at the sky. "Am I ever going to get to see my parents again?"

"We'll figure something out. Once things settle down, we'll find a way to get a message to them and meet on a beach somewhere."

"You promise? I miss them."

Tony shifted over onto the cushion next to her. He put his hand on top of hers. "I promise." He laid down next to her and they stared at the sky together.

A few minutes later, he sat up and stretched. "Why don't we spend the night here and head out to Swan Cay in the morning. I'll go see if I can find us some lobster." He stood up and headed toward the back of the boat to get geared up.

Chapter Fourteen

"The scenery is incredible down here. I could stay on this island the whole week and be happy," said Elisa.

"Just wait for the next leg. Cruising across crystal-clear water on our way to Swan Cay. That is what made Bryce and I fall in love with this place," said Val.

They unloaded from the vans and climbed aboard a large power boat. It had a large rigid top to protect the occupants from the Caribbean sun.

Rebecca Sharpe hurried toward the boat; her arms full of items purchased from the vendors near the dock. "Sorry, their stuff looked so amazing. I wasn't sure we'd have time to shop anywhere on this trip, so I wanted to get my souvenirs now."

"Ma'am, you're on island time now. Take as long as you want," said the captain.

Val accepted the bags handed down onto the boat, and Tom offered his wife a hand to safely step down onto the boat.

"It's hard to not support the locals who make these crafts, isn't it?" said Val.

"Exactly. I wanted to buy one of everything."

The captain started the engines, then began removing dock lines to get underway.

"Hang on, there's one more item being delivered," said Rebecca. She pointed to a man hurrying toward the boat with a blue and yellow cardboard box.

"We definitely can't leave until that is on board," said the captain.

Peter leaned over and accepted the case of beer with a broad smile. "Now we're talking! I wondered what we were going to do for an hour on the boat."

The captain gave a quick safety briefing and then tossed the final dock line. He eased the throttle forward to pull away from the dock and then pushed it forward.

The group shared beer and laughter as they took in the beautiful scenery along the path. Dozens of islands full of sand and palm trees passed by on each side of the boat. Less than half of them had structures on them. Some of the larger islands had short runways for their owner's plane.

Before anyone noticed how much time had passed, the captain pointed straight ahead at a beautiful island rising out of the Caribbean. "There she is, Swan Key".

"I thought it was Swan Cay," said Jackie.

"That's how it is spelled, but we pronounce it 'key'," said the captain. "I hope you find it is the key to your happiness."

Once the captain pulled the boat into a slip, Edward secured a line around a piling. The captain attached one at the stern and the group disembarked. Edward directed several staff members to accept the bags and load up golf carts for transport back to the villas.

"Do you know which villas you will each be staying in?" asked Edward.

Bryce looked at the group and back at Edward. "I was thinking we'd take the main villa with Tom and Peter. Jackie and Elisa's families can have the other villa."

"Fine by us," said Elisa. "I'll sleep on the beach for all I care. Unless there are bugs. I hate bugs."

No one else objected, so the staff split the luggage to the proper cart and headed up the path toward the villas.

Edward offered to come back for Sal and Jackie, but they declined the offer.

"I can walk. If I don't keep walking, I won't be able to." He walked up the path slowly and deliberately, holding the crutch in his right arm and Jackie's hand in his left.

The rest of the group walked up toward the house, but Peter lingered behind. "You guys go ahead. I'm going to check out the beach for a bit."

The rest of the group continued toward the villa, and Peter walked down to the edge of the water. He laid his backpack on the beach, removed his shirt and laid down on the sand, resting his head on the bag. *This is what I needed. A fresh start. No ex-girlfriend tying me to a bed. No random nurse sleeping next to me every weekend. Time for a new Peter.* He laughed out loud. *Glad Bryce didn't hear that.*

He scrolled through his social media briefly while he listened to the soft sound of the small waves breaking on the shore and quickly drifted off to sleep.

"Everyone should take some time to get settled in. In one hour, I'll give a quick tour of the island. Sunset will be in about three hours. Staff will have an hors d'oeuvres spread setup near the dock to enjoy with your first sunset. If you desire any snacks, you will find them in your pantry. We will make the first round of drinks to your liking; just tell us what you'd like to have," said Edward.

A hostess made two pitchers of a frozen rum drink and then left for the other villa, where she made a single pitcher. Each couple retreated to their room to get unpacked.

Val led the kids into the room assigned to her and Bryce. It had a large king bed in the middle with a sofa bed against the far wall. Noah sprinted at the bed and dove onto it, spreading his arms and legs out wide before landing on his face. Hannah climbed up and took a position on the other side.

"Kids, you'll be sleeping on the couch, but you can stay here for now. Why don't we get you in swimsuits and check out the pool?"

"Yes!" said Noah, hopping up and ripping his shirt off. Val put them in suits and then Bryce coated them in sunscreen.

"You both will need sunscreen several times a day down here. The sun is a lot stronger than it is back home," he said.

"Why, is it a different sun?" asked Noah.

"No, same sun. But the light hits earth at a steeper angle closer to the equator, so it is more intense."

"What? I haven't even seen a tent down here," said Noah.

"Bryce, I appreciate you trying to teach your kids science, but let's just go out and relax. There will be plenty of time for astronomy later," said Val.

After they put sunblock on the kids, she ushered them out of the room while she and Bryce put their suits on.

"Need any help with your suit?" asked Bryce.

"No, I'm good. Thanks."

"Are you sure? I have specialty training in anatomy. I can make sure everything is where it's supposed to be."

"And I have specialty training in engineering. I think I can figure out a suit." She pulled her arms through the shoulder straps and adjusted the fit slightly.

Bryce dropped his head and exhaled. He pulled his suit up and reached for the strings to secure it. "Well, let me know if you need any help tomorrow. We're on vacation, you know."

Val walked over to him and took the strings from his swimsuit out of his hands. She pulled hard on the strings, stretching his suit out in the front and drawing him toward her.

"Hey, easy there," he said.

"I'm well aware we're on vacation. I am also aware we have two children with us." She began tying his strings into a knot. "But what you don't know," she said as she pulled the strings tight, "is I already asked Rebecca to listen for our kids tonight while we go for a swim after everyone else falls asleep."

"Oh, really?"

"Yep. And we won't have to worry about the suits still being wet in the morning, because we won't be wearing them."

Bryce pulled Val in for a tight hug as she finished with his bathing suit. "That sounds outstanding."

Val smiled back at him. "Are you happy again, Mr. Grumpy?"

"First, it's Dr. Grumpy. And second, yes. Let's take the kids to the pool."

Chapter Fifteen

"As beautiful as Anguilla was, I think the water is nicer here," said Emily. She dipped a bite of lobster tail in liquid butter and slipped it into her mouth. A thin line of butter dripped down her chin, racing for her lap but was cut off by a quick swipe of her finger which was promptly licked. "Tastes better too."

"How many lobsters do you think we've eaten by now?"

"Not enough, but I wish you'd find another hogfish. That was better than the grouper you caught." She dipped another piece and continued speaking with her mouth full. "Lobster for breakfast is fantastic."

"Maybe that's what we'll do. Become suppliers of fish and lobsters for local restaurants on some little island. I could do that for a while and be happy," said Tony.

"Well, we need to get past this first. Is it time to begin phase two?"

"Almost. I need to get my exercise in first. A hundred push ups and two hundred sit-ups. Want to swim in and do them with me?"

"In the last month, how many times have I said yes?"

"A few times."

"But then what did I do when I got to shore?"

"You laid down on a towel and took a nap."

"Right. Have a great time. I'll guard the boat."

She watched him dive into the water and swim toward shore. *Take your time. I'm going to find the access codes one of these times. Then I don't need you anymore.* Emily dipped the last bit of lobster in butter and placed it in her mouth before standing up and continuing her search.

Chapter Sixteen

At the scheduled time, Edward gathered the guests around the pool to begin the tour.

"As you have seen, we have two primary residences here on either side of the pool. Both give excellent views of the water and are afforded privacy by the tropical foliage. Wherever you wish to go, there is a path that will take you there. There is a jogging path around the perimeter with a few trails to the beach, but the road we took from the dock services the main beach." He pointed away from the villas and continued. "Over on this end of the island are the crew quarters. Their responsibilities end after dinner, but someone is always available if you have specific needs."

He began walking down the path back toward the dock. "If you'll follow me, I'll explain the boats and watersport activities."

"Why don't you take the tour and I'll stay here with the kids," said Val. "I don't think they want to get out yet."

Bryce agreed and grabbed a towel before catching up with the others on the path. He could hear them ahead, but jumped sideways when he heard a short honk behind him and to his left.

"Want a ride?" asked Jackie from the driver's seat of a golf cart.

"Sure, thanks."

Sal pointed over his shoulder. "Plenty of room in back."

Bryce slapped him on the shoulder and climbed on before Jackie floored it and they cruised down the asphalt path.

When they made it to the dock, Elisa was laughing hysterically as Peter struggled to get off the beach.

"Rookie move, Thrasher!" said Elisa, leaning on Julio for support as she continued to laugh.

Peter looked down at his chest and saw he had an impressive sunburn, as well as a perfect outline of his phone across his abs. "Be nice Elisa, this hurts pretty bad."

"Sorry, but the phone outline is just too much."

"Hey Bryce, open that cooler next to you. I think Peter needs a drink," said Jackie.

He obeyed and pulled out a cold can of Carib beer and walked it over to Peter

"Thanks. Guess I should have put sunblock on before lying down." He rubbed the cold can across his chest, trying to relieve the discomfort.

"I'm going to show you off to my kids as an example of why we wear sunscreen. Thanks for the life lesson," said Bryce.

Edward got their attention again and continued speaking. "Folks, we have two boats here for you to use; Boston Whaler Dauntless 220s with a 250hp engine. They hold nine passengers and only have a fifteen-inch draft, so you can go pretty much wherever you want. They designed the hull for open ocean travel, but I wouldn't go more than a few miles offshore."

He pointed to a metal box on the end of the dock between the two slips. "Here is your fuel should you need to refill the boat. Most guests do not go through the eighty-gallon gas tank on the boat, but I recommend filling up if you plan to go on the outside. In the protected harbor here, you'll be fine with at least a quarter tank."

"Can we keep what we catch?" asked Tom.

"Yes, but there are a few protected species. There are cards in each boat showing daily limits, seasons, and which species cannot be harvested," said Edward.

"What about mahi mahi?" asked Sal.

"Mahi, wahoo, king mackerel, all of those are open season. If you catch fresh fish, our chefs will prepare them for you. Just call ahead when you're coming back and they will meet you to collect your cooler. There is an ice machine next to the pool. Be sure to load up before you head out; it would be a shame to waste such tasty fish."

He stepped down onto a boat and pointed out several of the features. "These come equipped with Raymarine chartplotters, VHF radios, a portable toilet, and an EPIRB. I recommend picking a few islands every day and checking them out. We even have an underwater metal detector you may use. The children love looking for forgotten treasure."

"Is there any down here?" asked Peter.

"Oh yes. People find gold coins every year. They usually come to the surface after storms as the sand shifts around. Remember, the tropical storm will arrive in two days. Once it's gone, that would be a perfect time to look for treasure."

Edward pointed at a small shed just off the end of the dock. "That building has your fishing supplies and watersport equipment. Dive masks, snorkels, fishing gear, and a few other items are inside. Does anyone have questions for me?" asked Edward.

He waited a few moments until he was satisfied there were none. "Very well. I am available via phone any time, and our staff will be here on the island. I will return daily and check in on you."

"Thanks Edward, we appreciate it. We're a pretty laid back group and I think we'll be fine," said Bryce. "Your resort is beautiful."

"Sir, may I ask you one personal favor? My son loved the video of you and Mrs. Chapman saving that man who drowned. Would it be too much of an imposition if I brought him with me tomorrow to meet you? You are a bit of a local celebrity around here now."

Bryce puffed up a bit taller at the compliment and smiled back at Edward. He began to reply but was cut off by Elisa.

"Oh, don't tell him stuff like that. He already thinks he's some sort of superhero," she said, groaning.

"Well, that's okay, because we do as well."

"Edward, bring your son. We would love to meet him," said Bryce.

"Excellent. We will be by after breakfast." He glanced at his watch and then addressed the group again. "Dinner is in about ninety minutes. Please enjoy the resort and reach out with any questions."

He stepped out of the Dauntless and walked to his smaller boat that was tied up at the end of the dock. Bryce and Julio helped remove the dock lines once Edward had the engine running. He gently pulled away from the dock and offered a smile and a wave before engaging the throttle.

"What a life. Can you imagine taking a boat to work? And islands like these are your office?" asked Tom.

"Yes, I can. And I do. Almost every single day," said Bryce, his voice trailing off. He continued to stare at Edward's boat as it cruised through the crystal-clear water.

Chapter Seventeen

The staff prepared a gourmet meal for the group, arranging the tables to accommodate everyone in the larger villa.

After dinner, Peter offered to make the first round of drinks. The others setup the kitchen table for a game of Texas hold 'em and created multiple stacks of colored chips for each player.

"Bryce, you in for twenty dollars?" asked Tom.

"You know it. Be there in a few."

Val made eye contact with him and raised her eyebrows. She pointed at Bryce and then at herself before making a subtle swimming motion. Bryce's eyes widened suddenly.

"Sorry Tom, I'm actually going to skip the first few hands. Put the blinds in for me and fold until I'm back." He stepped into their bedroom and returned with two towels. Hannah and Noah were sitting on the couch watching an animated movie. He gave each of them a hug and met Val by the door. She waved at Rebecca and mouthed 'thank you' before stepping outside to follow Bryce.

Once they shut the door, the only sounds were the wind in the palm trees and the waves gently breaking against the shore. Val linked her arm in Bryce's as they walked down the path toward the beach.

"What do you think of the place so far?" he asked.

"It's incredible. I want to see the kids snorkel and fall in love with the water like I did when I was their age. Will you take Noah fishing tomorrow?"

"Yep. We're going to go right after breakfast. With any luck we'll bring back some mahi."

"The kids and I want to head to a different island after lunch to do some exploring and searching for treasure." She pulled Bryce in close. "I want to enjoy every moment of this trip. Let's not waste any of our time down here."

"Then we'd better not waste time walking. Last one there has to put aloe on Peter!" He started sprinting with a few words remaining in his sentence and made it about ten feet ahead by the time Val realized she was in a race.

She leaned forward and sprinted toward the water. Bryce's lead held steady as he cleared the edge of the dock and jumped down onto the sand. He lifted his arms overhead in a victory pose while in the air. Then he landed and continued running toward the water.

Val crouched low off the end of the dock but continued running, as if clearing a hurdle in a track meet. Bryce was twenty feet from the water when he turned around and switched to a backward shuffle. He pointed both hands at her and smiled, celebrating the victory, until his left heel struck a mound of sand and he fell backward as if someone swiped his legs out from under him. He tried to recover by skipping a few times but failed and landed on his back.

She laughed and continued running, rapidly closing the distance between them.

Bryce landed hard but didn't stop moving. *Screw it, I'm going to roll my way in.* He completed a backward somersault and twisted around as his feet came back toward the sand. When he was upright, he was only six feet from the water. *One more leap*! He used his momentum to launch his body toward the water, but watched it retreat as he neared it. He stretched an arm out, extending as far as he could to reach the water and secure victory.

Val kept running until she caught up to the receding wave and stopped in ankle-deep water. Bryce landed with a thud in the wet sand a few feet shy of the water.

She leaned back and clasped her hands behind her head, panting. Bryce groaned and lifted his face up, just as the next wave smacked into him. He rolled over and sat up, spitting the sand and salt water out of his mouth.

"You should have seen that!" said Val, now leaning forward laughing. "That entire sequence. First you cheat on the start, then you showboat your end zone entrance and then trip before diving face first into the sand. Then the saltwater facial. Oh, what I would give for that to be on video!"

Bryce got himself up on his knees and then stood up entirely. "That's not fair. I lost because the wave was going out."

"No, you lost because you just had to gloat. But you didn't want me putting aloe on Peter anyway, did you?"

"Of course not. That's why I lost on purpose." Bryce brought his fingers through his hair, shaking out sand as they passed through. "Peter will never let me put aloe on him, anyway. He's too macho."

Val started walking through the water, flicking her hands through it and sending drops toward Bryce. "Are you about done preening? I didn't run all the way down here to not have sex in the ocean."

"Now that you mention it, I think I got all the sand out of me. I'm all yours."

"Lovely. Let's try to keep the sand out of me too." She grabbed Bryce's suit and leaned back, pulling both of them down into the water.

Chapter Eighteen

"Morning Chap. Did you sleep well?"

Bryce stretched a bit and looked around the room. "Yes, I did. What are you doing up, Tom? It's not even seven o'clock."

"I crashed hard last night. Travel always takes it out of me. You missed a beautiful sunrise this morning."

"I'm sure I did. I thought about getting up, but my pillow made a convincing argument not to. We may not get a sunrise tomorrow with the storm coming, but for now, the coffee smells amazing."

"Who all is up for fishing today?"

"Sounds like it's a guy's trip. Julio, Sal, Peter, and us. After lunch Val wants to take the kids to a different island and explore a bit."

The rest of the villa woke up slowly over the next hour and ate a quick breakfast of eggs, bacon, and fresh fruit. Val and Rebecca helped pack a bag of snacks for them, along with a cooler of drinks. Bryce and Tom filled a large cooler with ice and drove it down to load into the boat.

They found Julio at the dock loading poles and the other fishing gear onto the boat. "I think we're going to be trolling today. I don't see any bottom features on the map. Is that okay with you guys?"

"Sure. Hard to bottom fish when it's over a thousand feet deep, anyway."

"Julio, is that a gaff?" asked Tom, pointing at what looked like a half-length fishing pole with a large metal hook on the end.

"This thing? Yeah. We should be able to drag our catch right into the boat."

"Where's Peter? He was really looking forward to the trip today," said Bryce.

Julio shook his head and looked down. "That is one grumpy hombre. He can't really move much without pain from the sunburn. Said he'll be fine later, but he's skipping this first trip to hang out in the pool."

"I'm going to head back to get Noah and Sal. Are we forgetting anything?" said Bryce.

"I don't think so. Boat should be ready. We have life jackets, the radio works, we have food, water and ice," said Julio.

"Poles, lures, gaff. Good to go," said Tom.

Bryce nodded and drove up the path, returning in a few minutes with Sal and Noah. The adults helped Sal into the boat and he chose a seat in front of the console. Noah sat next to his dad on the bench seat behind the helm.

Bryce put his hand on his son's back, double checking the life jacket position. *This is exactly what I wanted out of this trip. I hope you love this as much as I do.* "Buddy, do you want to start the engine?"

Noah nodded excitedly. Bryce showed him where the key was and how to turn it. The deep purr of the four-stroke engine quickly followed. In a few minutes, they had cleared the northern end of the island and were cruising over the moderate swells of open ocean. The swells were a few feet taller than normal and an occasional white cap foreshadowed the approaching weather system.

"How deep do you want to fish?" asked Tom, holding on to the hardtop and leaning in toward Bryce.

"The pelagics like it at least a hundred feet deep. Let's try to find the drop and then follow it," said Bryce. He turned toward Noah and continued. "See this number on the depth finder? That's how deep the water is. Let me know when it gets to a hundred."

"What's a pelagic?" asked Tom.

Julio leaned in and yelled across to Tom. "They're fish that live in the water column. Not reef fish, not bottom feeders. Out here it's the mahi, mackerel, wahoo, marlin, tuna and a few others. I'll eat any of them."

"There's a hundred!" yelled Noah, pointing at the screen. "Wait, two hundred. Now it's just blinking. What happened? Did it break?"

Bryce pulled back on the throttle and slowed the boat down to idle speed. "No buddy, this is the drop off. It goes from fifty feet to a quarter mile deep pretty quickly. This creates a lot of upward current that attracts fish. We're going to try to fish along the drop and see what we can find."

Julio put a rod in into each holder at the stern of the boat. He attached a lure to each and tossed the line over the transom. He pulled line from one reel to allow the lure to float back further from the boat. Tom did the same on the other side.

Bryce took a small action camera out of his bag and strapped it to a stainless-steel support tube for the hardtop. "I'm setting this for time lapse recording. Maybe we'll get some cool pictures of us catching fish." He moved his hand to the throttle to start trolling when a shout from the front of the boat made him turn around.

"Fish on!" yelled Sal. He was laughing and cranking on a small rod from the front of the boat. "I found this under the seat and figured I'd give it a try. Looks like I'm about to go up one to nothing!"

Julio ran to the front and helped support the rod in Sal's weakened right arm.

"Thanks. This thing is pulling pretty good, but he's almost back to the boat. I don't think we'll need the gaff for it. Seems pretty small."

Noah leaned over the side and yelled, "I see it!"

A few seconds later, Sal lifted his arm and pulled a long thin fish over the side of the boat.

"What is that, a catfish?" asked Tom. "What's that thing on its head?"

"That's a remora!" said Julio. "These are so much fun. Who's got a camera?" He reached down and picked up the fish, removing the lure from its mouth.

Bryce pulled his phone out and snapped a picture of Sal grinning as Julio held up the fish in front of him. "Okay, Sal is first on the leaderboard. How did you catch that, anyway?"

"I have no idea. Just figured maybe a fish would hang out in the shade under the boat. I thought maybe I'd catch a barracuda or something. Not one of these."

"Watch this," said Julio. He held his arm out sideways and placed the head of the fish against it. The fish opened and closed its gills a few times and then held still. Julio removed his arm from the fish and spun around slowly.

"How is he doing that? The fish is stuck to him!" said Noah, holding his mouth open at the end of his comment.

"That's what they do Noah. They stick on to larger fish and follow them around. When the big fish eats something, they hope for a few crumbs. Does anyone else want to hold him before I toss him back?"

No one volunteered their arms, so Julio leaned over the side and released the fish. "Nice work Sal. Now let's get something that we can eat."

Bryce put the boat in gear and soon they were cruising forward around six knots. "I'll try to keep us around this depth for a while." He zoomed out on the chart to see the depth markings better. "Hey, this boat has blue tooth audio. Anyone have some tropical music on their phone we can play?"

"I got this," said Sal. He moved back toward the console and paired his phone to the sound system. Soon, Bob Marley filled the boat with a gentle reggae beat. Everyone found a place to relax on the boat and listen to the music as the boat made its way north along the edge of the continental shelf.

A sudden clicking noise came from the rod on the port side as the line was pulled off the reel. Julio raced to the back and lifted the rod out of the holder, beating Tom be a step. "Sorry, amigo, this one is all mine." He tightened the drag down and turned off the clicker. The rod tip bent down toward the water as the fish pulled against the force of the line. "Slow down!" he yelled, and Bryce quickly pulled back on the throttle to comply.

Julio fought the fish for thirty seconds until they saw a flash of green and yellow in the water. "Mahi!" he yelled. "Get the gaff!"

Tom turned around to find the gaff but saw Sal coming at him with it. Tom reached his hand out to take it, but Sal brushed him aside. "I can do this," he said.

Julio brought the fish along the starboard side, where Sal was waiting with the gaff. Tom was standing next to him, ready to grab on and help if needed. Julio reeled a few more times until Sal pulled his left arm quickly backward and stabbed the pointed tip of the gaff into the side of the fish. He lifted it over the side of the boat to a chorus of cheers from everyone on the boat. Julio fed a rope through its mouth and out the gill before holding it over his head. "Put my name on the leaderboard next to Sal!"

"Let's get some quick pictures before he loses his color," said Bryce.

They passed the fish around posing for pictures while holding the fish and then put it in the cooler.

"Dad, how big was that?" asked Noah.

"Probably about fifteen pounds. That fish will be enough food for all of us at dinner tonight. But you know what?" Bryce waited for the obvious follow-up question before continuing. "What about lunch tomorrow? Think we should try to get another fish?"

Noah smiled broadly and nodded.

"Hey, do you know what time it is?" said Tom.

"I hope it's beer thirty," said Sal.

"I thought Italians drank wine Sal, what gives?" said Bryce.

"They do. But I'm Italian-American. Thanks Mom. Now toss me a beer."

Tom grabbed three beers and a Diet Coke from the cooler and passed them around.

Bryce turned the boat around to run the drop back toward the house.

"Woah, some bigger waves all of a sudden," said Tom.

"I turned the boat around to head back toward the house so we're into the wind and swell. Ever hear the phrase 'Fair winds and following seas'?"

"Yes, but I didn't know what it meant," said Tom.

Bryce grinned at his friend and mentor. "Well, you do now. Welcome to taking waves on the nose."

After a few minutes of trolling into the swells, the motion was taking its toll on the crew.

"Hey, maybe we should head with the waves and duck in behind the islands for the return trip," said Julio. "Sal and Tom aren't looking so hot."

"Good idea. I'll get us turned around." Bryce began a slow turn to avoid wrapping the fishing line in the prop when the now familiar sound of the line being pulled from a reel came from the starboard rod. Sal was the closest to it, and he dropped his beer can on the deck of the boat before grabbing the rod. He held it in his left hand and tightened the drag down, which immediately pulled him to the edge of the boat.

"Woah, careful there Sal," said Julio. "Whatever you have on is pretty good size. You got this?"

Sal nodded and began to slowly crank the reel with his weak right hand. Bryce slowed the boat to idle.

"Do you want to put it in neutral?" asked Tom.

"If I do that, then the fish can run at us and shake the hook easily. We need to keep a little tension on the fish."

Sal continued to reel as everyone followed the line into the water with their eyes, trying to get a glimpse of the monster fish that was hooked.

"Woah!" said several people at once as the fish jumped out of the water. A large pointed nose clearing the surface first before the rest of the blue body followed. It flipped back and forth several times before landing back in the water.

"Marlin!" yelled Julio.

"No freaking way! You hooked a marlin!" shouted Bryce. He left the helm and grabbed the other rod, quickly reeling in the line to avoid any potential for an entanglement.

Sal continued to crank on the reel, slowly making progress against the large billfish. Julio helped hold the rod in place while Tom recorded video on his phone.

Several minutes passed and Sal continued to bring the fish closer to the boat. Occasionally, a large wave would hit the boat and interrupt the progress as everyone fought to maintain their footing.

"I'm getting tired. Time to increase the drag and get this guy to the boat," said Sal. He twisted the drag wheel and suddenly the fish was pulling harder each time it tried to run. Tom continued to record and Julio supported the rod as Sal cranked ever slowly on the reel.

"I see it!" said Noah. "It's right under the boat!"

"Okay, step back Noah. Those things can jump into the boat. We don't want anyone hit by its bill," said Bryce.

He stepped to the side and looked over just as the fish was rolling to the surface. It flipped hard and dove away from the boat at the same time a wave struck, knocking everyone off balance. Sal was pushed toward the edge of the boat by the force of the wave and then the fish pulled hard on his arm, which was above his center of gravity and also above the side of the boat. He did not let go of the rod and instead was pulled straight over the gunwale and into the water. Julio had been holding the rod and instinctively grabbed on tighter when Sal began tipping over. His left arm grabbed Sal's shirt, but he too was falling over the edge along with the fishing rod.

Tom saw this unfolding in slow motion through his phone and dropped it to clear his hands. He dove forward to grab Sal, hooking his fingers into Sal's waistband, which pulled him over the edge as well. Bryce watched as several of his passengers were falling out of the boat and reacted as most would in the same situation. He dove forward, trying to hold on to Tom, but slipped on the slime from the mahi that was still on the deck. He skidded forward and hit the edge of the boat before flipping over the side. In less than five seconds, every adult had fallen off the boat, leaving Noah alone on a boat that was in gear and pointed out to sea.

Chapter Nineteen

"Oh, this water feels great," said Peter, easing himself into the pool.

"How's the sunburn?" asked Elisa, who sat on the edge of the deep end holding her ebook reader.

"Better in the pool. I didn't blister, so that's good. I think I'll be wearing a shirt today and hanging out in the shade." He looked up at the clouds filling more of the sky as the day progressed. "Looks like I'll get a break from the sun this afternoon when the storm gets closer."

Val pushed Hannah on a round raft in the shallow end where Rebecca was also floating. "Valerie, are you still planning to go out after lunch and explore a bit? The waves look like they're picking up out there."

"We're going to try. I think it will still be calm enough on the bay side of the island. We probably won't get out of the house tomorrow, so we need to get some adventure in today. I hope the boys are having fun and bring us back some fresh fish."

"Just be careful."

"Oh, we will. Bryce is very cautious on the water. He's seen enough in the ER to make him nervous about nearly everything. He tries to tow the the fine line between safety and exhilaration. Usually he does pretty well with it but once in a while he goes a bit overboard and then we have too much excitement for a while."

"I bet that keeps life interesting though, doesn't it?" she added with a wink.

"Sure does. Life with Bryce is anything but boring."

Noah stared at the side of the boat where his dad and the others had just been standing. *What happened? They're all in the water and I'm the only one on the boat!*

"Dad!" he screamed and ran to the back of the boat.

The men righted themselves in the water and watched as the boat slowly pulled away into the oncoming swells.

"Noah, throw out the life jackets!" screamed Bryce. "They're under the front seat!"

Noah ran to the front of the boat and removed several life jackets. He ran to the back and threw them into the water. He was now over fifty feet away from his dad and the others.

Sal was floating on his back, keeping his lungs full of air for added buoyancy. Tom was close by, ready to support him as needed.

Julio was face down in the water, swimming toward the boat as fast as he could.

"Turn the boat around!" yelled Bryce. "It's just like the go karts. Turn the wheel!"

The boat continued to pull Noah away from his father. *I can't do this. I'm only six!* The engine and sound of waves on the boat were drowning out the words his dad was shouting at him. He turned and looked at the steering wheel and then back at his father and started to cry.

"I don't know how to do it!" he screamed. He walked back and forth from the helm to the rear of the boat, each time noting how much further away he was from his father. There was one man swimming toward him, but he wasn't getting any closer.

Noah looked up at the sky and prayed, "Jesus, help me save my dad and his friends. I don't know how to do it on my own."

Once he said the words, he glanced back at his father one more time. He could only see him when a swell came through and lifted him above the height of the wave ahead of it. *I need to try.*

He walked to the helm and sat on the cushion he had shared with his father ten minutes prior. The depth finder was still blinking its error on the depth. He took a big breath and let it out before grabbing the steering wheel with both hands.

Bryce watched the boat continue to pull away. Julio was trying desperately to catch it but stood no change against the wind, waves and the boat engine.

"Julio, save your energy!" he yelled. "Sal, you okay?"

"Yes, I'm fine," said Sal.

"Let's stick together and hope Noah can get the boat turned around. At least we're drifting toward land. I'm going to grab those life jackets and we should raft ourselves together."

Julio returned to the group carrying two life jackets, and Bryce swam for the other two. They worked to get a jacket on Sal and the others got into them, no easy feat when already in the water.

"What are we going to do?" said Tom.

"What can we do? Get back to shore, get help, and see if the Bahamian Coast Guard can grab Noah. As long as he stays on the boat, he should be fine. The waves aren't that bad yet and he has food and water," said Bryce.

"But the storm is coming," said Julio.

"I know it is. So let's get back to shore. It's what, maybe a mile away?" said Bryce.

"Probably, but with the wind and current, we're swimming the hypotenuse. So figure two or three miles. Save your energy, let's just keep slowly making progress," said Julio.

In a few minutes, the team had figured out a rhythm that allowed them to move as one without hitting each other constantly.

Noah gripped the wheel and turned it as far to the right as it would go. The boat turned sharply and began doing slow, tight circles. *No, that's not right!* He turned the wheel back a bit, and the boat turned in much wider circles. He adjusted a bit more until he had the boat pointed toward the island chain and was maintaining a somewhat stable heading.

But which one should I aim at? I can't see anyone! He moved to the bow and looked out over the water, but could not locate the group.

Noah went back to the helm and kept the boat pointed at the closest land he could see.

Bryce alternated between looking at the shore he was swimming for and glancing back at the boat as it became smaller in the distance. He would lose sight of it while in the trough of a wave and then usually find it again on the next swell. *Wait, it looks different now.* He waited for another swell to get a better look. *Yes! It looks like the boat is turning!*

"Guys, Noah is turning the boat!" he said.

The other three cheered and turned around to look.

"What's he doing? It looks like he's turning in circles," said Sal.

"Well, at least he won't get very far out to sea if he does that," said Tom.

"Hang on, the rotations seem to be slowing. I think he's correcting his steering. Give him a few minutes to figure it out. Come on Noah, you got this," said Julio.

The group stopped swimming and focused their attention on the boat. Another round of cheers went up as Noah straightened the boat out and maintained a heading.

"He did it!" yelled Bryce. "That's my boy! Now come pick us up."

"Do you think he can see us?" asked Tom.

"He's not pointed at us. He's actually a little upwind of us," said Julio.

"Perfect. The leeway will drift him right down on top of us then," said Bryce.

Sal spoke up with another concern. "As one who doesn't swim quickly, does he know how to shut off the engine or put the transmission in neutral? I would like to keep my insides inside, if you know what I mean."

"I had him start the engine this morning. He should be able to do the same thing in reverse. If he gets close enough for me to shout directions at him," said Bryce.

They waited in silence as Noah brought the boat ever closer.

"Hey Sal," said Julio. "That billfish doesn't count. You never got it to the boat. Still tied 1-1."

The group shared a laugh as tensions eased for the time being.

Minute by minute, Noah brought the boat closer.

Noah scanned the water, looking for his dad. Tears began welling up again and running down his cheeks. "Where are you?" he yelled.

He left the helm and went back to the front of the boat to look around. *There! I think I see them!* He stared at the same spot until he knew he was looking at several people in orange life jackets.

He kept his eyes on them and returned to the helm, adjusting the wheel slightly to the right. "I'm coming, Dad!" he yelled, wiping the tears away with both hands before gripping the wheel again.

"He just turned again, maybe only ten degrees, but it looked intentional. He must see us because he's headed directly at us," said Julio.

"Come on Noah, you got this," whispered Bryce.

A minute later, Noah raised his right arm and waved at them. Everyone waved back with smiles on their faces.

"Noah," yelled Bryce. "You need to shut off the engine. Just turn the key the opposite way you did to turn it on."

Noah looked down for a bit and then looked back at Bryce. "It's not working. I don't know how to do it."

The boat was nearly on them and about to pass directly by.

"Find the metal key and turn it. If it doesn't work one way, twist it the other way," said Bryce.

Again Noah tried, but failed. The boat was sliding past them.

"Turn the boat around and come back again. Just keep trying."

"Shame he can't just toss a line to us. It would just pull us into the prop as the boat kept going," said Tom.

"Hey Noah, do you see a long red string by the instruments?" asked Sal.

"Yes," he replied.

"Can you grab it and show it to me?"

Bryce grinned and gave Sal's shoulder a squeeze. "Brilliant."

Noah's head ducked down again, and then the engine abruptly died. Noah held his arm out, holding a red string attached to the kill switch.

Bryce and Julio swam toward the boat and reached it quickly. They pulled down the swim ladder and quickly climbed back aboard. In a few minutes, they had everyone back on board and breathed a collective sigh of relief.

"Noah, you were amazing. Thank you for saving us," said Bryce, hugging his son tightly.

"So I did a good job? I was so scared."

"You were perfect. Way better than any of us did, that's for sure," said Julio.

"This calls for a beer," said Tom, reaching into the cooler and grabbing three cans.

"Anyone mind calling it a morning? I say we head back to the dock and figure out what we're going to say to the ladies," said Bryce.

"Do we tell them about the one that got away, or the one that nearly did?" asked Tom.

"Exactly," said Bryce. He looked at the chart plotter and the wavy line drawn across it. He pulled out his phone and took a picture of their track. "Noah, these lines show where the boat has been today. I am saving a picture as a souvenir of when you became a superhero."

Bryce replaced the kill switch, fired up the engine, and pointed the boat back toward their island.

Chapter Twenty

The group arrived safely back at the dock and secured the dock lines. They passed the cooler up onto the dock and carried the food and drinks to the golf cart. Sal was chuckling to himself the entire time.

"I'll drive Sal and Noah up and bring in the fish. You two can think about what to say when we get up there," said Tom.

The other two watched the golf cart pull away and head back toward the villa.

Bryce turned to Julio and extended his right hand. "Hey, I wanted to offer a sincere thank you for the help back there. You helped keep everyone calm and were a big part of us coming back safely. I owe you."

Julio grinned and shook Bryce's hand forcefully. "Don't mention it. Please. Elisa will make fun of me for years. Seriously though, I was pretty scared there for a minute. I thought we could get back to shore but it looked like it would take some help from the Coasties to get Noah back."

"That was way too close of a call. I try to be more careful than that. We try to do whatever we can to stop bad things from happening to people, even risking our own safety in the process."

"Hey, you just summed up the military, amigo."

"I wouldn't compare the two. The risks I take are drastically different than the ones you guys do."

"The concepts are the same, just a different scale I guess."

"We'd better get going. I need to control the narrative before Noah brags about saving our sorry butts."

Bryce and Julio began walking up the path toward the house in silence.

Julio spoke first. "You know, Elisa really does like you guys. She'll never tell you, but she tells me how much better your group is than the last hospital she worked at."

"Really? I mean I'm sure we are, but she actually said that?" said Bryce.

"All the time. Don't worry, she never compliments me either. She just expects perfection out of everyone around her. Where she comes from there is no praise from doing your job. Only punishment for failure."

"Now she's sounding like an ER doctor. People like to give us a hard time for ordering CT scans on everyone but I've never once been given an award for limiting at patient's exposure to radiation. But when I miss something important, here comes the lawsuit."

"I'm glad that one with Kent is over with. She was pretty pissed off about it. Oh, and the donut move Tom pulled? Do you have any idea how hard it was to not laugh when she was telling me the story? She was so mad and all I wanted to do was bust out laughing. I need to tell him about it."

"That case about cost me my marriage and my life," said Bryce. *And ultimately Clay's as well.*

They arrived back at the villa and walked in to a flurry of conversations. Noah was standing on a chair with his hand on his forehead like he was searching for something.

He saw Bryce and pointed at him. "There! I see them again!" He turned and looked at his mom. "Then once I saw them I turned the boat and went over to pick them up. I had to turn off the engine so I didn't chop them up with the motor." To accent the point he made quick chopping movements with his hands. "Then, we came back home. Dad said I'm a superhero now!" As he finished the last sentence he jumped off the chair and ran toward the couch, launching himself face first onto the couch in full extension.

Tom was standing behind Val and mouthed the word 'sorry' to Bryce.

Val turned to look at Bryce with raised eyebrows. "Is that so? You left my son alone in the middle of the ocean on a boat that was in gear?"

"That did happen, but it's not like we intended to do it. We caught this huge marlin and while trying to get it to the boat we all sorta fell in."

"Every one of you?"

"Except me Mom," said Noah.

"True, Noah stayed on the boat. Then he did come and rescue us. But we had a plan to get him back. We just had to swim to shore first."

"And what about poor Sal? He could have drowned. Did he even have a life jacket on?"

"No I didn't. But that's my fault. I could have thought about that on my own but I didn't plan on getting in the water." Sal stood up and faced the room. "Look, accidents happen. No one was hurt and everyone learned something. And because of that, I can tell you that it was the most alive I have felt since the stroke. I have missed that feeling every day over the last few years. The camaraderie. Friends who let me reel in a huge fish. Being pulled into the ocean by a marlin."

His voice cracked as he tried to keep his composure. "If we could guarantee no one would get hurt, I would do that every day for the rest of my life. I forgot I was disabled. All I could focus on was getting that fish on board, and then figuring out a plan to get back on the boat. You guys gave me that, and I'm eternally grateful."

Jackie stood up and hugged him from behind.

"Lunch is ready," called a voice from the kitchen. "Conch salad, Johnny cake, and fresh fruit." The chef assigned to their villa laid out a beautiful spread of local cuisine on the counter along with plates and silverware.

"Oh that sounds delicious," said Elisa. "Let's focus on the good things today. You caught a mahi mahi, everyone came back safe, and you have another story to tell."

Tom held up his phone. "And a video to watch. I recorded the start of it and then dropped my phone when I fell over. It landed with the camera up and then out of nowhere Bryce flies in, hits the rail, and falls over. I'm warning you, don't watch this with anything in your mouth. It's freaking hilarious."

The group sat around the table and passed Tom's phone around while they ate. By the end of the meal the tension had eased and it was time to enjoy the afternoon.

"Can we go explore the other islands now?" asked Noah.

"You want to get back on the boat right away again?" asked Val.

"Sure, why not? And can I drive?"

Val and Bryce each said "no" at the same time, and both then followed up with "I'm driving."

Bryce saw the expression on Val's face and sighed. "Fine, you drive." He looked around the room. "Anyone else want to head out with us?"

"That's like the Donner Party survivors asking if anyone wanted to join them on next year's trip," said Peter. "Just joking, I'll join you guys. I feel bad for having missed out earlier. It's unlikely all five of us would have fallen in."

"Well then, let's roll. We still have the drink coolers packed. Noah grab the metal detector if you want to search for some treasure," said Bryce.

"I'll catch up, I need to grab something from my room," said Peter.

"What, sunblock?" asked Elisa, laughing.

Chapter Twenty-One

Val pulled the boat out of the slip and headed for the closest uninhabited island. The boat handled the smaller waves on the lee side of the island very well.

"It's sure getting windy," she said. "Let's stay close and make this our last trip until the storm has passed."

She pulled the boat as close to shore as she felt comfortable with. The shallow draft of the boat came in handy as Bryce jumped off the bow and landed in knee-deep water. He carried the anchor out a ways and set it manually, before the rest unloaded and headed ashore.

Peter turned on the metal detector for Noah and used his watch as an example of what he would hear if it found something. Noah thanked him and ran off, sweeping it back and forth ahead of him.

"Do you think he'll find anything?" asked Bryce.

Peter reached into his pocket and pulled out several gold coins. He tossed one to Bryce. "I guarantee it."

"You brought treasure for him to find? That is so thoughtful of you, Peter. Thank you so much," said Val.

"They're just dollar coins, but he'll be pretty stoked when he finds them."

Peter piled several coins together and buried them in a few inches of water. He then spread several more in random places around the larger stack. Bryce tossed the other coin down and kicked some sand over it, smoothing away the evidence of sand manipulation.

Hannah began digging shallow holes in the sand while singing a song. Val put her bag down and spread out the towels before tossing a bottle of aloe to Bryce. She pointed at Peter and said, "A bet's a bet."

Are you kidding me? I don't want to do this. Bryce walked over to Peter and flipped open the top. He squired some lotion onto Peter's back, triggering him to jump forward and turn around.

"Hey, that's cold! What are you doing?"

"I lost a bet with Val and now I have to put aloe on you," said Bryce, his hands spread out in front of him.

"Uh, you don't. Besides, it's cloudy out today. Thanks though." He wiped the block off his shoulder with the palm of his hand and then spread it around his chest and abs.

"And leave me out of your wagers. It's sort of weird."

"Sorry, the bet just sort of came out of my mouth when we were racing toward the beach last night."

"It's fine, but I can put lotion on myself." He looked down at the outline of his phone on his abdomen. "Well, at least I know how to."

"Check out that yacht," said Bryce. "Wouldn't you love to be on that in this water?" He pointed at a large boat moving up the channel. "How long do you think it is?"

"Long enough that I can't afford it," said Peter.

Val laughed at husband. "Bryce, I don't get you sometimes. We used to be on trips to the beach and you'd dream about being on all the boats you saw offshore. So we got certified to captain our own bareboat sailing charters and then you spent the weeks dreaming of being on the beaches we saw.

Now here we are on a beach and you're back to dreaming of boats again."

"Yeah, yeah, yeah. The point is we keep dreaming and then making them reality. See if you can read the name on the back. Most of those boats are available for charter and we can get all the information that way."

The three stood and stared at the boat, shielding their eyes to get a better view. Bryce took out his phone and zoomed in with the camera, trying to get a picture of the transom.

"Oh, that's convenient," said Val. "They're turning away from us to give you a better look at the name."

"Just a few more miles and we'll be there," said Tony. "This storm is really kicking things up. We should get anchored before it gets too nasty or we'll really be in a tough spot. The last thing I want to do is change anchorages in a tropical storm."

"I think this area is the prettiest we've seen yet. I keep saying that at every stop, but I don't see how the water can get any better," said Emily.

"Look over there," said Tony, pointing off the port bow. "Is that Bryce and his family?"

Emily picked up the binoculars and found them standing on the shore. "Sure is. And Peter is with them. Should we just go grab him now? We could be gone before the storm hits."

"Maybe. What do you think? We can't get very close because of how shallow that water is." He paused for a moment, pondering their options. "I guess we could take the jet ski in. We'd have to tie him up to do that."

"You have a gun. There's no chance they have a weapon out there. We could put on hats and other clothes and disguise ourselves so they don't know it's us until it's too late."

Tony leaned back in the captain's seat and pondered the situation. "What the hell, let's do it. Let me anchor this thing and we'll run in on the jet ski. We'll have to disable their radio and take their phone. I don't want them calling for help before we're long gone."

"What about the boat?" asked Emily.

"Good call. We'll have to take the key, too. But there's the issue with Valerie and the kids. There's a storm coming and they'll be trapped on the island," said Emily.

"Not a problem. The resort will watch for the boat to return by evening and go out looking for it when they don't show up. They'll only be there a few hours."

"Val was some swimming phenom in college. Do you think she could just swim back?" asked Emily.

"I suppose she could, since the tide is going out now. But would you leave two young children with Peter on an island for a few hours with a storm approaching?"

Tony turned the boat to point into the wind and crossed the channel into shallow water. He dropped the anchor and put the transmission in reverse to set it in the sand. Emily went below to grab large floppy hats and large sunglasses as disguise.

Tony turned to open the rear door and prepare the jet ski when he paused, turned, and ducked down. "Hang on, they're staring right at us. It looks like Bryce has his camera out. I think we're busted."

"There's no way they recognized us through tinted glass at this distance. We're fine. But maybe we shouldn't make a run at them if they're already interested in who is on the boat. They could get to a radio or their phone before we were close enough to stop them."

"Yeah, I guess you're right. Damn. This would have been a lot easier. He's going to love the name of the boat if he can make it out from that distance."

Small raindrops began hitting the windows on the Cantius and a gust of wind twisted the boat on the anchor.

"The storm is here. We need to move behind Swan Cay and get into position before the waves get too bad."

Chapter Twenty-Two

Bryce snapped a picture with his phone and then spread his fingers out to zoom in on the image. "No way. Guess what the name of this boat is?"

"What?" asked Val.

"Emergent Sea Medicine. How cool is that?"

A loud beep sounded behind them, followed shortly by an excited boy's voice. "Dad, I found something!" said Noah.

"Oh yeah? What is it?"

"I don't know. It just beeped here." Noah moved the large round disc back and forth several more times until it beeped repeatedly over the same spot. He tossed the detector to the side and fell down onto his knees, digging quickly at the sand with his fingers.

"Be careful Noah, you don't know what's under there. It could be sharp," said Val.

He dug slowly and deliberately until his fingers brushed past a shiny object. "There!" He picked it up and looked at it closely. "It's a gold coin! I found treasure!"

Hannah stopped digging and came over to see what her brother had found. He stuck it in her face, too close to focus on, before running over to his parents.

"Look at it!"

"That's outstanding Noah, you're having quite the day," said his dad.

"If there's one, there may be another one close by. Maybe a pirate had a hole in his pocket."

"You're right, Mr. Thrasher, thanks!" Noah handed his dad the coin and picked up the metal detector. He started searching again in the same area. In a few minutes, he had dug out several more coins and even let Hannah pull one out.

"Uh oh, here comes the rain. See it coming on the water," said Bryce, pointing to the southeast. "Looks like it got here a bit early. We'd better get our stuff and head back to the house. I think we're done exploring until after the storm passes."

Thirty seconds later, they were scurrying faster to collect their gear and stow it back on the boat. The gentle sprinkle had turned into a tropical downpour. Bryce fired up the engine and stepped aside to let Val drive back, but she was busy putting life jackets on kids.

"Just go. And please stay on the boat this time."

He obeyed and brought the boat up on plane for the quick trip back to the dock. Everyone was crouched behind the small windshield under the hard top for protection. As soon as he pulled the boat into the slip, the rain stopped.

"Of course it does," said Bryce, looking up at the sky. "But whatever, let's just call it a day." He reached into his pocket and handed the coins to Noah. "Everyone get on the golf cart and we'll drive back up."

"I'll meet you there!" said Noah, running up toward the house. His right hand held out in front of him, clutching his prize as he went.

"That was such a good idea. We should do something like that every trip," said Bryce.

The trio drove back toward the house and parked the cart in its shed behind the main villa.

"Did you see the pool? All the cushions are gone," said Val.

"And they put up storm shutters on most of the windows," added Peter.

Once inside the villa, conversations centered on the storm.

Julio met Bryce near the front door. "Man, this storm is picking up. The staff made us a quick dinner and then they all took off. Said they'll be back tomorrow, assuming the storm is through."

"Okay, let's get some food in and try to track down Edward. Should we evacuate or shelter in place?"

Chapter Twenty-Three

Edward pounded on the door to the main villa and then opened it quickly. A rush of wind came in with him and blew a few napkins off the table. He pulled the door closed behind him and turned to face the table, where all the heads were already facing him.

"Everyone, I have bad news regarding the weather. The storm has officially been upgraded to a category one hurricane."

A chorus of groans and mumbling rose from the group in unison. The kids looked at their parents and followed with similar responses.

"Now, there is no reason to panic. They have designed our facilities here for inclement weather. The structures are built to withstand a category five storm and the utilities are all buried to ensure no interruption in power, so long as the generator is functioning. We have enough fuel on hand to last for several weeks. This storm is moving quickly and should only affect the island for about a day. After that, we'll have the grounds crew here and will have the place in shape for you to enjoy the rest of your stay."

"Do you think it would be better if we'd evacuate before the storm?" asked Tom.

"I'm afraid that's not possible. The airports shut down a few hours ago. We do not have boats equipped for the expected sea state, either. I can assure you, this resort is one of the safest places to be at the moment. As your local guide, I will stay here with you to offer any assistance needed during the storm."

"What about your family? Where are they staying?" asked Valerie.

"They are at our home a few miles away. My wife understands the necessity of my job and we have made arrangements for someone to check in on them. I have sent the rest of the staff home to prepare their own homes for the storm."

Bryce looked around the room and saw the individual families sitting together, concerned looks on faces and hands clasped in mutual support. He shook his head and stood up.

"Edward, you've been great to us here so far. But there's no reason for you to stay on the island. You should be with your family. We have everything that we need and we're all very capable of handling whatever might come up."

Edward clapped his hands together in front of his chest and scanned the room. "Are you certain? My wife would be relieved if I were home, but I don't want to abandon my guests if you need me."

"We insist. But you'd better ship out quickly, it will not get any calmer out there. Do you have a boat?" said Julio.

"No, I sent the staff away in our company vessel. I will need to borrow one of yours, if that's permissible."

"Dude, we will not be using them. Looking out there now, I'd probably puke within ten minutes of riding through those waves," said Peter. "We'll be hunkered down in the air conditioning, drinking and playing games." He stood up and tapped Julio on the shoulder. "Let's go help him bust out of here."

Edward exited the building with Peter and Julio trailing him. They walked down the path toward the dock, passing the generator along the way. Edward pointed to it and said, "If power goes out, you may need to restart the generator. It should kick back on automatically, but there's a breaker you may need to reset if it does not."

They reached the boat dock and helped Edward prepare for departure.

"You may want to wear a life jacket on this trip, just in case," said Julio.

"Good idea, thank you. The cell phones will probably go down at some point, but you should be able to use the VHF as long as you have power. Not that anyone can make it out in a hurricane, but you can at least talk. I'll be back as soon as conditions allow. Good luck!"

He started the engine and idled it up to ensure it was running well. Peter and Julio removed the dock lines and tossed them into the boat as Edward put the throttle into reverse and backed out of the slip. He gave a last wave before turning the bow toward home and accelerating the boat up onto plane. He passed within fifty yards of the large motor yacht anchored offshore.

"Nice dude, I hope he gets home okay," said Peter. "What do you think about that other boat out there? Strange that they haven't sought shelter from the storm."

"I know. But really, where would it go? There are a few marinas back on Great Exuma and some in Nassau, but those are probably full already. The bottom is pure sand here. As long as their anchor holds, I think they'll be fine."

"Should we offer to have them crash with us during the storm?"

"That's actually not a bad idea. I'll try to reach them on the VHF." Julio stepped onto one of the remaining boats and turned on the radio. "Swan Cay to motor yacht anchored in our lee, Swan Cay to motor yacht anchored in our lee." He released the transmit button and waited for a response.

"Who is that on the radio? I don't recognize the voice," said Emily from the cockpit on board the Cantius.

Tony picked up the binoculars and looked through the windshield. "I don't know, some buff looking skinny guy. But he's standing next to Peter. No way we can respond. What if they recognize our voice?"

"Then let's just sit here and pretend we didn't hear them. We'll be seeing them soon enough," said Emily.

"Did someone in there pick up binoculars and look at us?" asked Peter.

"I think so. That's odd. They didn't respond on the radio, but certainly moved to look at us when we reached out. Maybe they don't speak English."

"They've been parked there a while. Seems strange that we haven't seen them yet."

Julio turned and looked at Peter. "If you had a two-million-dollar yacht, would you spend your days meeting the neighbors?"

"No, but I also wouldn't park it off someone's inhabited island, either."

"So, what do you want to do? We could go out there on this boat and ask them directly," said Julio.

"I say we just leave it alone. A boat like that is going to have plenty of communication equipment and access to weather forecasts. They know what is coming. If they won't talk to us on the radio, I doubt they'd talk to us in person," said Peter.

Julio tried calling on the VHF one more time and again received no response. He hung the radio back in its cradle and stepped up off the boat. Peter helped him hang the rest of the fenders between the boat and the dock, as well as make sure the dock lines had enough slack to account for a storm surge should it occur.

The two walked back along the stone path toward the main building. Julio looked up at the sky and said, "Man, this sky reminds of me of growing up in Miami. We'd get hurricanes all the time. Always so much fun to hit the beach right before it landed. Best waves you'd ever see."

"What about after? Was it still pretty nuts?" asked Peter.

"Nah, the energy is all out in front of a hurricane. It calms down pretty quickly afterward. But then there's often so much debris in the water. You don't want to get hit with a nail on a board coming at you in a wave."

They reached the main house and opened the door right as the rain began to fall.

"Welcome back, guys. Did Edward make it out okay?" asked Tom Sharpe.

"Yeah, flew out of here in a hurry. He's probably tied up at home already. He mentioned to watch out for the generator. Said it should auto restart, but there's a breaker that sometimes needs to be reset," said Peter.

"Well, dinner is in the oven. Should be ready in about thirty minutes. We're starting another game of Texas hold 'em. Do you want to be dealt in?" asked Bryce.

"Yes," said Julio and Peter in unison. They grabbed beer from the fridge and passed them out to those around the table. The kids were sitting on the couch, engrossed in videos on their various devices.

Valerie popped her beer open and held it up. "Here's to a fun storm party, and then back to enjoying the rest of our trip."

The group joined her in the toast and talk amongst themselves as stacks of chips were counted and distributed.

Chapter Twenty-Four

"Do you think they have any idea who we are?" asked Tony.

"No, there's no way. We're just a luxury yacht killing some time in the Bahamas." Emily looked out from the boat at the rising swell. Many of the waves now had white caps on them. "Do you think this boat will be fine in the storm?"

"Absolutely. It's built for open ocean passages. This is nothing. We've had the anchor set all day and we haven't moved an inch." As he said that, a wave struck the boat, making him lose his footing. He threw an arm behind him and grabbed onto the counter for support.

Emily raised her eyebrows and looked back at him. "You're sure?"

Tony nodded. "Yeah, you've seen the size of that anchor, right? We will not move. Let's get our bags ready. I want to head ashore as soon as it gets dark. No sense waiting for it to get rougher than it already is."

Emily put down her glass and turned toward the cabin. She paused and grabbed her lower abdomen, wincing. *Damn it, this is not getting better.*

"You okay?"

She breathed shallowly for a few moments while nodding her head up and down. "I think I may have appendicitis. We need to get this over with and me to a hospital. I started taking antibiotics yesterday, but it's still getting worse. I'll be okay for another day or two, but we really need to be in Nassau or the Dominican by then."

"Talk about bad timing. Do you want to stay on the boat and let me handle things on shore? I'll have the element of surprise and the only gun on the island."

"Maybe. But I really want to be there. I want to see the look on Peter's face when we march his buddy out at gunpoint. But I really do feel like crap." She glanced at the floor before returning her gaze to his. "Do you think you can handle it on your own? I'm hoping the antibiotics kick in and I'll start feeling better tomorrow. Right now spending a few hours lying flat on my back sounds amazing."

"I can handle all of them. You stay here. I'll bring our prize back when the storm calms down and we can be the first boat out. There's a deep-water channel on the north end of the island. Once we clear the sandbar, it'll be clear sailing. We can dump Bryce and then head straight to a hospital with our new identities."

Emily followed Tony down into their cab. The king-sized bed sat under a long horizontal window. Raindrops pelted the plexiglass in a rhythmic pattern. Quicker as the gust arrived, slower as the wind calmed for a moment before preparing for the next rush.

Tony laid out several items on the bed and then began tucking them into a small dry bag. A roll of duct tape, a knife, a beach towel and finally a black handgun, along with a spare magazine and holster.

"I think thirty-two rounds should be enough, don't you think?" he asked Emily, grinning.

"But we're only going to kill Bryce, right? As much as I hate Peter, I think he's been through enough. This Bryce thing is all for you. Just leave the women and kids alone, will you?"

Tony shook his head as he packed the items into the bag and closed it tightly. While leaning down to pick up the bag, he looked up at Emily. "I'm not a monster. I don't hurt people for fun. Bryce literally killed me and left me with impulse control and memory problems. I'll never be the same. Why should he be able to lead a perfect life with his perfect family? I'm just balancing out the universe. Then we can be free together. To start over. To start a family if we want." He pulled the bag over his head and tightened the strap, securing the bag to his chest. "I'm doing this for us."

Emily smiled at him and reached out to squeeze his hand. "Be careful. I'll be here waiting for you." *And continuing my search for the private keys and access to a hundred million dollars.*

"I'll have the portable VHF radio. If you need me, my call sign is El Diablo. I don't want to use our names. I'll call you La Niña."

Tony squeezed her hand and kissed it before walking up the stairs and through the salon to the rear door. He grabbed a baseball hat and pulled it low over his head. Looking out the window, he saw huge white cap waves and torrential rain. Suddenly, the shore seemed a lot further than a few hundred yards. He opened the door and walked onto the deck, leaning hard against the wind. Opening a locker, he removed a swim mask and life jacket before spinning his baseball hat around backward and pulling the swim mask on. He pulled the life jacket over the dry bag and clipped it in place. Next, he released the clamps that held the jet ski on its cradle on the swim platform. He held down the button to lower the platform and soon the jet ski was floating, buffeted by the wave action. Once the jet ski was clear of the cradle, he released the button and grabbed the rope connected to the metal eye on the bow of the watercraft.

The boat had swung on the anchor to face the wind coming from the west, placing the stern of the boat closer to shore. Tony pulled the bow line until the jet ski was close enough and then stepped on. He fired up the engine and then unclipped the line.

As soon as he pulled forward, a massive wave struck the side of the craft and nearly flipped him off. He had expected the impact, though, and gave the craft full throttle, which allowed him to steer into the wave and stay upright. He pointed toward the sandy beach and tried to time bursts of throttle with the back side of the waves. After a few slow, agonizing minutes, he was close enough to consider how he was going to land.

Tony waited for a wave to approach and then gunned the throttle, riding the wave onto the shore, using the momentum of the jet ski and the wave power to push the jet ski up onto shore. He hopped off and pulled it a few feet further to keep it out of the waves. He reached into the forward locker and removed a small anchor, which he dug into the ground as far from the water as the rope would allow.

Tony turned back towards the boat but could barely make it out through the large waves and blowing spray. He removed the swim mask and life jacket and clipped them to the jet ski. He watched for a few minutes to ensure that it wasn't going to get washed away, and then made his way up the stone path toward the main villa.

Chapter Twenty-Five

"Mom, can you make us another smoothie?" yelled Noah from his corner position on the couch.

Valerie excused herself from the poker table and walked over to Noah, sitting down next to him.

"What are you watching?" she asked.

"Big Hero 6. It's the one with Dad in it."

"What do you mean? Your dad's not in this movie."

"Yes, he is. He always says he doesn't get to decide anything anymore in the hospital. He says the government has turned him into a robot and tells him how he's supposed to help people. That's exactly what Baymax does."

Valerie laughed at her son's logic. "You know, you may be on to something. Plus, he sorta looks a bit like Baymax too, doesn't he?"

Noah smiled back at his mother, but refused to answer the loaded question. "Hannah and I were wondering if you could make us another smoothie."

"Of course. Mango again?" she asked.

"Yep!" said Noah as he handed over an empty glass.

Valerie rubbed his leg and headed toward the kitchen. She paused at the poker game and asked, "I'm making mango smoothies. Anyone interested in an adult version?"

The rising wind and rain were no match for the resounding chorus of the group. "Yes!" She quickly counted seven more drinks to be made, everyone except Bryce. She reached into the fridge and grabbed a Diet Coke, dropping that off in front of Bryce before getting down to the mango daiquiri business.

Val counted backward in her head. It had been nearly a year since Bryce had touched alcohol. The last time almost ended his life during an episode of severe depression brought on by an onslaught of struggles that have since improved. Oddly enough, it was his severe intoxication that both led him to consider suicide and also stopped him from being successful as he passed out before taking the pills. Through ongoing counseling at church and Val's support, he was doing much better.

Bryce caught Val's eye as she was preparing the blender and gave her a wink.

Emily watched Tony's jet ski move slowly toward shore, smashing through waves as it went. The force of the impacts slammed his body in every direction, but his strength allowed him to hang on. When he had beached the craft and secured the anchor, she got out of bed and resumed her search.

Tony stepped off the path and into the vegetation as he approached the main house. Where are you, super doc? He found a dark window and snuck a quick glance through. The view was through a small bathroom, but he could see most of the group sitting around a table, enjoying cards and frozen drinks. *Go ahead, drink up. It will only make this easier.*

"Where did you hide those private keys? There's no way you can remember sixty-four random letters. You can barely remember your name some days," she said, scanning the room. Her eyes stopped on a shelf containing several nautical-themed books. She grabbed the first one. *Passage Making*, by Tom Cunliffe. She flipped through the book but found no list of access codes. She examined the rest of the books, finding nothing but some highlighted text in a few of them. *Come on, where are they? I've searched nearly the entire boat while you have been playing underwater.*

She leaned forward to replace the last book on the shelf when a sudden and profound sense of nausea washed over her. Her hand went to her mouth as she looked around for something to vomit into. Finding nothing, she jumped out of bed and moved toward the stairs.

As soon as she was vertical, her vision started to fade. Sounds became muted and time seemed to slow. *I'm going to pass out, but why?* Emily stumbled backward toward the bed and, with the help of a well-timed wave, was able to fall into bed as she passed out.

Tony backed away from the window and started walking toward the next villa. He was somewhat protected from the wind, but had to keep his hat pulled low because of the leaves and other debris flying around. Arriving at the villa, he found several lights on but no sign that anyone was inside. He waited a few minutes to be sure and then knocked loudly. Hearing no response, he pounded more aggressively on the door. After a minute of waiting, he opened the door and stepped inside.

He quickly scanned the rooms, confirming that no one was inside. Once satisfied, he removed the dry bag and opened it on the long table in the dining room. He dried his hands on the towel and then laid the gun and spare magazine on it. While ensuring the handgun had a round in the chamber, he said, "Okay Bryce, are you going to be a man and just come with me? Or are you going to put your family in danger by trying to avoid the inevitable?"

Confident the gun was loaded and ready to fire, he placed it in the holster and tucked it inside the waistband of his shorts. He put the rest of the items back in the dry bag and slung it over his shoulder, before turning and walking toward the front door.

Chapter Twenty-Six

"Pair of aces," said Bryce, flipping over one of his hole cards. "Can anyone beat that?"

Julio, Sal, Peter, Tom, and Val all groaned and tossed their cards onto the table. Bryce leaned in to retrieve the pot, but instead received a slap on the arm from his right side.

"Back off ER, I have two pair," said Elisa. She flipped her hole cards onto the table, showing an ace and an eight. "Aces and eights, thank you very much." She stood up and scraped the pile of chips from the center of the table over toward her seat.

"Aces and eights? The Dead Man's Hand?" said Tom. "How can you play a hand like that in the middle of a hurricane? That's like saying 'it sure is slow tonight' during an ER shift. You just don't do it."

Elisa looked up at Tom over her recently acquired pile of chips. "What, so I should have just folded?"

"No, you could have split the pot with Bryce. Your top five cards would have been the same if you didn't use your other hole card."

"Luck and superstition were invented by people not talented enough to control their own outcomes. When an opportunity presents itself, those with the ability to succeed, do," said Elisa, stacking her chips into orderly piles. "When you miss a shot it's just bad luck now instead of a failure. I don't rely on luck. I use ability."

"So you don't think there's anything to the superstition that the crazy people come out on full moons? You take trauma call, you know what a warm summer weekend night with a full moon means."

"Yeah, there is truth to that. I'll agree with you there. But it is not due to superstition. It's just fact. People are nuts, and their belief in superstition allows them to blame their behavior on something stupid like the phase of moon. It's an excuse, not a cause. I also notice it's much slower when the weather is bad. No one seems to get appendicitis when it's sleeting."

Tom's laugh broke the awkward tension at the table. "Now that is true. I heard someone say that smoking is better than sex. I asked what he meant and he said it dawned on him while he was driving into work in a sleet storm. He passed numerous people standing outside in the sleet smoking, but didn't see a single person outside having sex in it."

The table nodded in agreement at the wisdom shared by Tom. Everyone except Bryce. "That's not entirely true. I seem to recall one wintry evening back in residency when–".

"Shut up Bryce," said Val, laughing. "I haven't had enough rum for that story. And besides, the kids are here."

Peter, Sal, Tom and Julio turned to look at Bryce with envious smiles on their faces. Peter said what everyone was thinking. "Again Bryce, why do we find ourselves envious of the guy with the worst luck of anyone we know?"

"Peter, it's not luck. That's invented by people not talented enough to control their own outcomes. It takes skill to have this many bad things happen."

"Hey Bryce, any stories of amorous encounters outside in the middle of a hurricane?" asked Julio.

"No. Not yet." He looked at Valerie and winked. "Ask me again tomorrow though."

"The answer will be the same, I promise," said Val, bringing another round of laughter from the table. "Who needs another drink?"

Every hand raised quickly, prompting Val to head back toward the kitchen to fire up the blender.

Julio leaned over and whispered something to Elisa that no one else could hear.

"Hell no. Stop getting ideas from the ER crew. I don't do sleet and I don't do hurricanes," she said. "Sunny and eighty degrees only."

The harsh noise of the blender drowned out conversation as Val began the next round of frozen drinks. The group expected a minute of noise like last time, but it cut out after ten seconds, along with every light in the building.

"Hey, what happened?" yelled Noah from in front of the bathroom door. "Who turned out the lights? I need to use the bathroom!"

"Looks like the power went out. Edward said the generator should kick back on automatically, let's give it a minute or two," said Julio.

Several people had turned the lights on their phones on used these to illuminate the room.

"If the power doesn't come back on, we may be forced to enjoy our drinks on the rocks instead of frozen," said Val.

"When I signed up for this free trip to paradise, I was promised frozen drinks. I want my money back," joked Peter.

Jackie looked at Sal and rubbed his leg. "Well, we need power for Sal's CPAP machine. We didn't think to bring a battery backup."

Bryce stood and walked over to check on Hannah. Her tablet was at full charge and she was still watching the shows downloaded on the device. "I'll be right back. I need to go reset the generator. I'll let you know if it's still storming."

Noah looked at his dad with a confused face. "Dad, I can hear the wind and rain on the window. Pretty sure it's still a hurricane."

Bryce smiled back at him. "Yeah, but we'll know for sure soon enough. It would be embarrassing if we were stuck in here and didn't know the storm had passed."

Peter stood and walked toward the door. "I'll go with you. Edward showed us where the circuit breaker is before he left. Shouldn't take more than a minute or two."

Julio stood to join them but Bryce held up his hand. "It's okay Julio, we got this. You and Tom can take the next trip out if needed. No sense all of us getting soaked right now."

Julio nodded and sat back down. "Sounds good man, be careful. Those winds are nasty. I'd put on some sort of eye protection so you don't catch a leaf in the eye."

Bryce and Peter each grabbed a snorkel mask from the tub of swim gear near the door and pulled it tight on their faces. "Be back soon," said Bryce with a distinctly nasal sound to his voice.

Peter opened the door and instantly a blast of warm moist air entered the room, along with sand and other debris. The two quickly exited and pulled the door shut behind them. They leaned in toward the wind and strode quickly toward the generator enclosure.

Peter reached the fenced-in generator first and lifted the metal latch to swing open the gate. Bryce stood behind him and caught the gate as the wind blasted it open. He slowly allowed it to open completely and then secured it with another latch in the open position. Then he joined Peter and they both entered the enclosure.

Peter located the sub panel on the side of the generator and opened the plastic door. Inside was a large single circuit breaker that was tripped. He rocked it further to off and then back to the on position. A few seconds later a few lights on the generator turned on and a starter engine whirred to life. Shortly thereafter, a deep grumble rose from the car-sized machine and soon they were bathed in bright light from an LED lamp mounted on a pole above the generator. Peter raised his hand toward Bryce who completed the high-five and then checked the fuel tank that was mounted on a concrete block slightly higher than the generator. The indicator read nearly full. He checked the supply line and ensured the shut-off valve was fully open. Satisfied, he turned and helped Peter shut the gate.

Once secured, they turned back toward the house but did not even take a first step. A large man stood in their way, holding a handgun pointed directly at Bryce.

Chapter Twenty-Seven

He yelled something at the pair but it was drowned out by the noise of the wind and rain. He repeated the command but this also wasn't heard over the noise of the storm.

He used his left hand and pointed at the two, then pointed toward the house.

Bryce put his hand in front of Peter's chest and shook his head no. *Hell no, we're not taking you back to our families.*

Bryce squinted through the mask to make out who was holding them at gunpoint. It was difficult to tell through the fogged lens, but he looked somewhat familiar. *Tony! How did he find us? How did he get to us in the middle of a hurricane?*

Tony's body language became more aggressive. He again pointed at the two and pointed toward the house. Bryce replied with a raised middle finger and shook his head no.

Tony fired the gun, hitting the ground between Bryce and Peter. The spent brass flying to the right, before the wind took over and blew it far to the left. He again pointed to the house, and this time the pair complied. Once Bryce and

Peter had passed him, Tony followed about ten feet behind. Far enough back to react if they turned to attack him.

Bryce's mind raced as he tried to devise a plan. *I can't let Tony take everyone hostage. He only wants me. How can I keep him away from the kids and everyone else?*

He was running out of time. They were almost back to the house. His eyes scanned back and forth across the path, looking for anything that he could use as a weapon. A short palm tree with long fronds was on the right, its leaves blown backward toward the house. At the base of the palm was a fist-sized white rock.

Bryce coughed loudly, causing Peter to glance to his right, just in time to see Bryce stumble and fall to the ground. He instinctively reached down to catch him, but his hands caught only air.

Tony stopped and pointed his gun at Bryce, yelling at him to get up. After a few seconds to collect himself, Bryce stood up, facing Peter, his left shoulder pointed toward Tony.

"Move!" screamed Tony, pointing at the house with the gun. As soon as the gun moved away from him, Bryce snapped his right arm up into a throwing position and launched the rock as hard as he could right at Tony's head.

Peter hadn't seen Bryce pick up the rock and was slow to react. But once Bryce had released the rock, he turned and raced toward Tony.

Bryce's aim was decent, but not perfect. The rock struck Tony on the side of his head, glancing off rather than delivering a direct blow. He stumbled backward and a step to the side, his arms flailing behind to steady himself. This gave Peter enough time to close within arm's length.

Tony recovered his balance and saw Peter nearly on him. He brought the gun up and fired without aiming, stopping Peter's advance.

Peter waited for the searing pain to set in after being shot, but it never materialized. He spun around and saw Bryce laying on the ground again, holding his left leg. Streaks of blood covered Bryce's hands and leg.

"You bastard, you shot him!" yelled Peter, glaring at Tony.

"Do you believe I'm serious now? Stop messing around and get your asses inside." He gestured toward Bryce. "Help him up."

Peter leaned down and helped him stand on his good leg. He leaned down to support Bryce's weight and helped him hop toward the house.

"I'm sorry Bryce, I was too slow. Let's get you inside and look at your leg."

Peter reached forward and opened the door. The crowd inside cheered their return, happy for the restoration of power. But the cheers ended quickly when Bryce hobbled through, holding his bloody leg. Silence turned to gasps and screams when Tony came through the door and slammed it shut.

"Everyone, stay right where you are. Hands on the table."

Chapter Twenty-Eight

"Bryce, what happened?" asked Valerie as she stood up quickly and took a step toward him.

"Stop!" screamed Tony. He pointed the gun at Valerie, who stopped where she was. Tony's appearance was made even more frightening by the blood dripping down his face from the wound the rock had inflicted.

"Mommy!" said Hannah. She jumped off the couch and ran toward her mother.

Tony turned and pointed the gun at her, his mouth open as if he was about to scream a command.

"Don't you dare point a gun at my kid, you bastard," said Bryce.

Tony turned to look at Bryce, the gun swinging around as his body shifted. Tony pointed the gun at Bryce's head and then looked back toward the rest of the group.

Sal had scooted forward on the couch and was leaning in front of Jackie.

"Looks like there's about ten people here. That means I have three bullets for each one of you. Bryce just took one that was meant for Peter while we were still outside. If you come at me, I'll shoot you. Understand?"

The room nodded in response.

"Who are you, and what do you want?" asked Julio.

"Who gives a shit who I am. What I want, is Bryce at the bottom of the ocean like I was; thanks to him. It didn't work out last time, but nothing can stop it this time. Once the storm has passed, I'm taking him back to my boat and we're leaving. Enjoy your last few hours with your friend."

Tony scanned the room, and then did again quickly. "Bryce, where's your son? Where is he hiding?"

"He didn't come on this trip. He came down with chicken pox so we left him at home with my parents," said Bryce, thinking quickly.

"Do you think I'm stupid? If you lie to me again, I'll add a hole to your right leg too."

"I'm not lying, he didn't come down," said Bryce, staring directly at Tony.

"That is your one free pass. I saw your family out exploring an island yesterday when I came up the channel. I know your son is here, so where is he?"

"Tony, leave our kids out of this. He's six. He can't do anything to harm you. Don't traumatize more people than you have to."

"Okay, whatever. We're just going to sit tight here until the storm passes. No one else will get hurt as long as you play nicely and follow my rules."

"What are the rules?" asked Tom.

"Sit down, shut up, and don't move," replied Tony.

Valerie hugged Hannah tightly and walked with her back toward the table. She sat down and pulled Hannah onto her lap. She placed her lips near Hannah's ear and whispered, "it's going to be okay, sweetie."

A silence settled over the room, interrupted only by the sound of rain and wind battering the side of the building. Everything else was quiet. Until the toilet flushed.

"Noah, run and hide!" screamed Bryce.

Tony whipped around and smashed Bryce in the face with the back of his hand, knocking him to the ground.

Tony turned back toward the group with the gun and slowly walked sideways toward the bathroom.

"Kid, come on out of there. Your mom needs you," he said. He took a few more steps toward the bathroom door that remained closed. "Noah, we really need you out here with the rest of your family." Tony listened for a moment but no sounds came from behind the door. "If you don't open the door I'm going to come in and get you. Don't make me do that."

Tony grabbed the handle of the door and pulled down hard, but the handle didn't move. "Kid, you have two choices. Either unlock the door and come out, or stand back because in ten seconds I'm going to kick the door down."

"Tony, don't do this," pleaded Bryce, who had raised up onto his knees with assistance from Peter.

"Time's up. Stand back," said Tony. He took a step back from the door and launched his right foot forward, striking the door just inside the handle.

Chapter Twenty-Nine

The expensive hardwood door had enough integrity to withstand the kick, but the frame did not. The strike plate ripped free and the door swung open. Tony recoiled from a blast of wind and sand coming from an open window next to the toilet. He kept his arm pointed at the kitchen table while he quickly scanned the shower and closet, finding them empty as well. After the quick search he closed the window and returned to the main area.

"Looks like whoever was in the bathroom is now out in a hurricane. Not a smart decision. He must take after you, Bryce." Tony pointed back toward the table. "Why don't you and Peter go have a seat?"

Bryce locked eyes with Valerie and tried to communicate telepathically. *It's okay, Noah is tough. He'll find a safe place to hide.*

Tony walked back toward the group and leaned against the kitchen counter. "Looks like we have a few hours to kill. So tell me, who is enjoying the vacation so far?"

No one replied to the taunt.

"I see. You'd rather wait it out in silence." Tony glanced around the kitchen and stopped when he saw the half full blender. "Frozen drinks? Nice. I think I will. Something to ease the headache I suddenly have after Bryce threw a rock at me." He poured the frozen slush into a glass and took a large drink before putting down the glass and making a face. "No alcohol? You guys suck at vacationing." He grabbed the bottle of rum and turned it upside down on top of the glass for a few seconds. He dropped a spoon in and mixed the rum into the drink before taking another swallow. "Now that is much better. Who doesn't love a nice mango daiquiri on a tropical island?"

Tom Sharpe cleared his throat and then said, "Tony, there is a first-aid kit under the kitchen sink. Can we use that to patch Bryce up a bit?"

"What's it matter? He'll be dead tomorrow," said Tony.

"Maybe. But seeing the wound is distressing his daughter. It's a simple thing that would help show her you're not a monster."

"A monster? Me?" His forehead creased as a confused look took over his face. "I wouldn't even be here if it wasn't for your buddy Bryce. He had to pick a fight with me last year that led to me drowning. Then the world calls him a hero for saving my life. My dad basically cut me off of any future with his company because I'm a little slower than I used to be. He treats me like some special needs kid. I'm no monster." He paused and took a drink of mango daiquiri. "But I'm no pariah either. Once Bryce is dead, the universe will be balanced out and I can move forward with my plans. I still control the crypto accounts and will be welcomed as a king in Central America."

"What about your queen? Where's Emily?" asked Peter.

"Emily? She left me a few weeks ago. She's probably lying out on some beach getting ready to ruin the life of some other guy. What a black widow."

Peter's attempt to keep a straight face failed, and a quick laugh escaped.

"Oh, it's funny she left me tough guy?" asked Tony.

"No, it's not funny. But it's the best thing that ever happened to me. I'm sure you'll see it in time also. That is one crazy lunatic. Anyone who is stupid enough to stay with her deserves everything she brings into their life. It's a shame you're throwing away your second chance by showing up here."

Tony pointed the gun directly at Peter. "Just because she left me, doesn't mean I don't have feelings for her. Say something like that again and you'll beat Bryce to Heaven."

Peter raised his hands up, palms facing Tony. "Hey, relax man. I was just trying to make you feel better."

Tony lowered the gun. "Just because we're not together doesn't mean I don't have feelings for her. You talk pretty tough for a man not holding a gun."

"Like I said, I'm sorry man."

"Do you honestly not have feelings for her anymore? After as long as you two were together?"

"She helped kidnap me and left me handcuffed to a bed for a day. I had underwear stuffed in my mouth and I pissed into a cup. No, I have no feelings for her after that. Well, at least not positive ones."

Elisa's eyes widened and she glanced toward her husband Julio. She mouthed words that looked like 'what the fudge?'

"Tony, can we please have the first aid kit?" said Valerie. "It's right there under the sink."

Tony mumbled something unintelligible while he opened the cabinet door and retrieved the kit. He set it on the counter and dumped out the contents, removing the scissors and a scalpel, before repacking and throwing the kit to Tom. He kept a piece of gauze and a strip of tape for himself.

"Have at it. And make sure you tell the authorities I helped treat Bryce's wound."

"That you caused," added Bryce.

"Like you're one to talk. You caused me to drown and then became a hero for saving me. Am I a hero now for letting them take care of your wound?" He laughed before allowing anyone a chance to respond.

"Bryce, your rock trick didn't help my head injury. I have this killer headache now. Gonna take a bit more rum to get through it, I think." He wiped the wound with a paper towel and then taped the gauze over it. He placed his baseball hat back on his head to hold the bandage in place.

Tony faced the group again. "Here's the deal. Anyone who needs the bathroom is going to do so with the door open. No more escaping. If you try to leave, I will shoot you. If you try to rush me, I shoot you. Understood?"

His question was answered by silence and universal glares of fury. Julio sat upright, gently rolling his head and shoulders. Elisa put her hand on his arm, which caused him to tighten that hand into a fist.

Noah heard his dad scream the warning and reacted immediately. They had practiced getting to safety when in public in case something ever happened, and he put that training into action now. He looked around the room quickly and ruled all potential hiding places as too easy to be found. A hiding spot can quickly become a trap.

He looked at the window and the darkness beyond it. He heard the wind blowing the rain into the glass and knew. I have to go outside. He ran to the window and opened it as far as he could. He turned back toward the door when he heard Tony gave a ten second warning, then climbed onto the toilet seat and leaned out into the storm. He saw the ground three feet below and continued to push his body through the window until his hands touched the wet, sandy ground. He pulled his feet forward and landed in a runner's stance. A loud crash followed him out the window as Tony kicked the door in. Noah used it as the starter's pistol and sprinted off into the storm.

Chapter Thirty

What happened? Where am I? Emily tried to gather herself together and determine where she was. She found herself in a bed that was violently rocking back and forth. She tried to sit up but a searing pain in her lower abdomen caused her hand to brace the area and her body to fall back onto the bed.

I must have passed out. "Tony," she called. After a few seconds, she yelled louder only to be met with more silence. *Oh no, he's on the island going after Bryce. Something's wrong with me, horribly wrong. I can't even sit up. I think my appendix ruptured and I'm septic. My blood pressure's too low and that's why I can't stand up.*

She crawled out of the bed and moved toward the bathroom. Once near the sink she reached up onto a shelf and found the pill bottle she was looking for. *Augmentin, don't fail me now.* She opened the lid and placed two tablets in her mouth, then swallowed them with a drink from a water bottle she kept next to the sink. *Bolus and titrate, isn't that what those idiots say? I'll start with a double dose and then maintain.*

She crawled up the stairs into the main cockpit and looked out the window. Large white cap waves continued to blow past the boat, rocking it in a quick, uneven pattern.

Most of the beach had disappeared as the wind blew the sea up onto the shore in an impressive tidal surge. The rain had slowed down a bit and she was able to make out the jet ski still safely resting on the beach, out of reach of the waves. At least for now.

Emily put her hand on her forehead and then formed a thin smile. *I don't even have a fever. I'm going to be fine. They usually don't operate on acute appendicitis in Europe anymore. As long as I stay on the antibiotics, I should be fine. But I need to stay hydrated.*

She slowly moved toward the fridge and removed a bottle of water. She searched through cabinets until she found the Gatorade powder. After pouring a few scoops into the water, she shook the bottle, leaned back in the chair and took a long satisfying drink. *I'll be fine. I don't need a degree to be able to diagnose and treat myself. Medical school would be a waste of time at this point anyway.* She allowed a smile to return to her face as she slumped into the chair and relaxed. Her eyes drifted down to the floor where she had crawled a few minutes before. She saw a wide streak of blood coming up the stairs, head toward the fridge, and end at her feet. She looked down and saw blood staining the front of her pants. *Oh shit.*

The Gatorade she had just drank made a stunning re-emergence as she vomited onto the floor and then passed out again.

"El Diablo, this is La Niña. Do you copy?" The communication was muted but audible throughout the room. Tony looked down at his jacket and reached inside to remove the radio. He turned the volume down and looked back at the group.

"She left you, eh El Diablo?" said Julio, his voice thick with sarcasm. "You can't use Spanish nicknames, especially when you're a villain. That's cultural appropriation and negative stereotyping."

"Screw you," said Tony as he walked toward the bathroom on the far side of the room. "Stay seated, I'll be right back."

They watched him put the radio up to his mouth and speak into it, but couldn't make out what was said. He put the radio up to his ear to listen without letting anyone else catch what was being said. Despite his increased distance, he still kept the gun aimed at the table.

"We need to come up with a plan, fast. I think he's serious about killing me," said Bryce in a whisper.

"No kidding, Bryce. That dude is crazy," said Elisa.

"We are going to have to rush him. Does anyone have any weapons on them?" asked Julio.

No one responded in the affirmative. "Then we're going to have to either make some, or rush him during a distraction."

"Hang on," said Bryce. "He's made it clear he's only here for me. If we do something and it causes someone else to get hurt, I will feel awful. This is my mess, let me just face it alone and if I get a chance to do something, I'll take it."

"No way Bryce. There's no guarantee he's only going to take you. And we're basically family. I won't sit by and watch you get hauled off to die," said Tom, to the immediate agreement of everyone at the table.

"I love you guys. I won't ask you to do this, but I won't say no either. He's a trained boxer and strong as a horse. He's going to be hard to fight," said Bryce.

"Then we don't fight fair. Who cares how we do it, we just have to win," said Julio. "I'm a soldier but I'll kick a guy in the balls if it will help me stay alive. There are no rules in battle when the other guy has a gun pointed at you."

"I owe Tony a few punches. I don't care if I'm the first to hit him, or the last. But I'm going to hit him," said Peter.

"Get in line," said Valerie from behind Hannah's head. "And he's lying. We saw Emily on the boat with him when they came up the channel."

Sal raised his crutch and jabbed it toward Tony. "Let's kick his ass."

"Stop talking!" roared Tony as he exited the bathroom. His tone quieted the conversation immediately. He walked quickly back into the kitchen but rather than leaning on the counter, he paced back and forth. He removed the baseball hat and threw it against the cabinets.

"New plan. Two of you are going to out to the boat and get Emily. She's sick."

"Go out on the water? In a hurricane? It's not possible," said Peter.

Tony lashed his left hand out and punched clean through a cabinet door, fortunately missing a shelf on the other side. "I don't care if it's impossible, someone is going to do it." He looked around the table and pointed at Peter and Julio. "You two. I have a jet ski down on the beach. Take it to the boat and bring her back. She's sick. She hasn't felt well for a few days and now has passed out twice. She's bleeding. You need to get her back here and fix whatever is wrong with her."

Valerie considered the selection of the two men and shook her head. "Tony, I should go instead of Julio. I'm the best swimmer here and there's a good chance we're going to be in the water. Peter's strength will help keep us on the jet ski, but if something happens, I'm the most likely to be able to swim her back to shore."

"Val, don't do this. Stay here with Hannah," pleaded Bryce.

"Getting Emily back here is the best thing we can do to keep you alive right now, Bryce." She lifted Hannah off her lap and gave her a hug. "Mommy's going to go out for a bit, I'll be back soon."

"Fine, but don't try anything. Remember I have your husband and daughter at gunpoint," said Tony. "Get her back here quickly."

"And then what?" asked Tom. "We are stranded on an island in the middle of a storm. We have no resources."

"Well you'd better come up with something. If she dies, so does one of you. Now get out there. The key is on the life jacket clipped to the handlebars. Take my swim mask, you'll need it to see." He tossed the swim mask to Peter.

"When you reach the boat, contact me on the radio. No names. Call me El Diablo."

Peter turned to the group and waved. "Wish us luck." He opened the door and waited for Val to exit before following her out into the storm.

"Now, the rest of you. Time to start figuring out what's wrong with Emily," said Tony.

"Great, this sounds like an oral boards question," said Tom. "Okay, how long has she been sick?"

"She wasn't really feeling sick, just having pain. It started a few days ago but has been getting worse every day. She thought it was appendicitis and started taking antibiotics. She was supposed to come ashore with me but we decided to let her stay on the boat because she was hurting a lot."

"Was she running a fever? Still eating and drinking?" asked Elisa, leaning forward in her seat.

"No, no fever that I know of. She still had an appetite."

"Anything else? Trauma? Eat something that may have been bad? Does she have any medical problems?" asked Tom.

"No, no injuries. She was healthy as could be. She knows a lot about medicine and is basically a doctor after working in the ER for years."

The doctors in the room shared a quick glance at that comment but were able to suppress their laughter.

"When was her last menstrual period?" asked Bryce.

"How the hell would I know that?" asked Tony. "But anyway, it doesn't matter because it just started. I think she may have been a few weeks late but she's bleeding now so it's not relevant."

"Unless she's having a miscarriage, or a ruptured ectopic pregnancy," said Bryce.

"What's a ruptured ectopic pregnancy?" asked Tony.

"It's where the baby never made it to the uterus before implanting, and grows on the ovary or the fallopian tube. These organs are not meant to hold a baby, and eventually it grows too large, ruptures through the organ, and causes potentially life-threatening bleeding. If that's what she has, she'll need surgery to fix it," said Elisa.

"How soon would she need surgery?" asked Tony.

"Immediately. Something that we cannot do here on an island during a hurricane."

"If that's what she has, then you'd better find a way to make it happen. You're not going to just let her die," he said. "Aren't you guys supposed to be miracle workers? You brought me back without any supplies, didn't you?"

"That was different," said Bryce. "You didn't need surgery, you just needed CPR. This can't be done."

"I hope you're wrong. If she dies, I guarantee the death count from this storm will be more than two," said Tony. He reached out and poured himself another drink. After taking a large swallow he picked up the radio. "La Niña, this is El Diablo. Rescue crew on their way to pick you up. We'll have you here in a few minutes. Let me know when they arrive."

"Tell them to hurry," came the crackling response.

Chapter Thirty-One

Peter and Val walked quickly away from the house, holding their hands up near their head to block the wind and debris. They were headed down the path toward the beach when Val pulled him to a stop. She leaned in close to be heard over the noise of the storm.

"My son is out here somewhere. I need to look for him before we get in the water."

Peter nodded his head in agreement. "Okay, I'll help. But we don't have a lot of time. Where do you want to start?"

Val answered by turning and running toward the other home on the island. *I bet he went to the other house to get out of the storm.*

They quickly approached the other building, staying well clear of the home with Tony and the rest of their party.

"The front door's open!" yelled Peter. He beat Valerie to the threshold and stepped inside. "Noah, are you in here? It's your dad's friend Peter."

Valerie rushed past Peter into the house and called out for Noah. She searched every room but did not find him. Surely he would have come out if he heard my voice. God, keep my boy safe.

"We really need to get down to the water. I think Tony is timing us and he's in communication with Emily. I'm sure Noah found somewhere safe to hide out."

Valerie's shoulders slumped. She spun around in a circle one more time calling for Noah without success. "Fine, let's do this."

They left the house at a jog and ran all the way to the shore. They could hear waves crashing on the beach as they approached. The dock was submerged but the remaining boat was still tied to it, the lines stretching tight between waves.

The storm surge had deposited a large amount of debris on the beach, slightly higher than the current water level. "Maybe the storm is moving past. The water seems like it's starting to recede. Maybe this is about over," said Peter.

Valerie glared at him. "My son is missing. My husband has been shot and is scheduled to die tomorrow, and everyone else is being held at gunpoint. This is not even close to over."

"You're right, sorry. That's not what I meant. We still have a chance to win this. I swear to you I'll do whatever I can do fix it. It's my fault Emily was brought into this mess."

Peter took the life jacket off the jet ski and handed it to Valerie. She pushed it back at him.

"I appreciate the chivalry, but you should put that on yourself. The waves and wind are pushing ashore. I can hold my breath for ninety seconds and swim for over an hour. How confident are you in your abilities?"

"I can move a lot of weight, but cardio is not my thing," said Peter as he clipped the life jacket on himself. He lifted the front of the jet ski and turned it toward the frothy sea. Valerie helped him push it to the edge of the water.

"This is going to be tricky. We can't get sideways to a breaking wave, and we can't hang out near shore very long. Why don't you get in front and start it up, then I'll jump on and sit behind you. I'll try to hold us both on."

Valerie agreed and took a few steps toward the watercraft before stopping. "I can't swim in all of this. I'm glad no one else is out here." She pulled the sweatshirt over her head and pulled off her shorts, revealing a matching set of lingerie. She looked at Peter and shrugged. "It was supposed to be a fun night, hadn't really planned on needing a swimsuit."

Peter's gaze quickly bounced off of Val's body and out into the surf toward the boat. "Once we get there, we'll need to secure it to the boat so we don't lose it." He walked toward the jet ski and dug the anchor out of the sand before dropping it in the storage compartment in front. The anchor line was still tied to the tow ring and he brought the other end over the front to the handlebars and handed it to Val. "Don't let this fall in the water, it might get sucked into the impeller."

He walked to the back and waited for a wave to break, sending a wall of water toward them that floated the jet ski briefly. "Ready?" he yelled.

After Val nodded, he pushed the craft forward into the water. She jumped on and fired up the engine. Peter used his legs to simultaneously push the craft forward and also jump on in a single move. Once he was up, Val pinched the throttle control, sending the jet ski forward into deeper water. Peter slid up behind her and grabbed onto the handlebars, trapping her like a child on an amusement park ride. A large wave lifted up the front and threatened to capsize them, but Val gunned the throttle and powered through it. Their destination was a hundred yards away.

Val leaned forward and held on as hard as she could. *It going to take a miracle to get her back to shore.*

Chapter Thirty-Two

"While they're getting Emily, you guys had better think about how you're going to save her," said Tony. He was sitting on a stool in the kitchen, rubbing his head. "Damn, this hurts. Anyone have anything for headache other than alcohol?"

"There is some Tylenol in the bathroom," said Jackie. "Want me to go get it? I need to pee anyway."

Tony stood and walked toward the bathroom. "Okay, sure. But no funny business. If you try to climb out the window, I'm going to shoot you."

"Whatever. We can't even close the door anymore since you kicked it in. Fortunately, I'm an ER nurse. I can pee anywhere, anytime, with anyone around."

Jackie walked into the bathroom and found the Tylenol in her bathroom kit. She tossed the bottle on the ground outside the bathroom and then quickly used the toilet. She exited and found the pill bottle still laying on the floor.

"Pick it up and give me a few," said Tony.

She shrugged and picked up the bottle, handing him two extra-strength Tylenol. "You'll probably want to wash that down with something other than alcohol."

Tony ignored her advice as he chased the pills with a large dose of mango daiquiri.

"Elisa, you're the surgeon. How is this going to work?" asked Tom, getting the conversation back on track.

"It's not. I can't operate on someone's abdomen without anesthesia or supplies. I literally have nothing."

"Yes, you do," said Tony. "There's a nurse's station in the staff building. It has some basic medical supplies. They are setup for sutures and some other basic needs. My buddy got stitches last time we were here when he cut himself fishing."

"Okay fine, I have basic supplies. But no anesthesia. No sterile field. No blood products."

"Not even a surgeon's lounge stocked with snacks and a massage chair," added Bryce.

"Right? I could really go for a stale bagel and bag of chips right now. I can't believe I took that for granted all these years."

"I have a thought about anesthesia," said Bryce. "What if we did a spinal block?"

"Ooh, I like that idea," said Tom. "I'll stab her in the back with a long 14-gauge needle and destroy her spinal cord. Then she won't feel anything when Elisa cuts her open."

"Knock it off," said Tony. "Don't you dare talk about her like that. Any of you screw something up and I'll–"

"Shoot us? Yeah, we got it," said Julio. "It doesn't help to add that sort of pressure to a situation like this, you know."

Tony shook his head and rubbed it slowly. "Fine, continue."

"If they have lidocaine in the kit, we might be able to do a spinal," said Elisa. "That should give me enough time to peek inside and see what I can fix. If it's a ruptured ectopic, I should be able to just tie off that side and be done with it. She'd need an additional procedure, but it should buy her enough time to get off this island once the storm has passed."

"How are we going to monitor her during the case?" asked Jackie.

"I'm hoping there's a blood pressure cuff in the nursing area. We can use a smart watch for heart rate. Her oxygen shouldn't be a problem since we're doing a spinal block."

"What if we just get her really drunk and give her a stick to bite on?" offered Julio. "Then we wouldn't have to worry about the block. We have plenty of booze."

"There's no way she'd be able to tolerate the pain of me cutting into her. She'd be moving all over the place."

"And maybe puke from the pain. I hate when drunk people vomit," said Jackie.

"Yeah, I'd rather keep her stomach contents out of her lungs. Especially since we have no airway supplies," said Bryce.

He looked over at Tony. "Look, we can theorize about this all day long. But you need to realize the chance of success is extremely low. And even if it's successful, she can't just get up and walk out of here. She's going to need to be in a hospital to recover and get definitive treatment. This is just a bandage on a serious problem. What is tomorrow's plan?"

"It doesn't matter to you. This is your last night on earth, anyway. Don't ruin it by worrying about tomorrow."

"Halfway there, keep it up!" yelled Valerie over her shoulder.

Peter kept his eyes focused on the approaching waves while steering in the general direction of the boat. He managed to avoid several enormous waves and even a palm tree that was floating past. It was impossible to stay seated and balanced, so he was in a low squat over the bench seat. His body leaning into the oncoming waves to reduce the risk of capsizing.

Twenty more yards. How am I going to come up alongside?

The boat was facing the wind, its stern turned toward the shore. Peter saw the swim platform at the back of the boat and steered toward it. The long boat was rocking up and down with the swell. The swim platform alternating between two feet out of the water and two feet under.

Peter yelled over his right shoulder toward Val. "We're going to have to time it perfectly when we get close. I think you'll need to jump on when it's underwater and then get the line around a cleat. Then I'll pull myself close and jump on. We can let the jet ski float behind the boat."

"Sounds good. Let me get behind you now so I can jump off the back."

Valerie tried to turn around and get past Peter on the starboard side. Her weight to the side, combined with the wave action, nearly put both of them in the water. She leaned back to the middle, and Peter juiced the throttle to maintain balance.

"You're going to have to go under, I think," said Peter.

Valerie nodded and slid as far forward as she could. She held the rope in her right hand and kicked her feet up above the handlebars. Peter backed up to give her room to lie down and then lifted on his toes to give her clearance.

"Don't tell Bryce about this," yelled Valerie as she lifted her arms above her head, grabbed the seat, and pulled herself underneath Peter. With a few efforts, she had cleared his frame and sat up before spinning around and holding the seat strap behind her.

"Nice job. I'll try to get you close. Make your move when you feel it's right."

He turned the jet ski so it was perpendicular to the stern of the boat and crept toward it. The swim deck on the transom loomed almost head height, before smashing down into the water and spraying them with salty mist.

Come on Val, you can do this. Wait for the perfect moment, but not too long. I can't hold us here forever.

Val kept her eyes trained on the platform and waited for the right moment. When it came, she sprung off the jet ski and lept toward the moving platform as it was rising out of the water. Unfortunately, right before she jumped, a wave pushed the jet ski a foot further away, increasing the distance she had to cover in the air. She landed with her right foot on the platform, but her left only caught the toe rail before slipping into the water. She flailed for something to hold on to but only found wind and rain, before falling backward into the dark water.

"Val!" screamed Peter, scanning the water at the back of the boat where she had fallen in.

"Someone's going to go get the medical supplies. Any volunteers?" asked Tony.

"I'll go," said Julio. "I know where it is. I helped the staff carry some things there when we first arrived."

"Count me in too. There's a hurricane out there. We should use the buddy system," said Tom.

"Remember, I'm still here with your families. Don't get an idea in your head to try something. The only way we all get through this is helping Emily," said Tony. "I'll give you ten minutes to get back. After that, my trigger finger is going to get some exercise. Understand?"

They both nodded. Julio set a nine-minute timer on his watch and began the countdown.

"Grab everything they have. I don't want to fail because you didn't think something was necessary," said Elisa.

Julio led Tom out the door and into the storm. He pointed to the right and started off at a jog. Tom kept up the best he could, and they reached the staff building in under a minute.

Julio tried the door but found it locked. "Seems like the storm needs to do more damage." He scanned around quickly and found a rock that would do. Tom stepped aside as Julio threw the rock into the paneled glass door, shattering the glass and creating a bowling ball sized hole next to the handle. He gingerly reached through the jagged glass and unlocked the door.

"Nicely done. How much time do we have?" asked Tom.

"Seven and a half minutes on my watch. The stuff's in here. Grab a bag or something to carry it in."

Julio led Tom into a small room that contained a medical exam table and a cabinet stocked with supplies.

"This is the type of resort where the doctor comes to see you. Must be nice to have that kind of money to rent something like this," said Julio.

Tom opened a plastic garbage bag, and they began dumping supplies into it. IV tubing, fluids, a few suture kits, several vials of anesthetic, iodine swabs, scalpels, boxes of gloves.

They cleaned out everything that seemed useful and headed for the exit.

"Looks like we made good time. Let's get this stuff back to Elisa," said Tom.

"Wait, we can't just go back right away. This is our chance to find some weapons. And there's still a kid out there somewhere. Let's split up. I'll head to the fishing shack; you go check out the other villa. Grab knives or anything that looks like it'll do damage. We can probably sneak a small one in, but we'll need to stockpile them outside a door and find an excuse to leave again. Keep your eyes open for Noah."

Tom handed Julio the heavy bag and ran out into the night, headed toward the other villa. Julio hefted the bag on his shoulder and double timed it toward the dock and the water sports shed.

Valerie felt her left foot land just short of the platform. Her momentum was no match for the uplifting platform and it flipped her backward and into the water. The combination of wind and current swept her behind the jet ski before she could come up above the surface.

Looking around, she found herself about twenty feet behind the jet ski and quickly losing ground.

"Peter!" she screamed, but the combination of the wind, the engine, and the boat slapping in the waves drowned out her voice. She felt around for the rope, but couldn't find it.

Son of a bitch. I'm going to have to swim against this storm. Longest twenty-foot swim of my life.

She put her face in the water and began an aggressive freestyle technique. It had been nearly fifteen years since her relay team had set her alma mater's record in the 400m freestyle. She longed for that athleticism and endurance as she struggled against the waves.

After thirty seconds, she looked up and realized she had gotten no closer to the boat, but she could see Peter scanning the water and moving toward her in a random pattern.

Come on, look at me.

She put her face back in the water and swam another thirty seconds. The lack of lights and clouds made her nearly invisible amongst the white cap waves breaking around her.

Something rubbed against her arm, and she reflexively pulled away from it. *Was that a fish? Debris?*

It hit her again, this time in the leg. *The rope!* She twisted her body around and flailed through the water, trying to find it without drifting too far away.

Val's right arm whipped out and found the rope with the back side of her forearm. She twisted her arm and wrapped the rope around her forearm and wrist. She grasped it with her left hand and kicked her legs in a single motion to raise her head out of the water.

"Peter!" she screamed while yanking on the rope.

Peter felt the jet ski jerk to the side. He turned around and saw Val's face above the water, muscles tight from exertion. He followed the line between her hands and the jet ski and shoved his hand into the water, hoping to grab the rope. Nothing.

He waited for a large wave to pass, and then leaned as far as he felt comfortable. His hand dove deep underwater and came up clenching the line. He rapidly pulled Val toward the jet ski and lifted her out of the water when she was close enough.

"Are you okay?" he asked.

"Yes, just a bit tired. That current is intense."

"So what now?"

"What choice do we have? Get me close. We have to try again."

Chapter Thirty-Three

Noah shivered, crouched low a corner of the room. His clothes were soaked with a combination of rain and saltwater spray. He had initially fled to the other villa, but decided it was too obvious of a hiding place. He now found himself alone in a dark shack, hiding from the unknown man with a gun, and a violent tropical storm.

"God, I'm sorry I haven't prayed every day. I'm sorry I was mean to Hannah all those times. If you get my family through this, I promise I'll do better. Please, help us." His voice was solid through the first sentences, then he broke down into a sob. "Please!" he screamed, before tears overwhelmed him.

He stopped crying instantly when the door to the shack flew open. He slid as far underneath a bench as he could and tried to keep quiet.

Julio stepped through the door and pulled it shut behind him. He wiped the rain off his face and glanced at his watch. Four minutes left. He flipped on a light switch and began searching the equipment for anything they could use. Several tackle boxes were on a shelf, along with fishing line, lead weights, fishing poles, even a gaff. He opened a tackle box and smiled when he looked at the top shelf. A nine-inch fillet knife. He pulled the knife from the sheath and inspected the blade. He cut several three-foot lengths of the strongest fishing line he could find.

"Excuse me, can you help me?"

Julio spun around and extended the knife in front of him toward the voice. He looked down and saw Noah cringe and lean back away from him. He instantly sheathed the knife and walked over to the boy.

"Hey Noah, there you are. We've been looking for you." He leaned down and gave him a hug. "Your parents will be so happy I found you. Are you okay?"

Noah nodded back. "Yes sir, but I'm cold. And scared. Is that man gone yet?"

Julio winced and shook his head. "No, not yet. In fact, I need to get back there soon or he'll be very mad. Your parents and sister are doing fine and I hope you get to see them soon. Listen, why don't you help me carry this stuff back by the house. I'll show you where you can hide in the other house. It's dry and a lot more comfortable. No one will go in there again."

Noah stood up and followed Julio back to the bench. He picked up a few triangle-shaped lead weights and two spools of fishing line. Julio carried the gaff, the knife, some rope, and a small extra anchor.

"Let's get back quickly. We're about out of time. When we get to the house, we'll store it all outside for us to use later."

He pushed the door open, and they ran out the door, not bothering to close it behind them. In less than a minute, they were approaching the main house. Julio pointed to an area behind a palm tree and they placed all the equipment there, covering it with a few downed banana plant leaves. He then led Noah to the other villa and took him inside.

"Listen, no one should come in here until it's over. But just in case, hang out in a bedroom. If you hear anyone come, hide until you know it's one of us, okay?"

Noah nodded. "Thank you for getting me back inside. Tell my parents I'm safe."

Julio gave him a quick hug. "I will. I'm proud of you Noah, you are handling this very well. Can I ask you to do one more thing?"

Noah nodded. "Yep. I want to help. I can do a lot of things. I'm six."

"Of course you can. This will be a huge help. Do you know where the generator is?"

Noah nodded again.

"Okay good. Next to the generator is a small metal box. Inside that is a big switch. That will turn off the generator. If we're going to have a chance, we need a distraction. Can you turn the switch off in forty-five minutes? I'll give you my watch."

Julio removed his watch and set a timer for forty-five minutes. He handed it back to Noah. "When this beeps, hit this button to make it stop and then go flip the switch."

"I'll do it."

"Great, thank you. Once the power is off, run back here again as fast as you can and hide, okay? The lights are going to be off, so be careful where you walk."

He put his hand on Noah's head and smiled down at him. "I hope Elisa and I have a boy as tough as you are some day."

He turned and ran out of the room, knowing he had less than a minute to go. As he jogged, he tied the fishing line onto the triangular lead weights and tied a quick loop on the other end. He shoved them into the rear of his underwear and put the knife in the front, laying sideways across his groin.

He found Tom waiting for him outside the door just as his alarm went off. "There's my alarm. We have less than a minute. What did you find?"

"I found a small hammer and some steak knives. I never saw Noah, though," said Tom.

"No worries. I found him in the fishing shack. He's hiding in the other villa now. Let's put your stuff over by ours. I have a knife and a few lead weights we can try to sneak inside."

They quickly added the supplies to the other storage location and re-entered the main building, holding the plastic bag of supplies.

Tony looked at his watch. "Twenty seconds left. You guys sure cut it close. Lift your shirts up, pull out your pockets, and spin around."

Tom and Julio looked at each other and shrugged before complying. Tony seemed satisfied and motioned for them to rejoin the others at the table. He then walked over and emptied the plastic bag on the kitchen counter. After searching through it, he pointed to Elisa.

"You, come check out what you have to work with. Once they get back, I want to get started right away."

Elisa stood and examined what they brought. "This isn't enough to do much. Obviously, I want to save her, but you need to understand how difficult this is going to be. This is wholly inadequate for major abdominal surgery on a critically ill patient."

"Don't give me excuses. Just show me results," said Tony.

Elisa organized the equipment in the order wanted and then sat back down. "Shouldn't they be back soon?" she asked to no one in particular.

Chapter Thirty-Four

"Get me as close as you can. I will not miss this time," said Val.

Peter brought the jet ski just off the rear of the yacht. He turned to wish Valerie luck, but only glimpsed at her back as she landed in a deep squat with both feet on the swim platform. *Not wasting any time, I see.* She leaned forward and grabbed onto the handrail and tied a quick knot to secure the jet ski.

Peter maneuvered the craft close enough for Val to throw him the slack. He used it to pull as close as he dared before pulling hard on the rope and leaping toward the larger boat. He landed on his back with his hips below the edge of the swim platform. Searing pain moved across his lower back as the boat rose and slammed into his spine as he fell toward it. He pulled hard on the rope and slid his body onto the swim platform. Valerie grabbed his shorts and held him in place while he rolled onto his hands and knees and eventually stood up. Once he was stable, they climbed the stairs and entered the salon of the yacht.

"About time you guys got here. It's only a hundred yards away," said Emily, her voice just above a whisper. They found her slouched down in a chair, an expanding pool of blood dripping off the chair and spreading across the teak floor. Emily looked at Val's now nearly transparent outfit and gave a thin smile. "Nice look, lady. You always dress like that when swimming with Bryce's friends? We should have hung out more."

Peter looked at her as a physician would examine a patient in the Emergency Department. Young female, vaginal bleeding. Severe abdominal pain, passing out. Ruptured ectopic pregnancy until proven otherwise. "Emily, are you pregnant? This could be a ruptured ectopic. We need to get you back to shore immediately."

"Why? Do you want to be a daddy, Peter? If I am pregnant, it's not yours. Wouldn't that be funny? I try to move on from you and start a family, then my kid kills me?"

"That's not going to happen. Come on, let's get you on the jet ski and back to the house. We have a plan to save you," said Val.

"Where are the life jackets?" asked Peter.

"There's a storage compartment behind the helm," said Emily.

Peter spun and walked out the salon door to the cockpit and found the compartment. He lifted the cover and removed three life jackets. As he replaced the cover, a loud crash came from the rear of the boat. The deck of the boat shuddered as the noise repeated a few times with decreasing volume. He hurried to the stern and saw the jet ski in several pieces, bludgeoned apart by the swim deck of the yacht.

"Son of a…" Peter groaned and raised his face to the sky. *How can get this get any worse? Okay, you're an ER doctor. Just roll with it. Get new information, adjust the plan. There is always a different option.*

He turned and re-entered the relative calm of the enclosed salon and looked at the two women. "Bad news.

The boat annihilated the jet ski. The rope must have pulled it toward the swim deck, which promptly smashed it to pieces. We'll have to find a different way to shore."

"Every large boat we've been on had a life raft. Emily, do you know where it is?" said Val.

Emily shook her head sideways. "I was here for the adventure and the money. Not to learn how to become a captain."

Val took a jacket from Peter and exited the salon, looking for any potential compartment that might contain a life raft. Thirty seconds later, she lifted a bench seat and found a large plastic rectangular box that looked promising. It had rope handles on the end and said 'LIFE RAFT' in bright orange letters. She hauled it out of the compartment and flipped open the container. Inside was a folded-up heavy-duty vinyl life raft. A red plastic handle was on top with a sign that read 'pull to inflate'. In the back of the storage compartment sat two short oars.

"Guys, I found the life raft. We have two oars. I think it's our best chance. Let's get this inflated and get Emily to the house."

"Stay here while we get the raft ready. When it's time to go, I'll carry you out," said Peter.

He joined Val on the rear deck and hauled the raft toward the steps leading down to the swim platform, now halfway destroyed. "How big do you think this is going to get?" he asked.

"It says it's rated for six people, probably a lot larger than we need. Maybe tie a rope on it and pull the cord while it's hanging over the water?"

Peter nodded and grabbed a spare line that was coiled nearby. He tied it to the stainless-steel handrail and then to a metal ring on what appeared to be a corner of the raft. He pushed the life raft over the top of the stairs and held on to the inflation handle as it fell overboard. A loud pop signaled the CO_2 cannister had activated and the raft quickly inflated. Soon a hexagon-shaped yellow raft was floating twenty feet behind the boat. It had a tall canopy above, shielding the interior from rain and ocean spray.

"Perfect. Grab the oars. I'll get Emily and let's get to shore."

Val didn't acknowledge the comment. She was alternating her gaze between the shore and the life raft. She spun around and looked at the front of the boat and the approaching waves.

"We have a problem, Peter," she said. "The wind has shifted. I think the storm is moving past us, and now the wind is more out of the south. Look where the raft is floating. It's not pointing toward shore anymore."

Peter followed the rope and extended an imaginary line through the raft and beyond. It did not extend through the island, but rather straight out into the bay. "Do you think we can paddle to shore?"

"No. That canopy is like a huge sail. The current is still pushing toward the island for now, but the force of the wind will be stronger. We're going to need to be in the water, not on it," she said.

"Damn it," said Peter.

"Exactly," said Val before she put both palms together and then spread them across her face and out through her hair.

"It's a hundred yards. We can do this. Let's get some flotation and get out of here. Grab a few of those fenders. We'll tie them to Emily like a super life jacket and then pull her to shore. With the wind shifting, I'm afraid the current will change soon too."

"I think we may be closer than that now. Looks like the boat is dragging its anchor. I don't think we're more than sixty yards away now," said Peter.

"Oh, great. That will help," said Val. "Go get Emily, I'll get the fenders ready."

Peter entered the salon and quickly explained the situation to Emily. He put a life jacket on her and carried her out to the back of the boat where Valerie tied several fenders to the front of her jacket.

"You'll need to stay on your stomach so these lift you up out of the water. Bring a mask and a snorkel; they should make it easier to breathe," said Val. She then tied a short line to the front of Emily's life jacket. "I'll pull you to shore."

"Okay. Don't lose me." She handed a small radio to Peter. "Tell Tony we're headed back to shore. Don't use his name; call him El Diablo." Peter obliged and then clipped the waterproof radio to the top of his shorts.

Once they had everything in place, they moved to the stairs leading down to the swim deck.

"I think we should jump in. It will keep us clear of the boat and give us some momentum toward shore," said Val. The three prepared to jump when Val suddenly changed her stance.

"Wait! The boat is dragging anchor. I'm going to let out more chain on the windlass to stop it from being pushed ashore. The extra weight will help the anchor hold. I'll be right back."

She quickly made her way to the helm and found the switch for the windlass control. It was clearly marked which way was up and which was down. She breathed a sigh of relief and engaged the device. A loud clacking noise followed as chain moved through the windlass. A foot per second is the standard travel speed of a chain on a windlass. She held the lever for about a minute before removing her hand from the button and rejoining Peter.

"That should do it. Let's go."

She waited for the stern to lift into the air as the bow dipped into a wave and then leaped as far as she could. When Val resurfaced, she heard the splash of Peter and Emily entering the water. She turned around and grabbed the line attached to Emily, quickly tied it to the front of her jacket, and swam like her life and the lives of her family depended on it.

Chapter Thirty-Five

"I hate to sound cliche, but we should get a pot of water boiling. I may need to sterilize equipment if something happens," said Elisa.

"Fine, do it," said Tony.

Elisa grabbed a pot from the cabinet and filled it nearly full with hot water. She then put it over the largest burner on the gas stove and set it to high.

"El Diablo, this is Peter Pan. We're headed back with the patient."

The unexpected sound caused everyone to turn and look at Tony. He unclipped the radio and keyed the broadcast button. "Copy that. See you soon." He replaced the radio and then looked across the room. "It's almost your time to shine."

Tony leaned back in the chair and stretched. He sank down a bit lower in the chair and smiled through half-closed eyes. "It's a shame we're here under these circumstances. You guys sure are interesting. Between the rum and the meds, my headache is feeling better."

Tom tapped Bryce's foot under the table and whispered without moving his lips. "We 'ound Noah. He's OK. He is hiding in the other 'illa."

"Oh, thank God," said Bryce, his emotion overcoming his brain's desire to keep that knowledge secret.

"What's that?" said Tony, opening his eyes fully and leaning forward.

Bryce hesitated, but recovered quickly. "I'm glad they're on their way back. We need to get Emily fixed as soon as we can. I was nervous about them making it back and forth in this weather."

"What are you talking about? Are they on their way back? How do you know?"

The adults shared a quick sideways glance.

"Yes, they radioed in a few minutes ago and said they were on their way," said Tom.

Bryce's mind was spinning. *That rock I threw must have brought back his concussion. The alcohol is helping too. If I can give him another solid blow, maybe we can take him down.*

Valerie lifted her head up and took a quick glance to shore. Halfway there! She looked behind her and saw Peter a few yards back, but looking strong. Emily's head was above the water, but she wasn't moving her arms or legs and her body floated downwind.

Val leaned forward and continued swimming, her mind drifting back to her collegiate days. *You got this. Only four more laps to go. Win this race and you can go party with your team.* The mental image of her relay team cheering her on morphed into Bryce holding Hannah and Noah. *Come on,*

Mom, you got this! You're almost there! Once you touch the wall, the rest of your team will take over. Give it all you got!

Positive energy can only take a person so far, and Val was fatiguing. There's a difference between leisurely swimming for half an hour while listening to music, and giving maximum effort while dragging someone behind you. She rolled onto her back stretched her arms out, willing to surrender a little ground to the current in exchange for a much-needed break.

"Peter, I'm going to take a quick break. Let's float for a sec."

"Thanks, I'm dying," replied Peter. He continued swimming until he could hold on to a fender connected to Emily. "Let's take a minute and then give a final push."

They floated silently in the waves, willing their muscles to regenerate quickly. Val looked at Peter as he held on to Emily. *He's a good man. I'm glad he's part of our life, just wish he had better taste in women.* She was lost in thought when she saw Peter's face change. He lifted his head higher out of the water and then his eyes opened wide.

"We have to move, now! We're almost at the end of the island!"

Val glanced toward shore and saw the tip of the island far too close. The current had picked up and was trying to pull them out past the island and into the open ocean.

She took a breath and flattened her body out in the water, pulling with everything she had.

Peter stayed even with her as long as he could. After twenty seconds, they were considerably closer to the shore, and also the channel that led out of the ocean.

We're not going to make it. Val kicked harder but caught her leg in the rope. *Why am I kicking the rope now? What changed?* She kept swimming, not wanting to turn to find out what happened. A second later, a strong force pulled her underwater and then she tossed around by a wave. She waited for the jacket to bring her to the surface, but she felt the rope wrap tightly around her arms and neck. *I can't move! Peter!*

Peter felt a wave pick him up and bring him closer to shore. He briefly enjoyed the increased speed that helped close the distance to their goal. He looked over to see how Val was doing but couldn't see her. Emily was twisted sideways and not floating as high as she had before. He looked around quickly, searching for Val but finding only the foamy ocean.

"Val!" he screamed, without receiving an answer. He kicked his legs and pulled quickly to get closer to Emily, reaching her a few seconds. He twisted her around until he found the rope leading toward Val. It was stretched tight under Emily. He took a breath and dove under the water, following the rope in search of Val. Suddenly, a wave broke over him and tossed him around. He held on to the rope with one hand but was out of air and needed to surface. He kicked violently, his left foot finding water, his right foot finding sand. Peter's head broke the surface, and he sucked in a huge breath before diving back along the rope. He quickly felt Val trapped underneath Emily and felt the rope wrapped around her upper body.

Peter swam underneath them and felt the sandy bottom again. He grabbed Val like an Olympic weightlifting bar and pushed her up as high and as fast as he could.

Val's head broke the surface, followed immediately by her taking a quick breath in. She waited to make sure she was staying up before releasing that breath and taking another large one. Glancing down, she saw the rope twisted multiple times with no clear direction of how to unwind. She felt Peter's grip loosen and held her breath as she prepared to go under again.

Peter let go and kicked to the surface just as another wave broke over them. He was tossed into a somersault and ended up on his back under the water. He righted himself quickly and found he was in waist-deep water. The buoyant fenders had pushed Emily closer to shore and exposed Valerie's legs, kicking wildly and searching for purchase. He combined running and jumping to leap through the water toward the women.

When he reached the women, he lifted Val's head above the water. She took a deep breath in and coughed a few times, clearing the salt water from her mouth and lungs. He grabbed her in one arm and picked Emily up by her life jacket with the other. He dragged them through the water until they reached the shore above the breaking waves. Peter quickly untied the rope from Emily's life jacket and untangled Valerie, allowing her to stand again on her own.

Val quickly dropped to her hands and knees and struggled to regain her breath.

"Are you two okay?" Peter asked.

"Yeah, I will be in a minute. Thanks Peter, you saved my life back there. The waves spun me and wrapped the line around me like a boa constrictor."

Peter nodded his head but didn't trust his voice to reply without showing too much emotion. He looked down at Emily. She was pale and breathing shallowly. She had not answered his question.

"We need to get her back to the house. Can you walk?"

"Yes. I need to get dressed first, though. You go ahead, I'll catch up."

Peter unclipped the life jacket from around Emily and lifted her in his arms. He hurried up the beach and then broke into a jog once he hit the paved path.

Chapter Thirty-Six

"Let's get the table ready for when she's here. I want everything off of it and the chairs moved. Get a large towel and we'll lay out all the supplies," said Elisa. "Do we have anything to create a sterile field?"

"How about some rubbing alcohol and plastic wrap?" asked Jackie. "We use plastic wrap in the NICU to help keep the babies warm."

"Okay, sure. I'll prep her abdomen and then you wrap her a few times. Then I'll cut a window and operate through that." Elisa looked around at the other docs in the room. "Who is going to do the spinal?"

Tom shook his head no and pointed at Bryce. "When he was still a resident, I was asking him to bail me out of failed LPs. Bryce is your man for the job."

"What a time to be praised. Why couldn't you have nominated me for an award or something back home? I feel like my skills will not be fully appreciated here," said Bryce with a crooked smile. "Tony, I need to get my phone. It has a medication reference app on it and I have to look up the dose of lidocaine for a spinal block."

"Whatever, just make it happen," said Tony. He stood up and started pacing the room quickly.

A hard pounding on the front door caused heads to turn toward it. Peter was visible through the glass, outlined by a light on a pole. He was holding Emily.

Tony ran to the door and pulled it open, allowing Peter to carry her through the doorway and into the villa.

"Emily, how are you doing?" asked Tony, but he received no answer. She was breathing, but that was about it.

"What happened? Why isn't she talking?" asked Tony loudly.

"She's lost a lot of blood. Her blood pressure is probably very low. We need to get an IV started and give her fluids because we're running out of time," said Peter.

"Bring her over here and lay her on the table," said Elisa.

"Wait, we should put down some blankets. She can't lay on a hard table like that. She may get pressure wounds," said Jackie as she stood up and walked toward a bedroom.

"Where are you going?" screamed Tony.

Jackie stopped and turned back around. "Sorry, I wanted her to have a blanket under her while lying on the table. It's bad for her skin to lay on a hard surface that long and she's also at risk of hypothermia. I was going to get a comforter off a bed."

"Yes, thanks. Do that. Get it under her before you lay her down," said Tony. Once he finished speaking, he continued pacing the room.

Jackie retrieved the bedding and spread it on the table. Peter laid her on it and dried her as best he could.

"We have two IV catheters and two liters of fluid. That's it," said Jackie. "Want me to get the first liter started?"

"Yeah, we'd better. Try to get a set of vitals," said Tom.

Jackie took off her smart watch and placed it on Emily's wrist. She swiped her finger across the screen until the heart rate monitor app showed up. She selected the 'continuous' setting and waited for it to pick up the rate. "Her pulse is 150!" said Jackie. "I'll see if I can get a blood pressure."

Jackie placed the blood pressure cuff on Emily's arm and then paused. "I don't have a stethoscope. Did anyone bring one?"

"I doubt it. Just get a systolic. It's not like we can do a lot about the results, anyway. It's just good to have an idea of where we're at," said Bryce.

Jackie placed her fingers on Emily's radial artery and watched the pressure on the cuff as she inflated it. Her eyes widened, but she said nothing until she had rechecked it. "Her systolic is seventy. We need to get the fluids going." She glanced at the smart watch and read off the heart rate. "Pulse one-fifty."

"When I open her up, she may bleed more. The pressure in her abdomen may be slowing down the rate of blood loss. I wish we had a blood bank here."

"She's O negative, I can tell you that much. Again, not that it matters," said Peter.

"How do you know that?" asked Elisa.

"We used to donate together when the hospital would have a blood drive. Only needed one glass of wine for a few days after that," said Peter.

A thump and a crash drew attention back toward Tony. A small ottoman was falling away from the wall after having been sent flying by Tony's foot. "Quit talking and start cutting. She's running out of time," he warned.

"We know. It has to get done in the correct order. We all know the stakes. You've made that abundantly clear," said Elisa.

Bryce used his thumb to scroll through the app on his phone and found the dosing ranges for spinal anesthesia. "It says we should use lidocaine mixed with dextrose to help the dose stay in place and not migrate. We don't have that. It also recommends 60mg of 5% lidocaine, we have 20 milliliters of 1%. That's 200mg. It recommends 1.25 milliliter, but we'll have to use six milliliters to get the same dose. Anyone know what the increased volume will do?"

"Probably just give her a better block," said Tom. "Either way, we'll find out soon enough."

Jackie opened an IV start kit and began prepping Emily's left arm. She expertly placed a 20-gauge catheter in the bend of Emily's elbow. Once she pushed the catheter into the vein, she clicked a button to retract the needle on the IV catheter.

"Oh no, I wish you hadn't done that," said Bryce.

"What? Wish I hadn't done what?"

"Retracted that needle. We only have two catheters. I could have used that needle for the spinal block and left us a spare."

"Well, you should have said something before I started the line. It's a habit," said Jackie, clearly annoyed.

"I know, sorry. I didn't think of it. Let's try to think about saving supplies any step we can moving forward."

Jackie hooked up the first bag of fluids to Emily's arm and sat on the table next to her, holding the bag in the air and allowing gravity to drain the fluids into Emily's vein.

"You know, what she really needs is blood. Saline is just going to dilute her clotting factors even more and may make things worse," said Elisa.

"We're just hoping to perfuse her brain long enough for you to get the bleeding under control. What other choice do we have?" asked Bryce.

"You can give her a transfusion," said Tony. "You have one more catheter. Take someone's blood and give it to her."

"It's not that easy," said Peter. "If we give her the wrong blood type, it could kill her. There's a reason hospitals are so meticulous about blood products. It can be a serious problem if a transfusion is done incorrectly."

"So don't do it incorrectly," said Tony, staring back at Peter.

"That gun and your attitude will only get you so far in life, dude. It can't make magic happen."

"You're right. That's why I have all of you. I don't believe in magic. I believe in ability. Prowess. Human achievement. Figure it out."

"Can we autotransfuse her?" asked Elisa. "Her abdomen is likely full of sterile blood. If we could collect, it we could just run it back in."

"What about clots? There is no filter for the IV line. We would just be pouring clot into her," said Tom. "I was on a mission trip once where we did a direct blood transfusion. We placed an IV in the donor and drained blood into a bag of saline containing a bit of a blood thinner, and then gave that to the patient. It worked well."

"Stop arguing and just give me some damn blood." The words were spoken softly and came from Emily, laying on the dining room table.

"The fluids must be working. Her heart rate is down to 125 and she's starting to wake up," said Jackie.

Tony walked to Emily's side and rubbed her hair. "It's okay. We'll get you through this. Then I'll get you to a hospital and make sure you're taken care of."

Julio had to take a step back to allow Tony to pass and stand next to Emily. For a brief moment, he was behind Tony and tensed his body and prepare for an attack. At the last moment, he caught the gaze of his wife who shook her head no. "Wait," she mouthed.

Julio turned around in frustration took a few steps before sitting down in a chair. "Something needs to happen, and soon," he said.

Everyone in the room agreed, but for distinctly different reasons.

"So she's O negative. Who knows their blood type?" asked Peter.

Bryce sighed audibly. *I'm as good as dead anyway, may as well use my blood. Just leave my friends and family alone.* "I'm O positive. I can give her blood," he said.

"Great. Hey nurse, stick a line in him and get it started," said Tony.

"'Hey nurse'? I told you, my name is Jackie. Show some respect."

"Tony, not his blood. I'm O negative. I need negative blood so that I can still have kids later," said Emily.

"How does getting Bryce's blood stop you from having kids later?" asked Tony.

"It doesn't matter, just get me O negative blood," she said. "And fast. I feel like I'm going to pass out again."

Tony looked around the room. "Which one of you is it going to be? She needs O negative, whatever that means. Don't get cute with your doctor tricks either. If she gets the wrong blood and dies, I'm taking a lot more of you out with her." He stopped talking but continued to look from face to face.

Valerie raised her hand. "I'm O negative. Figures. I assumed those shots I got during the pregnancy were the worst part about my blood type. But once I donated blood the first time, it was the constant phone calls from the blood bank that became the worst. Thank you for getting me to the next level of hell with this blood type."

"OK, come over here and get it started. We're out of time," said Tony.

"Mommy, no! Don't go! Stay here with me," said Hannah, pulling at Val's arm.

Val turned around and knelt down next to her daughter. "Hannah, Mommy needs to do this last thing to help."

"But I don't want you to. Stay here. I'm scared."

"Honey, do you see how sick that lady over there is?"

Hannah followed her mother's gaze and looked at Emily for a few seconds. She looked back at Val and nodded her head. "But she's a bad person. She hurt Daddy."

"Yes, she did. But aren't we supposed to help people whenever we can? Don't we pray for God to show us how to help others we meet in our lives?"

Hannah nodded. "Yeah, but I don't want to help her."

"I know, Hannah. And I don't want to either. But do you think God wants me to?"

Hannah nodded again. "Yes."

Val leaned down and gave her a big hug. "I do too. Don't worry about me, I'll be fine. It's just like a blood donation. I have plenty more where that came from. Besides, maybe if they take some blood, your dad can finally beat me in a swimming race."

Hannah smiled back at her winking mother and then joined her dad at the table.

"OK, drain me," said Val with her left arm out in front of her.

Chapter Thirty-Seven

Jackie picked up the second IV catheter and raised her eyebrows. "You sure?

"Yep, just get it done so we can get the surgery started."

Tom stood up and walked over to the two women. "We need to stop Emily's fluids when there's about two hundred milliliters left. Then we move the tubing over to Val's IV and fill it with eight hundred milliliters of blood. That's more than a unit of blood, but it should be a good dose and tolerable for Val."

"We're there now," said Elisa, clamping off the fluids. "Every minute we wait makes her odds of surviving even less. Let's get moving." She handed the bag of fluids to Jackie, who set them on the floor.

"I really wish we had a blood thinner, even just a bit of heparin would go a long way," said Tom.

"If you give her heparin before I can stop the bleeding, that will not help things much. Plus, it'll make the spinal block more dangerous," said Elisa.

"Which is worse? Pouring clot into her lungs, or a little higher risk of bleeding?" asked Bryce.

"It doesn't matter, we don't have any heparin. We'll just try to be fast and limit the ability to clot."

"What if I take a few aspirins before the donation?" asked Val.

"No, that permanently inactivates platelets. She may not stop bleeding if you do that. Better to give a small amount of something that goes away than someone that lasts for days," said Tom. "But again, it doesn't matter, we don't have heparin."

"Peter does." The words were whispered, but grabbed the attention of everyone in the room. "Tell them," Emily continued.

Peter sighed and dropped his head to the floor. "I do have some Lovenox with me. We can use that."

"Why didn't you say something sooner? You wasted time, dumbass," said Tony.

"Because he's embarrassed. Tell them why you take it, Peter," said Emily.

Peter stood up and addressed the room, his face glowing red. "It's not important why, but I'll go get it. I need to go to my bedroom, Tony. It'll take thirty seconds."

Tony nodded his consent, and Peter walked into the room, returning with a small plastic syringe.

"He's worried about blood clots when he travels," said Emily. "Because he takes testosterone supplements. Those muscles aren't real, but the tiny balls are." She smiled and her stomach twitched a bit, though not enough for her laugh to be audible.

Peter handed the syringe to Tom. "It's a hundred milligrams. I have no idea how much to use here."

"Me either, but ten is a round number. That should be enough, but not too much." He removed the cap from the needle and injected ten milligrams of Lovenox into the bag of fluids before recapping the syringe and setting it aside.

Jackie quickly placed the remaining IV catheter in Val and was careful to leave the needle intact for the spinal block. She set that aside and hooked the IV tubing up to the catheter. Soon, blood was rapidly pouring out of Val's arm and into the bag of fluids on the ground.

"Val, you'll want to sit down. I think you're going to feel this pretty soon. And you should drink a few glasses of water. You're probably already behind on fluids after that swim," said Bryce.

Rebecca stood and filled two glasses with water. She handed them to Val and then began a slow massage of her neck. "Thank you," she whispered.

Val smiled at her and began gulping the water. "Bolus and titrate." She leaned back into the massage and closed her eyes, trying to avoid watching the blood flow out of her body.

"Bryce, get the spinal block ready. We need to get started," said Elisa. "I'm going to need her blocked up to about the tenth thoracic vertebrae, if that helps you with placement."

"I don't think it does. I have to insert the needle below where the spinal cord ends. The drug should mix with the CSF and give some ascending anesthesia. We can invert her to have gravity help us out a bit also," he replied.

"Emily, we're going to roll you onto your side. You remember the position for lumbar punctures, right? I want you to push your lower back out like a cat arcing its back."

The team rolled Emily onto her right side and helped draw her knees up to her chest. She curled her neck down and tried to flex her spine as much as possible. This opened the space between the vertebrae and allowed for easier placement of the spinal needle.

Bryce picked up one of the glass bottles of lidocaine and read the label, confirming the concentration. He lifted Emily's shirt and saw the bony prominences of her spine clearly against the skin. *Thank goodness she's not fat. I should be able to get into her CSF space without much trouble. But how much lidocaine is enough? Too little and she will not be numb. Too much and it could stop her from breathing or cause a seizure.*

"My app says to use sixty milligrams of 5% lidocaine to achieve anesthesia to the T10 level. If you wanted T4 level, we'd go up to eighty milligrams." *If I wanted to kill her, I'd use at least two hundred milligrams, but that would take two bottles. I wonder if we could take out her arms with a hundred?*

He picked up the lidocaine bottle and snapped the plastic lid off the top with his thumb before inverting and inserting the needle through the rubber membrane on the lid. He withdrew the entire ten milliliters, representing one hundred milligrams of anesthetic.

Bryce opened an alcohol swab and cleaned the area where he planned to inject. He started by wiping the area, and then spreading outward in an expanding circle. He repeated the procedure two more times until the area was as clean as it was going to get.

"Emily, you're going to feel a poke as I insert the needle. I'm going to give you seventy milligrams of lidocaine. I think this should get you numb to the point you can undergo the surgery, but not risk respiratory depression. Let me know if you have difficulty breathing, okay?"

She nodded her head in response.

Tony walked over and stood by Emily's head, watching Bryce closely. "Don't mess this up."

Bryce paused and looked up at Tony. "Tell me about it. I've never had to do a lumbar puncture after someone shot me. I hope that doesn't affect my ability. Maybe you shouldn't have shot me."

"Maybe you shouldn't have attacked me. Why do you always blame me for everything that happens to you?" said Tony.

Bryce let out a quick laugh. "Because generally it's all your fault."

He reached forward with his left hand and pushed his thumbnail into Emily's skin, feeling for the proper location to insert the needle. Once satisfied, he placed the tip of the needle on her skin and slowly inserted it. Once he felt the needle pop through the outer layer of skin, he slowly advanced toward where her spinal canal should be.

"Come on Bryce, you got this," said Val.

"Thanks babe." *But this will not be like the time in medical school. I'm going to push through and make this happen. Tony doesn't scare me. He may have a gun pointed at me and my family, but punishment will only come from failure, which will not happen.*

"What exactly is it you're trying to do?" asked Tony.

"The spinal cord is surrounded by cerebrospinal fluid, a thin fluid that provides support for the brain and spinal cord. Holding this is place is a few layers of membrane. During an epidural block for a procedure such as delivering a baby, the anesthesiologist will attempt to place the medication between these membranes. That takes a special needle and years of training, neither of which we have here. Spinal anesthesia is different. For this, we put the needle through both membranes and inject the anesthetic directly into the spinal fluid."

"How many of these have you done before?"

Bryce continued advancing the needle slowly. "I'll let you know once my first one is done."

Tony threw his hands up and turned away from Bryce. He ran his left hand through his hair and turned back around, his face drawn tight from a frown. "You've never even done one?"

This time, Bryce looked up to answer. "No, I haven't. But I put needles in the same location all the time. The only difference is we're going to inject medication instead of pulling fluid out." He pulled his hands off the needle and backed a step away from the table. He opened his hands and gestured toward the needle in Emily's back. "Do you want me to stop? Have someone else with less experience do it? Because honestly, standing on this leg is becoming uncomfortable. I wouldn't mind taking a break."

Tony stared at him, fuming. He raised the gun and then paused a moment before lowering it back down again. "No, continue. Please."

Bryce shrugged and walked back toward the table. "Okay then. No more comments about what we're doing. This is beyond the edge of what's possible Tony. Let us do what we do. You just sit there and shut up."

Bryce grasped the needle and advanced it further. He felt a slight pop as the needle penetrated a layer of membrane. "There's one." He advance a fraction of a millimeter at a time until he felt a second pop. "And the second one." The hub of the needle instantly filled with clear fluid and slowly dripped out onto the table.

"We're in. Time to inject."

He steadied the needle with his left hand and reached for the lidocaine syringe with his right hand. He unscrewed the cap with his thumb and index finger and adjusted the syringe in his hand. As he did so, the syringe caught a finger and spun out of his hand, landing on the table.

He groaned audibly. "Oh no, I dropped the syringe. It's not sterile anymore. I can't inject that into her spinal canal. It would be a huge risk of meningitis."

"Then get a new syringe!" screamed Tony.

"Relax, I told you to be quiet, remember? Peter, can you draw me up another syringe? I don't want to let go of this needle."

Peter jumped up and grabbed the other vial of lidocaine from the supplies. "This is the last one," he said as he flipped off the cap. He opened another syringe and drew up another ten milliliters. He reached out and handed it to Bryce. "Here's another hundred milligrams of Lidocaine."

"Thanks. I'll be careful with this one," said Bryce as he attached it to the hub of the needle. The syringe stopped the fluid from leaking out as it provided back pressure. He turned the syringe so he could see the markings on the side and depressed his thumb.

"We're doing eighty milligrams, so eight milliliters." He spoke the words out loud, knowing at least four people in the room would check his math using the known concentration of the medication.

Eighty is the right dose. But I have two hundred milligrams sitting here in syringes. I could have it injected before Tony even knew what happened. That would paralyze her diaphragm and her respiratory muscles. She'd be toast.

Bryce looked up at Tony and saw the concern on his face. Saw his left hand on Emily's head, gently stroking her hair.

Saw the gun in his right hand, pointed down at the ground. Saw his eyes locked on Emily's face.

I could do it; no problem. As soon as he realized something was wrong, he'd be distracted and maybe Peter, Julio, or Tom could take him out.

He debated his conscience for a moment and then adjusted his grip on the syringe.

Chapter Thirty-Eight

Bryce made his decision. His hand trembled as adrenaline brought on by the tension surged through his body. He reached back with his thumb, and depressed the plunger, slowly delivering the medication a milliliter at a time. Ten milligrams. Then twenty.

I'm no killer. I heal people. But she is going to kill me and is part of the reason my family is being held at gunpoint.

Thirty milligrams. Forty. Fifty.

But if I do this and Tony kills all of us in a fit of rage, then who have I helped? I killed someone directly, and indirectly killed my family and friends.

Sixty milligrams. Seventy. Eighty. His thumb relaxed, and the plunger stopped moving. He looked up at Tony, still fixated on Emily's discomfort. *Why do I feel sorry for him? He started all of this and is attacking my family.* Bryce closed his eyes and took a deep breath. He pulled his hand away from the syringe and looked up at Tony. "That's eighty milligrams. She should feel the effects soon."

"Do you feel anything, Emily?" asked Tony.

"I think so. My legs are feeling heavy and they're starting to tingle," she said.

"Good. I'm going to leave the needle in place until we see what level the anesthesia has gotten to. I don't want to make another attempt at this. Let me know if you start feeling any weakness in your arms or start having a hard time breathing, as that is a sign that the medicine is getting too high in your spinal column."

Elisa organized her equipment, preparing to begin the case. "Hey, we need some sort of suction. I'm going to have to empty the blood out of her abdomen."

"Where are we going to find that? We don't have a vacuum pump and no one uses a turkey baster anymore," said Peter.

Julio began looking around the room, searching for a solution.

"What if we used some kitchen towels to mop up the blood?" asked Valerie.

"You want me to take nasty towels and swab her abdomen? Why bother doing the surgery if we're going to kill her from infection afterward," said Elisa. "No, we need a tube or something."

"I got it," said Julio, walking toward the kitchen. He walked to the fridge and depressed the handle on the front of the door, releasing a stream of water. "This fridge has a water line, probably from the sink." He turned around and visually estimated the distance. "It's got to be at least twenty feet long."

"Great, but it's attached to the fridge. I need one end in my hand and the other end hooked to a pump generating suction. What do we have for that?"

"I could manually siphon it. I'll suck on the end and draw the blood up and spit it out. Maybe we can start a siphon effect if it's full of water," said Julio.

"Fine, whatever, just make it happen," said Elisa.

Peter stood up and walked toward the fridge to help Julio pull the appliance and disconnect the water line. A few minutes later, they had the nearly twenty-foot-long line removed.

"Hey, I can't breathe," said Emily in a weak voice. "And now my arms are heavy."

"The anesthetic is going to too high. If it gets much higher, she won't be able to breathe. Quick, help me set her up. Maybe gravity will pull the medicine down and stop the progression," said Bryce. He removed the needle from her spine and held pressure at the injection site while Tony lifted her up with one arm, the other holding the gun at the ready.

"How are you doing? Is it getting worse?" said Tony.

"I can't tell. Give me a minute," said Emily.

"Do you need to go higher? I can lift you up more. I'll hold you up forever if that's what it takes."

Val did her best to stifle a laugh, which came out as more of a cough. "I don't mean to distract anyone, but I think the bag is full of blood."

Jackie grabbed the IV tubing and slid down the roller to close off the tubing, stopping the flow of blood from Val's arm. She disconnected the tubing from her IV and picked up the bag of blood. "Val, I'm going to run some of this saline into your arm to flush the IV. You feeling okay?"

"Yeah, just great. I've never celebrated after a hard swim by donating two units of blood at once. I think it's nap time."

Jackie switched the bag of saline from Emily to Val and allowed enough to flow in to clear the IV catheter of blood so that it would not clot off. She then hooked up the tubing to Emily's IV and stood on a chair, the bag of blood resting on his shoulder. "We'll let gravity do its thing and pour the blood into her.

"It's not getting any worse. I think I'm okay for now," said Emily.

"Let's lay her down and get started. We only have so long until the anesthetic wears off," said Bryce.

"Yes, thank you. If we were back home, I'd have torn the OR staff a new one already. I don't do delays," said Elisa. "Julio, you're going to handle my manual suction? Disgusting, but thank you."

He nodded consent but showed no sign of liking it.

Elisa put on a pair of gloves and stood on Emily's right side. "I'm going to pinch you; tell me if you can feel this." She grabbed a bit of skin between her thumb and index finger and pinched them together. "Did you feel that?"

"No, I felt nothing," said Emily. "And I can't move my legs. I think the block is working."

"Good, I'm going to test you one more time. Tell me if you feel this." Elisa moved a few inches higher and grabbed a larger piece of skin. She grimaced as she pinched and twisted the skin as hard as she could. When she released her grip, there was a deep red mark on the skin and a small bruise forming already. "Did you feel that?"

"No, not at all."

"Good, let's get started. Julio, I'll need you on suction once I get in." Elisa picked up the scalpel like a pencil, pinched between her thumb and middle finger. She lowered it to the skin along Emily's right lower abdomen and used her index finger to push it into the skin. She moved her arm sideways across the lower abdomen, creating a long incision similar to beginning a Cesarean delivery. Blood immediately welled up from a few places and she pushed her finger down to stop it.

"Someone turn on the stove. We're going to need some cautery to stop this bleeding and heat is our only option. Get some oven mitts and heat a few kabob skewers. I'll use the tip to apply heat and cauterize the wounds."

Tom walked to the gas stove and turned the knob to ignite a burner. He set it to high and laid a few skewers down with their tips just resting inside the blue flame.

"Once they're red, bring them to me one at a time," said Elisa.

As soon as she finished the sentence, all the lights in the house went black, cloaking the room in darkness.

Chapter Thirty-Nine

"What the hell happened?" yelled Tony.

Several people used their cell phones and turned the flashlights on. The light of the burner illuminated Tom in the kitchen.

"I can't operate on a kitchen table on an island in a hurricane with the lights turned off. I mean, come on," said Elisa. "Someone go fix it."

Julio leaned over to Bryce and whispered, "I told your son to kill the power. I think he just did it. He's hiding in the other villa. I wanted to lure Tony outside to fix it and maybe we can overpower him out there. No chance he hurts anyone else if it's just us out there with him. What do you think? Still got that fishing weight on a string I gave you?"

Bryce nodded and replied without moving his lips. "Yeah, I got it."

"Good. Hit him in the head with it. Maybe a corner will penetrate that thick skull. There are some supplies behind a palm tree by the path as well. See if you can find something to use."

"Tony, I think the generator may have blown the fuse again. Why don't some of us go check it out?" said Julio.

"One person only. It doesn't take a village to check a circuit breaker." Tony pointed at Tom. "You. Go check it out."

Tom glanced at Bryce, who subtly shook his head no. "I really have no idea what I'm doing," he said. "I've never even seen it before and it's in the middle of a hurricane. Someone who has worked on it should go out there.

"I'll go," said Bryce. "I'm already injured. It's not like I can do a lot, anyway." *Except find my son and give him a hug, then tell him it's going to be okay.*

Tony looked at Bryce and then down to the bloody bandage on his leg. "Fine, go out and fix it. You have five minutes."

Bryce stood up immediately and walked over to Val. He leaned down to kiss her forehead and quietly whispered, "I'll find Noah and tell him to keep hiding. You guys will make it through this. If I don't, know that I love you."

He looked back at Tony. "Five minutes? No problem." He held up his watch and pointed at it before smiling and turning toward the door. A slight pull on the handle allowed the door to blow open. "Hey, I think it's letting up a bit," he said. "There isn't any sand blowing in my eyes."

Bryce pulled the door shut behind himself and headed out into the storm.

He followed the path through the foliage toward the other villa and found the front door with a broken pane of glass.

"Noah, are you in here? It's Dad," he yelled once inside.

Seconds later, a bedroom door flung open, and Noah came sprinting out of the room. He slammed into his dad at full speed, but his grip kept them combined as one.

"Dad, what's going on? Is everyone okay? I turned off the generator like Mr. Morales asked me to."

Bryce didn't answer right away, but he held Noah tight.

"Are you okay, Dad? You're crying."

"Yes, I'm fine. I have been worried about you, but this hug is exactly what I needed. We are doing fine. We're actually about to operate on a lady who is very sick and if we do it well, then everyone should get out of here okay because that bad man with the gun will be happy. You did a great job turning off the power. That is why I could come out here to see you. But he thinks I'm fixing the generator, so I need to get back. I want you to stay hidden in a room, but be ready to climb out of a window and run again if the bad man comes back. Do you understand?"

"Yes, I'm just scared. I'll wait here until someone comes to get me."

Bryce leaned down and kissed his cheek. "I know you're scared. And buddy, I am too. That doesn't mean we have to give up, though, does it?"

Noah shook his head.

"That's right. When you're scared, you actually get some super powers that you never knew you had. You run faster, you punch harder and you can do things you never thought you could before. Now I'm going to go do all of those things. I love you, Noah."

Bryce gave him a last squeeze and waved goodbye. He glanced at his watch. *Two minutes left.*

He ignored the pain in his leg and ran back toward the generator and passed right by it. *Why should I stop? I know what's wrong..* He searched for and quickly found the stash of supplies hidden under the palm tree. His eyes fixated on the sharp point of the gaff and his eyes widened. Laying next to the gaff was a roll of fishing line. Fluorocarbon, fifty-pound test. *Perfect. The guy is dumb as a tuna, maybe this will catch him too.*

Bryce grabbed the fishing line and tied a quick knot around the base of the palm tree. He ran across the path and pulled it taught, about twelve inches above the ground, and tied it to another tree. He took the gaff and stood it upright behind the second tree. *If I can just get him to fall, I'll stab this through his lung.*

He glanced at his watch. *Thirty seconds left!* He turned and jogged back toward the main villa.

Chapter Forty

Peter tapped his right heel up and down, attempting to relieve some of the nervous energy building up. ER doctors don't like to sit around and wait when action is called for.

"Tony, where does this all end? Let's assume Emily is going to make it through surgery and you guys get to leave on the boat. What's next? Where can you go? They will hunt you for the rest of your life. Wouldn't it make more sense to put the gun down and let us testify you had a change of heart and tried to make things right? You could help save a life which I'm sure the judge would appreciate. Bryce is a forgiving guy. Maybe you guys can work something out that allows you to serve a little jail time, and then you're free to continue your life?"

"Shut up, we're not going to talk about that," said Tony.

Tom jumped into the conversation. "Why not? I think it's a great idea. The jet ski is gone. We won't even know if the boat survived the storm until sometime tomorrow. What's going to happen if your boat is resting on the bottom? What then?"

Emily made a hissing sound as she exhaled. "Don't listen to them, Tony. The boat will be fine. It's huge and Valerie let out more chain before they left the boat. I even heard the windlass. There are plenty of places for two rich young people to blend in."

"She what? What exactly did you hear?" asked Tony, walking over to the table and standing next to Val, who turned her body and leaned away a bit from his large body.

"Right before we left the boat, she noticed the boat was drifting to shore. She went back into the cockpit and let more chain out. I heard the windlass run for about a minute. It kept starting and stopping, but it sounded like it moved the chain."

Julio shook his head and looked at the ground, his shoulders slumped down.

"What did you do?" screamed Tony, leaning close to Val's face. "I dumped all but ten feet of chain to help the anchor hold during the storm. There's no way you let the chain out for a minute. It would have been completely out after a few seconds."

Val turned back toward Tony, defiant. "What do you mean? I pulled down on the lever. Down for drop more chain, right? I tried to save your damn boat."

Peter and Julio stood and walked toward Tony. "Back off, man. She's the only one who could have brought Emily back from the boat, and she just gave her a huge blood transfusion. You're going to owe Emily's life to her," said Peter.

"Down means pull the chain back onto the boat! The starting and stopping was the windlass trying to pull the boat against the wind and the waves. If you ran it a minute, you probably took up at least fifty feet of chain in those conditions. There's a good chance that the anchor is going to fail now!"

Julio mostly suppressed a smile and tried to make eye contact with Val. Tony's leg kicked forward and sent a chair flying into the entryway. It snapped upon landing, sending splinters of wood across the tile.

When Tony turned to assess the wreckage, Val gave Julio a quick wink. "Oops, sorry. I was trying to help," she said.

"Looks like maybe you need to reassess your options, Tony. Maybe it's not guaranteed that there will be a boat to get you out of here in the morning. Maybe it's time to consider putting the gun away and making sure we all make it through this alive," said Julio.

Tony paused and looked back at Emily laying on the table. He ran his hand through his hair and took a few quick breaths. "Emily, my dad has a lot of money in the banks down here. He carries a lot of influence. I bet we can get reduced charges if we end this now."

"No, you moron. What about the kidnapping back in the States? That's not going to just go away. Keep your head together. Well, what's left of it anyway. That concussion must be messing with you. Just trust me and stick to the plan."

Peter jumped into the conversation using a conciliatory tone. "Hey, I was the one who was kidnapped. If you let us out of here, I won't press charges back home." He raised his right arm with a bend in the elbow. "I swear to God."

Emily laughed. "Tony, don't listen to him. He doesn't even believe in God. We used to laugh at how easy the shifts were on Christmas and Easter when the fake Christians tried to fool God into believing they were worthy of Heaven."

"A lot has changed since we last talked, Emily. I've been coming around slowly. Laying handcuffed to a bed with underwear shoved in your mouth really makes a man ponder the universe. This trip has driven that home even more."

"You mean it? You won't press charges back in the US?" Tony alternated looking at Peter nodding his head, and Emily shaking her head no. He took a big breath in and exhaled in a sigh.

"Emily, we can't run forever. That's not the life I want. I think we should consider it."

Just then, the front door opened, and a rush of wind blew through the villa. Bryce walked in soaking wet, limping hard on his injured leg. "Tony, it's not the circuit breaker and I couldn't figure out what the problem is. I need you to come out and look."

"If we don't get power on, I can't do anything. We're running out of time," said Elisa.

"Her heart rate is climbing again and her pulse is getting weaker," added Jackie. "We only have one more liter of fluid and the blood transfusion is already in."

"Okay, let's go. Come, show me what you tried," said Tony, looking at Bryce and walking toward the door.

"Wait, you can't just leave me here," said Emily. I can't move and they have knives. Leave me the gun. You don't need it. Bryce can hardly walk anyway."

"Do you think you can hold it?"

"Yes, just give it to me."

Tony walked over and held the gun out for Emily, who took it in her right hand. She felt the weight of it and put her finger on the trigger.

"I can handle it. I'm good."

"Just keep your finger off the trigger. Keep it off unless you're ready to fire. We've gone over that," said Tony.

"Whatever, I know what I'm doing." She waved the gun through the air and pointed at the door.

"Hey, don't point that at me!" said Tony, stepping to the side.

"Relax. It's not like I'm going to shoot you. Go get the power turned on. I feel like I'm getting weaker again."

"Fine, we'll be back in a few." He looked at Peter, Julio, Tom, and the rest of the crew. "Don't do anything stupid."

Bryce limped toward the door and pulled it open. A fresh blast of warm, humid air hit them in the face. Tony followed and pulled the door closed. Bryce did not see Julio shaking his head no and mouthing the word 'wait'.

Chapter Forty-One

Tony lowered his head and followed Bryce out of the villa.

Bryce was three steps ahead of him, head down as if leaning against the wind. Where is that tripwire? His eyes scanned forward and found the tree it was tied to. There! Just a few more steps.

"Bryce, I wanted to talk to you away from Emily. What would happen if–", his words cut out and changed to a grunt as his left foot caught on the tripwire and his body pitched forward.

Bryce was ready for the stumble and pulled the triangular fishing weight out of his pants. He gripped the loop of line in his right hand, allowed it to drop until the line was tight, and then swung his arm back.

Tony's momentum carried him forward, twisted him around, causing him to land on his right shoulder and roll onto his back. He looked up and saw Bryce's arm coming down in a fast arc and tried to raise his left arm to protect his head.

The weight slammed into Tony's pinky finger and shattered bone upon impact. It then continued past the finger, struck the side of his head, and ultimately impacted his right clavicle before coming to a stop.

Tony screamed in pain from three separate injuries, all occurring at approximately the same time. Bryce's momentum from the massive swing combined with wet leaves caused him to lose his footing and end up on his back next to Tony.

Bryce immediately rolled away as Tony's hand went to his head and then his collar bone, feeling for injuries. Tony flipped onto his stomach and tried to use his right arm to lift off the ground, but screamed in pain again. He rolled a bit and used his left arm to steady himself and stand up.

By this time, Bryce was on his feet and emerging from behind the palm tree, with a three-foot metal pole held vertical in front of him. Tony's eyes widened as he realized Bryce was holding a fishing gaff with a large, sharp hook on the end.

"You should not have done that, Bryce," said Tony, rubbing his right clavicle with his left hand. "I think you broke my collarbone." He held his hand up, trying to capture some light but finding very little. "And I think I can see bone sticking out of my finger."

What about that giant gash on your head? Have you noticed that yet, you moron?

"I will not let you just kill me, Tony." Bryce was closer to the generator, but Tony was closer to the villa. *I can't just let him walk back in there and grab the gun; I need to keep him out here.*

"What's the fun in that? I'm going to take you down with me, you jackass," said Bryce. He took a few steps to his right near the edge of the path and slowly advanced toward Tony, hoping to flush him in the other direction.

Tony reflexively turned and backed up a few steps, rotating around an imaginary axis between them.

That's it, keep turning.

"You don't understand. Peter and Julio had me convinced to end this standoff and let you go. Peter promised he would not press charges for the kidnapping, and I'm confident my father can get Emily and I reduced charges here in the Bahamas."

Bryce lowered the gaffe a few inches and cocked his head to the side, but continued rotating around the imaginary axis.

"That's right. It was going to be over once we turned the power back on. Your wife pulled up the anchor and my boat is probably crashing into the shore right now, so we have no chance of getting out of here. But no, you had to be the hero again. That offer is off the table. It's back to being personal." Tony laughed. "I don't even care about Emily anymore. She's psychotic. She was the one that pushed me to kidnap Peter and try to kidnap you." Tony put up a hand up to his temple and winced. "Damn you Bryce, my headaches are back worse than ever. I think I'm going–". His lips continued moving but instead of assisting his brain in getting words out, they helped his stomach empty itself on the ground in front of Bryce, who reflexively took a few steps backward. Every person who works in an ER knows how to get out of the way of vomit, urine, and stool. It's a learned reflex.

Bryce's movement stopped when his right foot caught on something and held the foot in place. He hadn't expected that and fell backwards, his arms flailing out behind him, palms open, searching for something to grab into. Finding nothing, he continued backward toward the ground, landing on his back with a thud. He waited for a second to see if any injuries were going to announce their presence with sharp pain.

Tony looked up and saw Bryce on his back again. He wiped his mouth and rushed toward him.

Bryce only had a second before Tony was on him. His right leg was still over the trip wire, so he planted his left foot and pushed it out to generate some backward momentum and create distance. Instant sharp pain penetrated his left tricep, worse than he had ever experienced. His right arm swatted at the source of pain and felt a cold stainless-steel object stuck in his arm.

Chapter Forty-Two

Tony laughed loudly at the scene before him. Bryce Chapman, his nemesis, having just impaled himself with the gaff in his left arm. His left foot was stuck through the looped handle on the end opposite the sharp hook.

"Nice move, genius. I'm going to take you inside and then go check on the power. Keep your foot inside that loop."

Tony reached down with his left arm and grabbed Bryce by the belt. He dragged him the ten feet back to the front door and pushed it open.

"Hi honey, I'm home!" he yelled. "And look what I dragged back with me. Think he's big enough to keep?"

Several lights turned to illuminate the entrance, after which an equal number of screams filled the room.

"Bryce, are you okay?" asked Valerie as she jumped up from her chair. She hurried to his side, but Tony pushed her away.

"Go sit back down. The little sneak is fine. He had set a trip wire for me and then attacked with something before trying to skewer me with the gaff. Fortunately, I was nauseous from the head injury and puked, which made him jump back and trip over the line himself." Tony began laughing again.

"But he just couldn't stop himself. He didn't even seem hurt. He also didn't realize his leg was inside the looped handle of the gaff, so when he kicked his leg out it stabbed that hook deep into his arm." Tony laughed again and then kicked the shaft laying next to Bryce, who followed with a scream of his own.

"Daddy!" cried Hannah, trying to run to him. Tom was close enough to grab her and hold her back.

"Emily, how are you feeling? I think it's time I take that gun back." He walked over and took the gun with his right hand, wincing as the weight pulled on his broken clavicle.

"I'm getting worse. Were you not able to get the power on? We need to get this started," said Emily.

"You're damn right," said Elisa. "This anesthesia doesn't last forever. We're going to lose our window to operate. And it looks like our anesthesiologist is out of commission for a while."

Tony pointed at Julio. "You, get out there and check the generator. We never even got to it. Watch out, there's a damn trip wire across the path." He paused and thought for a moment. "But you probably already knew that. You were one of the people who went outside a while ago. Did you hit the supply shack down by the docks?"

Julio started back at Tony but gave no indication of a reply. He responded with a straight face, "Do you want me to check the generator?"

"Yes, but I'm done messing around. You have three minutes. If you're late, I drag your friend here around by the arm. He comes with a convenient handle. Now get out there."

Julio stood up and hugged Elisa. "Be back soon," he whispered," before heading out the door.

Tony walked over to the couch and sat down gingerly. "Hey, nurse, come over here and wrap my finger up. I can see my bone and it's grossing me out."

Jackie sighed and grabbed a stack of gauze and some tape. "I told you, my name is Jackie." She examined the wound quickly and pieced it together the best she could before covering in gauze and taping it closed.

"Aren't you going to tape it to the one next to it? Even I know that's what you do to a broken finger. Don't start limiting care to me. I'm still the one with the gun." He looked down at Bryce and grinned. "And the one with the trophy catch."

Jackie quickly taped the fourth and fifth fingers together and then walked back to stand next to Elisa.

"Valerie, I want you to know that I had decided to give up. I didn't want to do this anymore, especially with our escape route likely destroyed. But then your husband did what he always does and made things worse. He put you, your family, and your friends directly back in harm's way. How's that make you feel, Bryce?"

Just then, the lights in the room flicked back on and the fans of the air conditioner units hummed.

"There we go. Now, let's get the surgery started," said Tony.

Julio re-entered the villa a minute later. "The storm is really letting up. The rain isn't constant, and the wind isn't as strong as it was, though it still gusts pretty hard. I think we're on the tail end of it."

"Good to hear," said Elisa. "Now get over here and get ready to suck all the blood out of her because I need to open her up."

Julio picked up the plastic water tubing from the fridge and took a position across the table from Elisa.

"First, help me wrap her abdomen with this plastic. I want to create a clean field around the incision." She ripped open several alcohol wipes and cleaned the skin vigorously around her planned incision. She used the first wipe to rub firmly in all directions, and then the subsequent ones to make ever expanding spirals outward. Once that was complete, she pulled several lengths of plastic wrap from the box and laid them across Emily's abdomen.

"It's not perfect, but it's the best I can do. We'll need to get her on antibiotics at some point," said Elisa.

"Bryce, you can't see anything down there, can you?" asked Tony. "How about I sit you up so you can see better?"

Tony walked over to Bryce and slowly turned in a circle. "Where can I put you where you won't be able to do anything else to mess this up, but I can still keep an eye on you?"

His eyes scanned around from place to place and finally landed on a solid appearing wooden beam mounted above the front window. "Yeah, that will do, I think."

Tony reached down and grabbed Bryce's right arm with his left. Bryce gripped his forearm and gingerly stood up. Once he was upright, Tony grabbed the shaft of the gaff, eliciting a groan from Bryce.

"Oh sorry, didn't mean to be so rough with you," said Tony, laughing. "Go stand under that curtain, just to the left of the window."

Bryce did his best to comply. The tip of the gaff was tenting the skin down by his elbow, having entered behind his triceps. The handle pointed down to the floor, with the loop still wrapped around his leg. It made for an awkward gait, one accented by sharp stabbing pain each time pressure was applied to the shaft.

Tony grabbed the thick curtains and pulled them between the gaff and Bryce's chest, looping them back over the beam and tying a quick knot. The end of the curtain was too high for Bryce to reach, and he couldn't move without the gaff pulling on the flesh of his left arm.

"I bet I could even use those curtains as a tow strap. No way that beam is coming out of the wall, either. Enjoy your perch Bryce."

Val looked over with a frown. She tried to convey as much empathy as possible as she took in the scene before her. Bryce, her husband and father of her children, hung up from his own body while the man who promised to kill him laughed hysterically.

"Enough, I'm cutting. Julio, get ready. If you can't clear out the blood, I can't see anything. When I open her up, she may bleed more because the pressure in her abdomen will go down. We will be in a race to get control of the hemorrhage before she bleeds out."

Elisa picked up the scalpel and drew an imaginary line across Emily's lower abdomen. "Let's hope you're numb, girl." She pressed the scalpel into her skin and pressed firmly as she pulled the blade through the tissue.

Chapter Forty-Three

Edward Ferguson paced around the family room in his small home several miles from Swan Cay.

"Honey, sit down. I'm worried you're going to trip on something in the dark," said his wife.

"Isabella, I can't stop worrying about our guests. I know the facilities can take it, but can the people? I wish there was some way I could get out there to them."

"Well, do you have a boat that can handle the sea state?"

"No, I don't."

"Do you have a helicopter and pilot who can fly in these conditions?"

"No, I don't."

"Then stop feeling guilty. You didn't force them to keep their plans when the storm was forecast. You didn't force them to stay on the island when it looked like it was getting worse, did you?"

Edward looked at his wife and sighed.

"No, I didn't."

"Then sit down. Worrying never calmed a storm."

"That's not entirely true," he said. "Remember when the disciples were in the boat during a storm? They were terrified and worried, then a bit later the storm abated?"

"You're right. I stand corrected. It happened one time. When Jesus told the storm to calm down. Do you happen to have Jesus here?"

"Well, not literally."

"Then sit down and stop worrying. You can get out there as soon as the storm has let up. Assuming the boat survives, of course. Let's open that bottle of wine we'd been saving. I think you could use some relaxation."

"My dear, if relaxed is how you want me to feel, I think we should be in the bedroom instead of the family room."

Isabelle laughed as she walked to the wine cabinet and retrieved a bottle of Pinot. "I see you haven't forgotten how to spend time during a power outage. I'm sure your friends are having just as much fun with their liquor cabinet and their spouses as well." She closed the cabinet door and walked into the bedroom, glancing back over her shoulder. "You coming?"

Chapter Forty-Four

Elisa's hand moved steadily across Emily's abdomen, extending the perfectly straight incision through her skin. She held pressure on several small areas of bleeding as she extended the incision deeper. Tom handed her red-hot skewers when requested to cauterize the small vessels she encountered.

"I'm going to need someone to retract for me. You need to keep the wound open so that I can see deeper into her abdomen. Any volunteers?"

"I'll do it. Just don't cut me with your scalpel. I'm not some medical student holding a retractor for you," said Tom as he pulled on a pair of gloves.

"Great, this will be just like the donut scene again. You know, I still catch hell for that from my colleagues?"

Elisa was referring to a presentation during the morbidity and mortality rounds where the surgery department discussed a case that Bryce, Tom and she were involved in. The ER team felt Elisa went too far in performing procedures on the patient and Tom drove that point home by ripping apart a jelly donut in front of the entire surgical staff.

"That was hilarious," added Bryce from over by the front door. "Hey, I'm trying to pay attention, but If I don't move, the pain's not too bad at this point. I'm not sure how long I can hold this position, though. If I pass out, will someone hold me up so the point doesn't dig deeper into me?"

"Sure buddy, I got you. Give me a warning before you pass out, though," said Peter.

"You can just hang on by your arm if you want. Those curtains and that beam could probably hold up three of you," said Tony.

"Emily, can you feel any of this?" asked Elisa.

"No, not really. I feel some tugging, but there's no pain."

"Okay, I'm opening the abdomen. We need to go quickly here. Julio, get ready on suction. Tom, hold back what I tell you to hold back."

She extended her incision deeper and separated the muscle layers and ultimately the slick peritoneal membrane, the final layer protecting and encasing the abdominal contents. As the blade opened the peritoneum, it released pressure from the cavity, sending a fountain of blood up through the opening.

"Julio, get in there and suction," commanded Elisa.

He quickly placed one end of the tube in the wound and placed the other into his mouth. He sucked on the end of the tube as hard as he could, but was making minimal progress. The blood would not enter the tube.

"Suck harder," yelled Tony.

"It's not working. I can't generate enough negative pressure to draw the blood up."

"Maybe the tube is too long. Can we cut it shorter?" asked Sal. "My speech therapist showed me it's easier to drink through a shorter straw."

"Great idea, shorter tube means less resistance," said Elisa.

Jackie ran to the kitchen and grabbed a pair of scissors, then cut off most of the tubing, leaving only a few feet sticking out of Emily. Tony reached his hand out and Jackie tried to hand him the scissors.

"No, never hand a sharp object to someone with the pointed end toward them. I swear, are you guys idiots or intentionally trying to hurt people?" said Tony.

She reversed the scissors and handed them over.

Julio tried again to draw blood up the tube and was slightly more successful, but not enough to make a difference.

"This isn't working. The tube isn't collapsing, we just don't have enough negative pressure. We need better suction or I can't continue," said Elisa. She picked up the small forceps and pinched the hole in Emily's abdomen closed, then clamped the instrument together. "Come on, we need another idea."

"Her heart rate is back to 140 and her pulse is getting weaker," said Jackie.

"Hang the second liter of fluid," said Tom.

"What she needs is blood," said Elisa. "And for me to stop her bleeding. Neither of which seems very likely at the moment."

"Think of something," screamed Tony. "You have to. She's going to die!" He was pacing the room again, holding the wound on his head.

"Where are we going to find a vacuum pump?" asked Elisa.

No one spoke for as they all considered the problem.

"What about using a vacuum?" asked Val. "There's one in the front closet."

"No, that's meant to pump air. It can't handle water, let alone blood," said Tom.

Another moment of silence began, interrupted only by the sound of rain on the glass and wind whistling under the front door.

"The washing machine."

All eyes turned toward Bryce.

"Remember when the drain pump on ours went out Val? I had to take the front access panel off and the pump was right there? I bet we could connect the tubing to that pump, turn the washer on the spin cycle and pump the blood right out."

"There's not enough tubing to reach that far," said Tony. "We'll have to move the table closer to it."

"I'll look at the machine. Where's it at?" asked Peter.

"It's in the laundry room, the door next to the bathroom. There's a junk drawer in the kitchen that has a few screwdrivers in it," said Val.

Peter grabbed the tools and found the washing machine. In a few minutes, he had the panel removed and the pump exposed. "There's a pipe going into the pump, and a pipe going out. Should be straightforward enough."

"We can't move her. She has an open abdomen, and the light is best right where we are. This fixture is outstanding. I'm getting light from a dozen angles," said Elisa.

"Then what do you suggest?" asked Tom, his voice trailing off out of frustration.

"Bring the washing machine over here."

Peter sighed. "Okay, I'm on it." He unhooked the hose connections and then unplugged the machine. He pulled it out of the wall and twisted it back and forth, walking it slowly toward the door. Julio came over and helped guide it through the door, then they both dragged it over to the kitchen table where Rebecca plugged it into an outlet.

"I don't want to just shoot blood all over the place, grab a bucket or something to stick the drain hose into," said Elisa.

Peter went back and found a plastic bucket from the laundry room. He put the drain hose from the washing machine into it and then took the end of the hose from Julio's hand and brought it to the pump.

"The water line for the fridge is smaller than the pump intake. We need an adapter."

"Never a hardware store when you need one," said Val. "Oh well, we tried. Good job everyone."

"You're not quitting. Figure something out," said Tony.

"Oh, yes I am." Val smashed her palm onto the table. "You can't simply will a miracle to happen, Tony, even if you're holding a gun. Frankly, it's amazing we've even gotten this far. But I'm tired of your bullshit. You shot Bryce and now he's hanging on the wall like some sick trophy. My son is out there, lost in a hurricane, and my daughter has to watch all of this. You've drained a lot of my blood and are planning to kill my husband, even if we're successful. You suck at motivating people, you evil bastard."

Tony started back at Val with an open mouth and a confused look for a few seconds before he recovered enough to speak. "I'm not evil. I'm out here trying to save my girlfriend's life. Do evil people do that?"

"And why are we doing that on this island at this very moment?" replied Val. "Because you tried to kidnap and kill my husband. You stalked us here by... actually, how did you even know we were here?" Val looked around the room and met all the blank stares. "Never mind, it doesn't matter. I never knew you before you drowned, but since you came back to life, you certainly have acted evil to my family."

"It was your Facebook post. 'See you in a week, Swan Cay'. That post told us all we needed to know."

Val's head dropped to her chest. "Damn social media," she mumbled.

"For your other comments, can you blame me? My dad heaps praise on the guy who caused me to drown, then blames me and my friends for what happened. He treats me like I'm damaged goods, someone he can't trust. Cuts me off from the family finances. This is how I'm treated by the guy who couldn't be bothered to make it to my birthday parties. To tuck me in at night. Sure, he hired people to do all of that. But actually be there? No way. Not him. Not for me."

"You realize Bryce isn't your dad, right?" asked Val. "You're saying this is your dad's fault now as well as Bryce's? Do you take any responsibility for getting drunk and then acting inappropriately toward me before you drowned?"

"I have no memory of anything that happened that day."

"Well, that's convenient. Just block out the bad things you've done and continue blaming everyone else."

"I didn't block them out; I lost memory when I drowned. I'm still not normal, and the doctors say I never will be. That's why I don't really care what happens anymore. I don't have fifty more years left. They tell me I'll probably have dementia in ten."

"So why take everyone down with you? Would it have been better if we just let you die that day?"

Tony's eyes filled with tears, and his speech faltered. "Do you know how many times I've wished that had happened? How many times I've screamed it to the sky? You don't know what I've been through since then. How hard life has been? Emily has been the one positive thing that's happened to me since I drowned. She cares about me. She makes me happy."

"Really? Who thought up the plan to kidnap Peter as a way to get Bryce? Whose idea was it to come down here and do this now? Is she really a good influence on you, Tony?"

"Enough," yelled Emily from the table. At least it was intended to be a yell. She leaned up a bit off the table to increase the volume of her voice, and in doing so, she forced more blood out past Elisa's clamp. "Tony, stop listening to them. I can't keep loving you if I'm dead. Figure out the pump and get me more blood."

Tony wiped his eyes with the back of his hand and regained his composure. "You heard the lady. How are we going to get the pump connected?"

"Just cut a piece of plastic from a lid and make an adapter. We can wrap it all in plastic to make it airtight."

Tom looked at Julio and smiled. "How do you come up with this stuff so quickly?"

Julio shrugged it off. "Years of being in the military and dealing with constant supply shortages. If you can't get what you need, you adapt and find a way." He stood up and walked toward the kitchen. Halfway there, he felt something shift inside his shorts and a metallic ping followed shortly after. He looked down at the fillet knife that had fallen out of his shorts.

"What is that? Were you hiding a knife in your pants? What else are you keeping from me?"

"Nothing. I forgot it was even in there. I always travel with a crotch knife."

"You guys even suck at lying. Okay, take your pants and underwear off. Turn the pockets inside out."

"Come on Tony, there are kids here," said Julio.

"I don't care. Just do it around the corner of the kitchen counter. You can put everything back on after you prove to me you're not hiding anything else. In fact, everyone else who has been outside, get in the kitchen and strip down."

Tom and Peter joined Julio in the kitchen and removed their clothes alongside him.

Julio put his right hand into his shorts pocket and cupped the fishing weight in his palm. He pinched the bottom of his pocket between two fingers and inverted it, showing the empty pocket to Tony. The others followed suit and showed their empty pockets.

"Fine, get dressed again. Oh, and Peter, I see what Emily meant about the steroids. Great look, buddy."

Peter fumed as he pulled his clothes back on again. "Just give me two seconds, that's all I need," he whispered to the others.

"When we act, it needs to be all of us as hard as we can. He can't shoot three directions at once," said Julio.

"I'm old, but pissed off. Just give me a signal I can't miss," added Tom.

Tom and Peter went back to their former positions and Julio searched the cabinets for an appropriate piece of plastic. He lifted a large lid from a container and showed it to Tony. "I think this is our best option. I need a knife or scissors or something."

"Just keep everything where I can see it."

Julio grabbed a pair of scissors and took the lid over to the washing machine. He cut the intake hose a few inches above the pump and held the lid against the tubing. He drew a quick outline of the pipe on the lid and repeated the process for the ice maker's water line. When finished, he had two concentric circles drawn on the translucent plastic lid.

He gingerly cut around the outside of the larger circle and then carved out the smaller circle with the tip of a knife.

When he put the knife down, he had a reasonably well constructed adapter.

"Let's see if it works." He pressed the custom piece over the drainpipe and then pushed the water tubing through the center hole. The fit was snug. He pulled some plastic wrap out of the box and wrapped it as tight as he could. "Anyone know how to get this thing to kick on?"

"It should kick on when the spin cycle starts. Just set it to spin and pour some water down the other end. We'll see what happens." Julio adjusted the dial and Jackie went to the sink to fill a glass with water. She poured it into the free end of the tubing until there was several feet of water in the line. Julio started the machine and everyone turned to watch the tubing. The drum started to spin and a second noise started, followed by the water level dropping in the tube. A slurping sound came from the adapter piece as air was sucked in around the edges of the tube. A few spurts of water dribbled out the far end of the tube and into the bucket.

"The seal isn't good enough. It's not going to work," said Julio.

Elisa dropped her head and swore under her breath.

Chapter Forty-Five

"We need to find a way to seal this connection," said Julio.

"And quickly," added Elisa.

"Peanut butter," said Sal. "Smear a lot of peanut butter around the connections. If thick enough, it should make a good enough seal for a few minutes."

"I love it," said Julio, hopping up and heading to the pantry. He opened the door and pulled out a large jar of creamy peanut butter. "If the kids weren't here, we probably wouldn't have bought this. Thank goodness for good fortune."

"Excuse me?" said Val. "I'd rather our kids were not here with us. I'm sure we could have used cream cheese or many other things. Our kids being here is not a good thing."

Julio lowered his voice. "You're right. It was a stupid thing to say. Sorry."

"It's fine. I know that's not what you meant. We're all sort of at peak stress level right now. I didn't mean to lash out at you. Thanks for trying so hard to solve the problems we're facing and maybe get us out of here."

Julio nodded to Val and removed the plastic wrap. He used his fingers to smear large amounts of peanut butter on each side of the adapter and then wrapped it tightly again with plastic. This time, he pinched the top and bottom of the plastic with his fingers.

"Try it again."

Jackie restarted the washer on the spin cycle and this time when the drain pump kicked on, it sucked the water quickly down the tube and launched out the back of the machine into the plastic bucket.

"Yes!" yelled Elisa. "Okay, let's move. Peter, I need you on suction. Julio is going to have to stay where he is."

Peter took the open end of the tubing and held it next to the clamped incision. Elisa took it from him and grabbed the clamp with her other hand. "Tom, be ready to hold the wound open once I release this clamp. Peter, after I clean out all the blood, I need you to hold the suction for me. Try to keep your fingers in front of it so it doesn't suck her bowel or bladder into the tube. I have a feeling it's going to suck more than Chapman."

"Hey, no fair!" yelled Bryce from the corner.

"Ready?" asked Elisa. When everyone nodded yes, she released the clamp and Tom pulled the wound open, extending the opening as far as he could with his fingers. Elisa cradled the suction tubing in her hand and lowered it into the pool of blood. Instantly the tubing turned red and two seconds later, the machine was spitting out a steady stream of blood.

"Oh, that is disgusting," said Tony, holding a hand to his mouth. He leaned against the wall and became pale and sweaty.

Julio quickly glanced at Tom and Peter, then at Tony.

Tony breathed heavily and sat down hard on the couch, but did not pass out. The feeling quickly passed and in less than a minute, he stood up again. The sweat on his forehead had already dried up.

Julio shook his head and continued to hold the tubing in place.

"I can nearly see the bottom of her abdominal cavity. How much blood is in the bucket?" asked Elisa.

Tony glanced down and his eyes widened in disbelief. "It's a two-gallon bucket, and it looks more than half full already."

"Damn it, I wish we had more blood. She's going to bleed out before we get her off this table."

"Then give her more blood. Val still has the IV in. Do another transfusion, now!" yelled Tony.

"Elisa, would you keep those thoughts in your head? Val can't do it twice. That's too much. Do you want two dead women?" said Bryce.

"I thought she was some kind of super athlete. She can handle it. Do it."

"Bryce, it's fine. This is the last time. I'll be all right." She looked at Jackie and nodded. "Drain me again."

Jackie stopped the fluids going into Emily and moved the tubing back to Val's IV. "You are one tough momma."

She added another small dose of Peter's blood thinner and then laid the bag on the floor, where it quickly filled with blood.

"I'm going to need a vacation after this vacation," said Val. "One with lots of iron pills and nowhere near the Bahamas."

"Babe, how about Jamaica? We've always wanted to go there."

Val closed her eyes and smiled. "Sounds great Chap. But I'm making the plans this time." She leaned back into the chair and tried to calm down as the next twenty percent of her blood volume drained away.

"We're nearly there. It's definitely coming from her right ovary." Elisa reached deep into Emily's pelvis and lifted clots out of the incision. "I need something to dump this clot into. I don't want to clog up the suction."

Jackie retrieved a pot from the kitchen and sat it on the table. Elisa started dropping fist-sized clots into it, each one landing with a soft splat.

"Thanks, that's better. Emily, I can see the problem. You definitely have a ruptured ectopic pregnancy that is inside your right fallopian tube. Do you understand what that means?"

"Yeah, I got it. I've been working in medicine for years," said Emily.

"Of course. Anyway, this baby is not viable, and it's killing you. I can see a small artery pumping blood out into your pelvis. Normally I would remove the entire fallopian tube, but I don't have confidence in our equipment here. I don't want to cut anything I don't have to, so I'm going to tie off the vessels on either side of the rupture which should stop the bleeding. You will still need another surgery to remove my sutures and this ectopic. Do you understand?"

"Yes, I get it. Just do what you have to in order to save me."

"Elisa, relax. You don't need verbal consent to save her life. We're alone on an island in the middle of a damn hurricane. You don't have to write an op note either," said Bryce.

"Shut up ER. There's a reason you guys aren't welcome in my operating room." The words sounded harsh, but both Elisa and Bryce had smiles on their faces. The back-and-forth banter had become as natural as saying hello.

"Is the next transfusion hanging yet?"

"Almost full. Should be up in a few minutes," said Jackie. She leaned down and put the pulse oximeter on Val's finger. "Hey, how are you feeling?" She looked down and noted a heart rate of nearly one hundred and fifty.

"Weak. Very weak," said Val.

Jackie looked at the IV bag, just over halfway full. She closed the valve and stopped the blood donation. She lifted the bag and tubing, careful to shield it from Tony's view. "I am hanging the next units of blood now."

Bryce could see the bag was only half full of blood and breathed a sigh of relief. *Thank you Jackie. I can always count on you to take care of my family. We owe you big time. Hopefully, I'll get a chance to repay you.*

"Jackie, can you hand me the suture? I'm ready to tie it off," said Elisa.

Jackie picked up one of the two suture packets and peeled back the two layers of plastic, exposing the cardboard packet with the suture inside. Elisa grabbed it from inside the plastic and pulled the needle out from its holder. She picked up the scissors and cut the needle off and set it to the side.

"I'm going to reach in and tie off the tube on either side of the ectopic. You may feel some tugging here." She reached in and wrapped the suture around the fallopian tube and created a knot, then pulled it snug. As she did so, the suture broke in her hand.

"Damn it. The suture broke. This is only 4-0 suture, we'd usually use at least 2-0 thread here. Even so, this shouldn't have broken so easily. How old is the package?"

Jackie looked at the other remaining suture and frowned. "It expired six years ago. Good thing QUACC isn't here.

Those administrative morons. They nearly shut our ER down over Emily's rats and expired products."

"What is it with you and expired products?" said Peter, directing his gaze and comment toward Emily.

Elisa regained control of the conversation. "That figures. Crappy equipment and expired products. I'll just have to be gentle and not pull so hard." She retied the knot, using less tension on the knot. She then repeated the procedure two more times for extra holding strength. "Hand me the last packet and I'll tie off the other side." A minute later, she had tied three more knots and leaned back, satisfied with her work.

"We're done. Now I just need to close. Shut off the washing machine. There's nothing bleeding right now and we have nothing to irrigate with, anyway."

Elisa looked down, and her mouth dropped open. "I can't believe it. I don't have any suture left to close her abdomen."

"What does that mean?" asked Tony.

"It means I don't have a way to close these layers of skin. I used the only suture on the fallopian tube."

"So what do we do? We can't leave her open like that."

"What about fishing line?" said Tom. "It's basically what most suture material is, anyway."

"It's not sterile. I can't put something inside her that isn't sterile."

"We have that pot of boiling water. We could sterilize it that way," said Tom.

"What is the melting point of fishing line? Will it be too weak after boiling it?" asked Peter.

"No, it should be fine," said Val. "My 3D printing filament doesn't melt until it's at least one hundred eighty degrees

Celsius. We're only getting up to one hundred with boiling water if we keep it off the bottom of the pot."

"Aren't you full of helpful knowledge," said Tony. "There's a roll of fishing line right outside. It's what made Bryce fall on his ass and poke himself with the gaff. Julio, go grab it. I have a feeling you had something to do with it being there anyway."

Julio retrieved the spool of fishing line and was still pulling pieces of leaves and other debris off it when he walked back in. "The storm is just about over. It's not even raining anymore." He held out the line. "Here you go. Where do you want it?"

Elisa pointed to the kitchen. "In there. We can't use it covered in crap. Cut off several sections about eighteen inches long, rinse them off, and then toss them in the boiling water. We'll let it boil for fifteen minutes and then I'll try to close her up. I'm going to need a needle or a hook or something to pull it through."

"If we have fifteen minutes to kill and the storm is slowing down, I'm going to go check out the boat. Emily, can you hold the gun again?"

"Yeah, I'm feeling better and they're just about done with me. I can feel a tingling sensation in my chest. If the block is wearing off, maybe I'll be walking in an hour or two."

"And then what, you just waltz on out of here?" asked Val.

"I was thinking we cruise out of here on our luxury yacht, actually. With any luck, she's still floating."

"She may be floating, but the storm surge is headed out. You're going to lose a few feet of water depth in the next few hours. Better hurry. Don't forget to write," said Bryce.

"You're coming with us, don't forget that," said Tony.

"How am I going to swim to a boat and climb on with this hooked to me?"

"Oh, I won't make you do that. We'll just tie a line to the gaff and drag you. Maybe we'll catch a king mackerel while we drag you behind us. Once we hit the drop, I'll clip my dive belt to you and cut the line. See? I'm no monster. I'd never make you try to climb on a boat."

Tony handed Emily the weapon, which she grabbed quickly.

"Wow, you seem stronger," said Tony.

"I really do feel better. Once she controlled the bleeding, I could feel a difference. Once they finish the transfusion and the spinal block wears off, I should be ready to go."

Tony leaned down to kiss her on the lips. She raised her arms to hug him, but he jumped back before she could complete the embrace.

"Hey, you just pointed the gun at me again!" he said. "Stop doing that!"

"Sorry, but my finger wasn't on the trigger. It's fine."

"Whatever, I'll be right back. Don't let them try anything. Bryce, stay right there."

Bryce smirked and nodded in reply. "Couldn't move if I wanted to."

Tony opened the door and stepped out into the night.

Chapter Forty-Six

He felt the rush of wind against his face, but much less intense than the last time he went out and fought Bryce. *The storm is ending. It's time to see if we can get off this damn island.*

He removed the trip wire from the palm tree and tossed the line into the brush. *That idiot. I was ready to shut this all down and walk away, but he had to push it. Just had to take another swipe at me. Damn him for that. Now how am I going to end this without going to jail?*

Tony followed the path down to the dock, avoiding downed palm fronds and random debris laying along the path.

I don't see a way out of here that lets me maintain a normal life. Emily is crazy. I can't keep her around any longer. She's most of the reason we're in this, anyway. I wish I could call my dad, but would he even talk to me?

His eyes had adjusted to the dark, allowing him to make out the path better as he neared the shore. Suddenly, the palm tree in front of him changed right before his eyes. *What is that? It's glowing!* He took a few more steps and looked around, finally looking at the sky. *The moon! The clouds are breaking up! That boat better still be floating.*

The light allowed him to increase his speed and soon he reached the beach, littered with debris and foam. His eyes swept the water, looking for the boat, locking on once he found it.

Finding the information he needed, Tony turned and ran back toward the villa.

Chapter Forty-Seven

"Emily, what is your goal in all of this? Why are you torturing my family?" Val asked in a tone of despair. She was fatigued from the events of the last few hours and eager for the situation to end.

"My goal? Same as yours. Happiness. Financial security. A family with healthy children."

"How does kidnapping Peter, trying to kidnap and kill Bryce, and holding all of us hostage, help you accomplish that?"

"To be honest, this isn't how I saw my life going. I thought I would get into medical school, meet some gorgeous resident or fellow and get married. When the medical school rejection letters started coming in one after the other, I started to lose hope. Then I stopped even getting interviews. It became clear that despite my impressive medical knowledge, it was going to be hard for me to become a doctor."

"There are a lot of other roles in medicine where you can provide care to patients. Did you consider a physician assistant program?" asked Val.

Emily scoffed. "A PA? Why would I want to do that? I watch them in the ER running around doing all the work while the doc sits around and just signs the chart. I don't want to be someone's servant."

"But they provide care to patients and make their own decisions in the moment. They make considerable differences in the lives of their patients. Bryce tells me stories about them all the time."

"It's not about making a difference. A hurricane makes a difference. It's about proving I can do it. It's about making a lot of money. Being respected." She held the gun up and turned it over in her hand. "I don't know if you've noticed, but I'm pretty close to accomplishing my goals at the moment."

"How can you say you want a family with healthy children while you hold someone else's kids at gunpoint? Isn't that just the slightest bit hypocritical?" asked Peter.

"Hypocrisy? How? What I want has nothing to do with anyone else. Life is a zero-sum game. Look at Tony's family. Where do you think all that money came from?"

Rebecca Sharpe had stayed silent through nearly the entire ordeal, but broke into the conversation. "Who taught you that nonsense? Life is not a zero-sum game. Have you ever been loved? When I hug Tom, it makes us both happy. Where does that happiness come from? Is there equal sadness that spawns somewhere to balance out reciprocal joy and pleasure? Oh sure, you can believe it's a zero-sum game. You can walk around waving a gun at people, taking pleasure in their misery. That creates a zero-sum situation. But if someone's sadness brings you joy, or someone's success makes you mad, then it speaks poorly of you, my dear."

"You don't know me. You don't know my situation," said Emily defensively.

"I know you well enough." Rebecca stood and took a step toward Emily. "You seem pretty good at destroying the lives of people around you. First Peter, then almost the entire Emergency Department with your little stunt. Now you seem hell-bent on destroying Tony."

"Destroy him? I saved him!" shouted Emily. "He couldn't see past tomorrow when I met him. All he wanted to do was get Bryce back for what had happened. Well, and talk to his counselor. Some on-line app he talked to all the time. I put a stop to that quickly. He didn't need that garbage. I've seen enough psych patients to know how to help him."

"Emily, you're a scribe. You have no formal medical training. You're no therapist. How could you do that to someone who was dealing with a traumatic brain injury?" asked Peter. "I mean, I'm no fan of Tony, but that's not the—"

A loud explosion cut Peter's comment off. The gun jerked in Emily's hands as she fired a bullet through the ceiling. Everyone jumped back, silent except for Hannah, who started screaming and holding her ears.

Emily waited for the shock to dissipate before continuing. "I am the one in control here. Peter, you do NOT get to lecture me about how to treat people. You dumped me and then immediately started dating the entire emergency department staff. You made me stand there and watch while you hit on them in the patient rooms. Funny how you never took lunch breaks when we worked together, but when your little nurse friends showed up early for their shift, you suddenly had to take a quick break. Did they care that the break only lasted a few minutes, Peter?"

"Can we talk about anything other than this?" asked Elisa. "I've never had a patient shoot a gun during a case, and I can tell you I'm not a fan. Anyone else's ears ringing?"

Several heads nodded yes.

"How much longer on the sterilization?"

The front door burst open suddenly and Tony jogged in. "I saw the moon!" he said excitedly. "And the boat. It's still floating but very close to the shore. I think it might be touching bottom, so we don't have a lot of time. Have they closed you up yet, Emily?"

"Not yet. We're almost done with the sterilization procedure," said Jackie.

"No, you're done now. We are out of time." He snapped his fingers and pointed at Jackie and then the pot of boiling water.

"You're such an ass," said Jackie as she pulled the fishing line from the water.

"I brought a few hooks from the fishing shack. Hopefully, they will work to suture with. I looked for the gaff but couldn't find it. I know it's hanging around here somewhere," said Tony with a confused look on his face.

"Hilarious. Really," said Bryce.

Tony held his hand out and displayed the hooks to Elisa. She took the smallest one and compared the size of the eye with the fishing line. "That's not going to fit. We'll have to use a larger needle. I'm glad the plastics team won't see this wound and mock me over it. I'd be embarrassed. Someone get me the vodka or rum."

Tom brought over a bottle of rum and poured it over the hook. "Better than nothing, I guess." He then put the bottle to his lips and took a big drink. "Bolus," he said.

"And titrate," added Val.

Elisa took the fishing line and fed it through the eye of a hook. She tied a quick knot and then straightened the hook the best she could. She took the hemostats and crushed the barb to make it as smooth as possible. Once satisfied, she closed the layers of tissue to finish the case.

"How long until she'll be able to walk?" asked Tony.

"Probably not for another few hours," said Tom. "She'll get sensation back before motor function will return."

Tony's smile faded as his eyes widened. "A few hours? We don't have that kind of time. The water is receding, and the boat is nearly aground as it is. We need to leave soon."

"Then just carry me. You're strong enough," said Emily.

"I have a broken collarbone and a broken left hand. I can't carry you. Plus, I need to get Bryce down there and maintain control of the gun," replied Tony.

"Well, isn't this a predicament?" asked Julio with a grin. "A real logistics challenge. Reminds me of the story of the farmer traveling with a chicken, a bag of feed, and a fox. He needed to cross the river, but he could only take one thing with him at a time. If he took the fox, the chicken would eat the seed. If he took the seed, the fox would eat the chicken. What are you going to do, Tony?"

Chapter Forty-Eight

There was no immediate answer. Tony sniffed the air and looked at Emily. "Did you fire the gun?"

"Yes, they were mouthing off and I couldn't take it anymore. I fired one bullet into the ceiling to shut them up."

"Okay, fine. But don't do it again." He turned back toward Julio. "To answer your question, this farmer is going to be creative. I can't carry Emily because of my injuries. Bryce can walk. The rest of you can carry Emily down to the beach and get her on the boat."

"Why would we do that? We just saved her life, isn't that enough? Figure out your own escape," said Julio.

"I'm done," said Elisa as she finished up the last suture. "The wound is closed. You need to rest and not lift anything for two weeks. But really you should have a repeat surgery in twenty-four hours for definitive management. I just put a band-aid on it."

"Fine. We'll do it when we can," said Tony. "Bryce, you're going to have to walk. I hope you can do that without ripping that hook into your arm any further."

"Maybe you could let me lean on you to steady myself as we walked to the shore? It's the least you could do."

"No way. I don't trust you. Every time you're close to me, I get injured and my head is already killing me. That run made it worse and my concussion is back full force. Besides, my arms will be full carrying your daughter. She's my last insurance policy to stop you guys from doing anything stupid. Once we're underway, I'll toss her back toward shore with a life jacket on and you can retrieve her."

"You bastard, you leave my daughter out of this," said Bryce.

"We agree with Bryce. We will not help if you involve Hannah," said Julio.

Val stood up and ripped the IV out of her arm. She grabbed a band-aid from the first-aid kit and used it to secure a folded piece of gauze over the access site. "Tony, you're just going to make this worse. I don't think anyone in this room is going to let you take my daughter out of the room. Take me instead. I'll just swim back. I promise I won't try to fight you. Not that you left me enough blood to do anything, even if I wanted to."

Tony looked around the room and took in the determined looks of the adults. The celebratory mood from having overcome so many challenges to perform an operation using limited resources gave way to one of grim reality. Everyone knew a showdown was coming. They just didn't know how it was going to start.

Bryce's face hardened as he considered what he could do. He looked up at the thick curtain tying him to the beam over the window. *There's no way I could rip that off the wall, even if I could stand the pain of the gaff poking further into me. There's one thing I could try, but it's going to hurt.*

Bryce whispered something quietly toward Tony, but it was too quiet to be understood. Tony turned to look at Bryce, who repeated the whisper and motioned with his arm for Tony to come closer.

"What is it?" asked Tony.

"I have another idea, but it's a decision I want you to make, not Emily." As he was speaking, he tried to make eye contact with Peter, Tom, or Julio. None of them connected with his gaze. *Well crap.*

Tony took a few steps closer and rotated his left arm out with the palm raised. "Well, what is it?"

Just one step closer. You are not leaving this room with my daughter.

"It is an escape plan. I think I can help you get out of here, but not if I'm dead."

Tony took another step closer and leaned forward a few inches. "Yeah? How so."

Bryce bent his knees as far as he could with the gaff in his arm and then jumped as hard as possible. He brought his left knee up and yanked down on his left arm simultaneously, ramming the sharp end of the gaff further into his arm, but generating upward momentum to lift his body off the ground. His right leg came up next with the hip extended and knee flexed, then whipped forward and extended his knee, catching Tony square in the side of his head with the heel of his foot.

Bryce screamed in pain and landed back on the ground, quickly standing up to take pressure off his arm. He looked sideways and saw the tip of the gaff now protruding through his skin. A wave of nausea came over him, along with an instant layer of sweat.

Tony stumbled backward from the blow but did not fall down. He held his head and howled in pain.

A second blow smacked Tony in the head as Sal brought his crutch down with all his might. The force of the swing pulled Sal forward and pitched him onto the ground. His right arm could not catch the weight of his falling body and his head smacked the ground with a thud.

Another loud explosion filled the room and the window next to Bryce shattered, letting in a rush of wind and humid air.

Tony screamed again and looked at his left forearm, that was now dripping blood from a fresh wound. "You shot me!" he screamed at Emily.

"Oh my God, I'm so sorry. I saw them attacking you, so I tried to shoot Bryce." Emily was trembling, but kept a firm grip on the gun.

Julio had moved toward the gun when Tony screamed, but stopped when Emily pointed to gun his direction.

"Now that you've seen I'll use it, I suggest you back the hell off," she said.

Julio raised his hands and backed up a few steps.

Jackie helped Sal off the ground and onto the couch. She checked him over for injuries before sitting down next to him and glaring at Emily.

Tony continued to moan and hold his arm. He walked over to Emily and took the gun from her, holding it in his right hand. "Why would you do that? He wasn't going to get a second hit on me. I could have crushed his little ass as he hung there from the wall. Now I've got two open wounds on that arm. Damn you!" He finished the last sentence at nearly full volume. "All you do is make things worse." He turned around and walked back toward the front door.

"Babe, I said I'm sorry. Let's get out of here and we'll pretend you were injured in the hurricane. No one will have any idea. Have them carry me to the boat and we'll leave right now."

Tony didn't turn around or respond. He walked over to Bryce, who stood up straighter, defiant despite the searing pain in his arm. Tony brought his right knee up and rammed it into Bryce's gut.

Bryce flexed forward and clenched his abs to absorb the impact, but still had the wind knocked out of him. He waited for the stabbing pain in his arm, but it never came. *Huh, now that the tip is through the skin, it actually doesn't hurt as bad.*

"That was a cheap shot," said Bryce after he could stand back up again. He saw Tony pulling on the curtain to undo the knot. "What are you doing?"

"I'm taking you down. It's time to head to the boat." Once he was free of the tether, Tony pushed him toward the door.

"What about me? How am I going to get to the boat?" shouted Emily.

Tony turned around and looked at her. "You're going to have to get your own boat. We're done. I've had enough of you."

Emily's mouth dropped open, and she gasped quickly a few times. "You can't leave me here! With them! I can't even move. They'll send me to prison for the rest of my life!

"Yep. You're psychotic. Probably the best place for you." Tony turned to Bryce and motioned to the door. "Your family stays here. You go with me."

"Thank you. I appreciate that." He slipped the loop out from under his leg and stabilized the gaffe with his arm. "I'll take that deal any day."

"To the rest of you, stay the hell away if you want to live. Do what you want with Emily. I don't care anymore." He shoved Bryce forward and followed him out the door, ignoring the screams and pleas from Emily.

Chapter Forty-Nine

With Tony and Bryce gone, the room took on a different tone. No longer in immediate threat of harm, everyone relaxed a bit, except for Emily. She continued to cry and scream for Tony, her words as wasted as her potential career in medicine.

"Let's tie her up and then get down to see what we can do for Bryce," said Julio. "Someone grab that fishing line."

"You guys handle her; I'm going to find Noah," said Val, standing up and heading for the door. "I'll bring him back here once I find him. Will someone be guarding Emily?"

"I can," said Rebecca. "I think she needs a good talking to, anyway." She picked up a large knife from the kitchen and sat down next to the kitchen table.

"Thanks. Can you keep an eye on Hannah also? I don't want her out there in this."

"No problem. Go get your son and save your husband. We'll be fine," said Rebecca. "I'm no stranger to knives. We'll see if Emily wants to test that or not."

Julio quickly bound her wrists behind her back and then tied her ankles together before joining the two bonds with several additional wraps of line. Emily struggled a few times before accepting the futility of her situation.

"I thought I knew you," said Peter, looking down at Emily. "What happened?"

Emily looked back at him and then looked away quickly. "Nothing ever happened. Literally nothing. Work and then go home. Repeat for a few months and then go somewhere else. The medical school rejection letters kept finding my new address, though. Again and again. Then you rejected me too, so what else did I have to look forward to? I thought if I could shut down Washington Memorial ER for a few months, you would have to go somewhere else and we could start over again. Then Tony tracked me down and it sort of fell apart from there."

"You need help, Emily. I'm talking counseling, medications, therapy. The good news is they should be able to provide all of that in prison. Hopefully, in twenty years, you'll be eligible for parole, maybe sooner if you volunteer in their medical clinic or find other ways to show you're not as bad of a person as you appear."

"You guys ready?" asked Tom, pacing by the front door. "Bryce may not have much time left."

They all verbally agreed and met Tom at the front door after securing a knife from the kitchen. If you're going to be at a gun fight, better have a knife than nothing.

Val walked quickly to the other villa and opened the door. "Noah, are you here? It's Mommy!" she yelled.

A few seconds later, a door flung open and Noah came running out. "Mom!" He ran to her and wrapped his arms around her waist, holding on as if he would fall off a cliff should he let go.

"Baby, it's me. It's okay. The bad guy isn't at the house anymore. Are you hurt?" She knelt down next to him and ran her hands across his head and down his body. She spun him around and continued to examine him.

"No. I think I'm okay. How are Dad and Hannah?"

"Your sister is fine, but Dad is still with the bad guy. The others are going to help him now. Once I take you back to the other house, I am going to go help too."

"Mom, you're bleeding! What happened?" said Noah, pointing at the blood-soaked bandage on her arm.

"I gave some blood to that woman who was sick. It left me a little weak from it, but it's not an injury. I promise you, I'm okay." She stood up and took his hand in hers. "Let's get you back to the other house. Mrs. Sharpe is watching your sister there. The woman who was sick is there too, but she can't move, so you won't need to worry about her."

"But I want to go try to help Dad. I don't want to stay in the house," he said.

"Noah, I love your heart. You're just like your father. But I don't want that woman to get away and I think Mrs. Sharpe would appreciate it if you would help guard her. Do you think you can do that for me?"

"Will it help Dad?"

"Yes, because it will let me know you two are safe, and then we can focus on getting your dad away from that man."

"Okay, I'll do it." He took Val's hand and started walking toward the door. "Do I get a gun?"

◈

Tony pushed Bryce ahead of him. "Does it feel good to know we're just about done with all of this?"

"Yeah, I'm thrilled."

"You know the feeling you get after you end a toxic relationship? I have that now, along with hoping I'm going to get out of here. I'll have a fortune in crypto and no one to tie me down."

"Looks like everything is going your way. I'm happy for you Tony. I'll join you for a few beers on the boat before we shove off and go find some islands to explore."

"I wish, Bryce, but that's not how it's going to end. You destroyed my life. And now I'm going to destroy yours."

"Why? How does that help anything? What is your motivation to kill me? You ruined a trip I had planned to save my marriage. I nearly lost my wife over the struggles that spawned from our first interaction with you. If I intentionally harmed you, I could understand why you hate me. But I just don't see it."

"You don't see it? Remember five minutes ago when you kicked me in the head? About an hour after breaking my hand and collarbone? Do you remember that, super genius?"

Bryce laughed. "Really? Why not take it back a little further? I did all of that because you were holding my friends and family at gunpoint. What was I supposed to do? Just shut up and die? That's not who I am."

They were halfway to the beach now. The moon was shining through the clouds more often than not, and the wind had died down considerably.

"How's your head feeling?" asked Bryce.

"Killing me, thanks to you. I am trying hard not to vomit again. Though it's hilarious that you speared yourself rather than get puked on."

"What can I say? It's a reflex to get out of the way of vomit. I don't usually have to think about dodging trip wires."

Bryce was getting nervous. He was running out of time before he was to be tied to a boat and dragged out to sea. *I need to get him talking and slow him down. Maybe Peter and the others will find a way to rescue me.*

"Aren't you worried Emily will steal all the crypto? Isn't that stuff easy to move from one account to another? What if she's already told Peter how to move the funds?"

"She has no idea how to access it. I kept the private keys on the boat, but I doubt she ever found them."

"But what if she did? Maybe she has a copy of them and will show Peter how to move the funds once the internet connection is active again. Then you'll have a boat but no money. Once your gas tank is empty, you're screwed."

"Emily had no interest in learning open water cruising. There's no way she found the codes in that book. I hid them inside the jacket cover. She would have had to remove the jacket cover to find them and I never even saw her glance at that book."

"Oh really, since you never saw it, that means it never happened? Were there times she was on the boat by herself and you couldn't see her?"

Tony pondered the question for a moment before replying. "Doesn't matter. She wouldn't take off the jacket cover, even if she found the correct book."

"No? This is the girl who bought dead rats on-line and used expired medical supplies from a former hospital in an attempt to get my ER shut down. I wouldn't trust her at all. Frankly, I'd assume she had the information. The question is whether you will get internet access before she will."

Tony scoffed at the comment. "She'll be in police custody. She can't do anything with it even if she had it."

"How sure are you? Want to bet a hundred million dollars?"

"Actually, it's a hundred twenty-five million now. I've done well with the funds my dad gave me to invest. Not that he cares."

They had reached the end of the path and were standing on the concrete dock. Bryce could see the boat extremely close to the shore, clearly floating but with an unnatural movement against the waves. He imagined the stern sitting on the sand; its propellers and drive shafts slamming into the bottom with each wave.

"Walk down the beach and lay on the ground behind the boat," said Tony. "Once I've tied you up, I'm going to get on the boat and try to pull it out a bit using the windlass. If you try to undo the knots, I'll shoot you. Got it?"

"Are you sure you want to do this? Maybe it's easier if I just help push the boat out and wave goodbye as you ride off into the sunrise?"

"You can't push a sixty-foot yacht against the wind and waves. I don't care how much of a badass you think you are. Get down there."

Bryce slowly walked toward the boat, trying to waste as much time as possible, hoping his friends would arrive and save him before Tony dragged him out to sea. He was holding the shaft of the gaff in his right arm to steady it.

The boat was barely floating; its the swim ladder rubbing against the sandy shore.

"Wait here," said Tony, pointing his gun at Bryce and stepping onto the swim platform. He reached onto the stern and retrieved one end of a quarter inch dock line that was attached to a cleat on the stern.

Damn it, is he actually going to save the boat and pull me out to sea? How did it not run harder aground? No way in hell am I allowing him to tie me to the boat.

Tony hopped off the boat and brought the line toward Bryce, who had turned back toward shore with his right shoulder pointed at Tony. When the distance between them was less than five feet, Bryce quickly spun clockwise, his hand firmly gripping the shaft of the gaffe as he rotated. The metal pole struck Tony on the right side of his head, directly over the laceration.

Tony fell to his knees, dropping the gun in the process. Bryce watched it fall and land in the sand several feet away. He released the gaff from his grip and dove forward for the gun. Halfway to the ground, he felt a sharp pain in his left arm and his movement toward the sand suddenly stopped. In the next moment, he was violently flipped onto his back.

Tony had recovered quickly and was back on his feet while Bryce was falling to the ground. He took two quick steps and planted a foot on top of the gaff sticking out of Bryce's arm, stopping his movement immediately.

Bryce screamed from the second impulse of pain and looked up to see Tony standing on top of him. Tony leaned down and picked up the gun, then picked up the gaff. He quickly tied a bowline knot through the looped handle to secure Bryce to the boat. He then dropped to one knee, planting it directly in Bryce's abdomen and knocking the wind out of him again. Bryce began a quick series of coughs trying to recover his breath.

"What? Don't like cheap shots?" asked Tony. "Don't worry, that's the last one either of us will deliver to each other."

Bryce looked down at the expertly tied knot securing him to the boat and smiled.

Tony took a step toward the boat but stumbled sideways. Nausea overcame him and he leaned forward to vomit several more times before standing up quickly and walking back toward Bryce.

"This head injury is making me stupid," he said. "Can't leave that knot so close to you. It would be a shame if you simply untied it." He untied the knot and pulled the slack through the loop on the gaffe. He then walked back toward the boat, tied a quick loop in the line near the boat and secured the end to this with another bowline. Tony turned toward the boat and swayed his body with the rhythm of the waves. After a few seconds, he leaped onto the swim platform and then climbing up onto the boat.

Bryce leaned his head back in the sand, exhaling in one sigh the air he could recover over the last few breaths. *Come on guys, where are you? I could really use some help right about now.* He turned his head over and looked at the boat. It was rocking up and down with the waves, clearly still floating and not yet hard aground. It wouldn't take Tony long to get the boat moving to deeper water.

Chapter Fifty

Peter, Tom, and Julio jogged down the path toward the boat dock. A dim glow of red brightened the eastern horizon as the sun rose, revealing clear skies to the east.

"Would you look at that?" said Julio, pointing toward the sun.

"Good, this has been the worst night shift I've ever worked," said Peter.

"Red sky in morning, sailor take warning," added Tom.

"Yeah, and that warning for Tony only refers to weather. It doesn't even take into account the three of us coming to kick his ass," said Peter.

"Remember, he still has a gun. He's like a caged animal who sees a chance for an escape. Who knows what he's capable of?" said Julio.

"He's a caged animal with a head injury, a broken hand, gunshot to the arm, and a broken collarbone," added Tom. "We'd better be able to overcome that."

The three arrived at the dock in time to see Tony tie a quick knot and jump onto the boat.

"Let's splint up a bit. He can't shoot all three of us," said Tom.

"Sure he can, just not with one bullet," said Julio. "His accuracy will be terrible from this distance. He's got a broken hand and is on a boat moving with the waves. But don't think for a second you're immune from a lucky shot."

They split up and kept about ten feet between themselves. Soon they could see Bryce laying in the sand, flat on his back.

"Bryce, you okay?" yelled Tom.

Bryce heard the call and rolled his head around to see where it came from. He breathed a sigh of relief when his eyes found his friends walking toward him. He rolled onto his stomach and started to stand up, but stopped when he heard a gunshot behind him and saw a puff of sand kick into the air a few feet to his left.

"Stay down or I keep shooting!" yelled Tony from the back of the boat cockpit. He pointed the gun at Peter and the others. "You three stay back!" and then disappeared back into the cabin. A rhythmic metallic clunking noise started from the front of the yacht.

"He's pulling on the anchor chain to drag the boat out into deeper water," said Julio.

"Bryce, how are you attached to the boat?" yelled Peter.

"There's a thick dock line through this gaffe handle. I'm tied to the stern."

"If we throw you a knife, do you think you can cut it?"

"I'll sure try. Just don't land that knife in my chest," yelled Bryce.

Peter flipped the knife around so he was holding the blade and swung his arm backward. "Just like corn hole," he said and released the knife as his arm extended past his hip. The onshore wind caught the knife and pushed it away from the water, landing in the sand well outside Bryce's reach. The heavy dock line and Tony's threat prevented him from making progress toward it.

"Damn it," said Peter. "I'm good at corn hole, but not in fifty mile-an-hour wind."

"I got it," said Tom, pulling his shirt over his head. He put his knife inside the shirt and then wrapped it tightly around the blade before tying the remained into a knot. He held up his makeshift football and hefted the weight. At his age, a thirty-yard toss in no wind with a real football would be a challenge; this was an impossibility.

"Let me make the toss," said Peter, taking the package from Tom.

"Hang on, did you play center field in high school? I used to throw people out at home all the time," said Julio, grabbing the package out of Peter's hand.

Julio moved his right arm through several wide circles, and then across his chest and back out wide. He then hoisted the balled-up shirt and tossed it toward Bryce, aiming far to the right. The package flew in a near perfect trajectory and landed about ten feet away from the target before rolling a few feet closer. It was resting on the sand between him and the water.

Bryce immediately started moving toward the package. He closed half of the distance before another gunshot halted his progress.

"I said stop!" came a yell from the boat.

Bryce raised his hands and stood still. After a count of ten, he slowly started inching sideways, trying to get closer without arousing suspicion.

"Nice toss Julio. Much better than I would have done," said Peter. "But we can't get to him without taking a chance at getting shot. It's going to be up to Bryce for now unless we can think of something else."

***

Val walked Noah back to the main villa and took him inside.

"Where is everyone?" he asked.

"They all went down to the beach to get your dad. I need you to stay here with Mrs. Sharpe. I'll be back with your dad in a bit."

Noah nodded and gave her a quick hug. "Good luck Mommy, I know you can save him."

"I hope I can. Here, take this," she said, handing him a small knife. "If Emily tries to move, poke her in the arm with this. She can't feel her legs, so don't bother poking her there."

Emily's eyes widened when she saw the determined looked on Noah's face and his right arm held out, the tip of a knife pointed directly at her.

"I'll be back soon," said Val as she turned and jogged out the front door. *I need to find a different way down to the water. Tony's going to be expecting us to come down the main path.*

She turned left out of the villa and jogged through the neatly trimmed grass along the previously well-maintained hedge of shrubs and tropical trees. *Where is that path at Noah? The one you showed me that had all the crabs on it. There was a light on a pole marking it.* She jogged a bit farther until she came to two large bushes, stripped nearly bare of their leaves and flowers. A few brilliant yellow flowers remained. *There! The yellow elder bush.* There was a long metal pole laying on the ground, struck down by a branch that fell and crushed the base, snapping it off and leaving one sharp edge. She picked it up and leveled it against her hip. *Not a great weapon, but better than nothing.*

She pushed through the limbs and found herself on a small path leading through the foliage. She jogged downhill, only slowing once to catch her breath. *Remind me to never exercise after donating blood twice.* Twenty seconds later, she was at the edge of the foliage and standing on the beach. The yacht was about fifty yards to her right, with Bryce standing behind it on the shore.

Run away Bryce! Get back to the villa! Unfortunately, her willed thoughts didn't result in the desired movement. She looked harder and saw the reason. A thick rope led from the boat along the beach and up to Bryce. Behind him, she could barely make out three shapes. Peter, Tom, and Julio. *Why are they just standing there? Do something!*

She watched Tom remove his shirt and then roll it around in his hand. First, Peter took it from him and then Julio ended up with it. She watched Julio throw it at Bryce, who started moving toward it before a loud gunshot stopped him abruptly. *No wonder they're not going to him. Tony is shooting at them!*

Val looked down at the metal pole she brought with her. "Looks like it's down to you and me. I'm not sure how, but we're going to save Bryce."

She looked at the waves crashing into the shore and saw they were much smaller than earlier when she and Peter brought Emily ashore. *I can probably get to the boat through the surf, but it's going to suck.*

Val carried the metal pole with her and walked out into the churning water, stumbling forward over a small drop off created by the wave action. She recovered quickly and leaned into the oncoming waves, plodding toward the boat.

Chapter Fifty-One

"Hey, did you guys see that? Someone just walked down the beach and into the water," said Peter.

"What? Who?" asked Julio.

"It's got to be Val. My wife is back guarding Emily, and it was too tall to be Elisa," said Tom.

"What was she carrying? It looked like a long rod of some sort. What's she going to do with it?" said Peter.

"I don't know, but we need to make sure Tony doesn't see her coming. Somehow, we need to keep him looking our way."

While they talked, Bryce continued to inch toward the knife bundled inside Tom's shirt. He was four feet away now.

The metallic ratcheting noise continued. Each iteration meant Tony was two inches closer to sailing away with Bryce in tow.

"I'm going to get in the water," said Peter. "No reason for us all to stand here on the beach."

"Strange time for a swim, man," said Tom.

"I have to try something. I brought Emily into this mess, so I feel somewhat responsible." Peter removed his shirt and shoes, then removed his shorts so he was standing in a pair of skintight boxer jocks. "Wish me luck." He ran the few feet to the water and sunk down to his knees to blend into the breaking waves, hoping Tony did not spot him.

Val continued to make her way toward the port side of the boat. She could hear the metallic clunk each time the windlass brought another link of chain on board. The boat was creeping away from shore and the line attached to Bryce was rising off the sand.

She was nearly halfway there, and making steady progress, when her ears picked up a distinct sound. *No! He got the engines started.* Val leaned into the waves and tried to jog against the pressure of the wind and current. She sped up a bit, but not as much as she had hoped. Still over thirty yards away. *Hang on Bryce, I'm coming.*

Tony pressed hard on the windlass lever to continue pulling the boat away from shore. The windlass is not designed to carry the full weight of the boat against the anchor, and it was a risk to use it to pull the boat out. The motor could burn up, the gears could fail, or the breaker could trip. Any of those meant a premature end to Tony's escape, but it was worth a try, rather than risking the destruction of the propellers that were likely buried in the sand.

He rocked up and down violently along with the boat as the tight anchor chain pulled the boat down into each coming wave. His concussion and the larger waves amplified his usual mild seasickness to the point he was having trouble standing.

After a minute of pulling on the chain, he looked back and saw the line attached to Bryce lift off the ground. The boat also rocked more completely to each side, suggesting less contact with the ground below. He reached his hand down and flipped on the fuel pumps to the twin diesel engines. Once he heard the beep confirming the pumps were on, he held down the starter buttons. Two seconds later, the deep rumble of twin diesel engines vibrated through the boat.

"Yes!" he yelled. "Once the rest of the chain is up, I'm out of here." He turned around and looked for Bryce's friends. "What the hell," he said. "Why are there only two? Where's the other one?" He glanced out the starboard side and saw no one. Off the port side, he noticed some movement that seemed out of place in the waves. "I see you," he said. "But it won't matter. You're too late."

Just then, the clanking sound stopped and a high pitch whine replaced it. Tony looked to the front and saw the chain wasn't being pulled onto the boat anymore. He swore and exited the rear of the cockpit, pausing to look back at Bryce and the others. He aimed between the two and fired another shot, hoping to keep everyone in place before continuing to the bow and lifting the cover over the chain locker. Looking in, he saw the chain was stacked up high and binding the windlass. He reached in with his left hand and ripped on the lower part, freeing the stack and allowing it to fall away. He shut the locker before hurrying back to the stern and re-entered the cockpit, where he again pulled on the windlass lever. The reassuring metallic ratchet noise filled the boat again.

"She put so much damn chain out, going to take a few more minutes, and then I'm gone," he said.

Bryce used Tony's distraction to close the distance to the knife and was kneeling down in the sand, trying to undo the bundle. The wet cloth knot was hard to untie, especially as tight as Tom had bound it together before Julio threw it toward him.

Chapter Fifty-Two

Val was nearing the boat but fatiguing quickly. She had rapidly lost about forty percent of her circulating blood volume in the last two hours, and it had taken a toll on her exercise capacity. *I'm coming Chap, hang in there.* She looked up and saw only two people standing on the beach other than Bryce. *Where is the other person? I better not be the only one trying to save him.*

She was within a boat length of the yacht when suddenly Tony was standing on the bow and grabbing the anchor chain. She dipped low in the water and ducked under waves as they passed her. He was only there a few moments and then was gone. She waited a few more seconds and then pushed hard to cover the final distance. As she got closer, she found herself on the lee side of the boat and the waves were noticeably smaller. She could stand up and walk instead of swim, finding the water just above her waistline.

The waves continued to raise and lower the boat with the swells; the hull creating its own wave as it fell back down into the water. She gripped the pole and pushed it out ahead of her like a pole vaulter lining up to approach the runway.

Julio saw Peter surface near the bow of the boat, take a few breaths, and continue swimming out further. The rising sun was bright enough to see Peter against the waves. If Julio could see Peter, then so could Tony. Julio turned and jogged back toward the vegetation and started picking up fist-size rocks. He held out his shirt and stacked them on the fabric, coming back to Tom after he had a dozen projectiles ready to go.

"We need to keep Tony's attention. Peter is doing something out in front of the boat and Val must be getting close on the other side. I'll start throwing these rocks at the boat. Can you keep handing them to me?"

"Can do," said Tom, stretching his shirt out and accepting the transferred stones.

Julio hefted the first one and threw it at the yacht, striking the cabin window next to the helm. They saw Tony's head whip around to investigate the source of the noise.

The rock toss was quickly answered with a few poorly aimed gunshots.

"How many shots has he taken now?" asked Julio.

"He shot Bryce, then Emily fired twice, and he's taken a few more at us. Maybe six or seven, I'd say," said Tom.

"I think you're right. How do you feel about trying to run him out of ammo?" asked Julio with a smile.

"Did you just ask me to try to get shot at on purpose?"

Julio answered with a shrug and a nod. "Why not? It's for a good cause. And as you said, his aim has to be terrible on that boat with a broken hand and collar bone. How are we going to do it?"

"Just keep throwing rocks. But we should split up and get closer to the boat. When he comes out to shoot at one of us, the other tries to hit him with a rock. That'll keep him distracted from Peter, Bryce, and Val as well."

Tom nodded and dropped the collection of rocks onto the sand. He picked two up and walked a few steps away before throwing one toward the boat. It landed twenty feet short.

Julio looked at Tom with a frown. "Maybe you should just keep handing rocks to me." He hefted a rock and launched it at the boat, striking the cabin door, and shattering the tempered glass into thousands of pieces. The door became opaque, but did not lose its integrity.

"Nice one!" yelled Tom.

Julio waited until the door pushed open and he saw Tony's head emerge, then launched another rock.

Val came up alongside the boat and put her hand against the hull. It was traveling several feet up and down with the waves, and was in about four feet of water. She took both hands and held the pole vertical, leaving roughly half of the ten-foot pole out of the water. Just then, the boat moved sideways with a wave and slammed into her, knocking the pole out of her hands and causing her to lose her footing. The wind and waves pushed the boat toward her quicker than she could move backward. Realizing the futility of flight, she took a deep breath and dropped underwater as the boat moved on top of her.

Tony's head whipped around when the glass door behind him exploded. He released the windlass control and kicked the door open. His eyes quickly found Julio standing back up from his pitcher's throw. Tony screamed and raised the gun, pulling the trigger repeatedly until the slide locked back, unable to find another round in the empty magazine. He searched his pockets but couldn't find the spare magazine.

The boat shuddered hard and nearly knocked him to the ground. He looked at the stern and saw it perilously close to the shore. "Why am I going backward?" he yelled to himself before running back to the helm. He looked out the front windows and saw the anchor chain still in the windlass. He pulled the control to drag in more chain and noticed it was much easier than before.

"What the hell? It's like the anchor isn't there anymore."

He looked out the window and saw Peter's head about thirty feet off the bow, swimming back toward the shore using one hand.

"You bastard!" yelled Tony. "Eat some prop!" He grabbed the dual throttle controls and slammed them forward, engaging full power on both engines. The stern shuddered as the props churned into the sandy bottom, but slowly the boat moved forward.

Bryce had the bundle nearly unwrapped and could see the handle of the knife when he dropped to the ground in response to the rapid gunfire. In doing so, the package rolled away from him, but he quickly went to retrieve it. As he was bending down to pick it up, the engine noise increased suddenly. Bryce looked up to see the boat pulling away. He grabbed the shirt and knife bundle a moment before the line pulled tight and made him jog toward the water to avoid being dragged by his arm. He struggled to untie it while running on his bad leg and trying to stop his arm from taking the pressure of the dock line.

He reached the drop off at the water level and fell forward, tumbling face first into the foamy water. His right hand shot out to find the bottom and lift his head out of the water. When he broke the surface, his hands were empty. Any hope of cutting the line vanished. He grabbed the rope with his right hand and tried to keep the pressure off the hook in his arm while staying on his back so he can breathe.

Val felt the engine noise increase drastically and realized Tony had put the transmission in forward gear. She estimated she had about twenty feet before twin brass propellers would cut through the water that she currently occupied.

She planted her feet in the sand and jumped backward, twisting her body and pulling against the water with all her strength. A second furious underwater stroke combined with the current pulled her out from under the boat. She felt the cavitation of the propellers as they turned the sea into a foamy mix of bubbles and water. Val pushed hard to escape, every moment expecting to feel sudden severe pain as the propellers chewed through her. But the pain never came. She surfaced to see the boat pull away and Bryce go face first into the water. "Bryce!" she screamed.

Chapter Fifty-Three

Peter watched the boat lift out of the water as the engines engaged, propelling it toward him rapidly. He continued to swim one-handed in a blunted side stroke, timing his pulls with the waves.

The wave action combined with little water movement across the rudders meant the boat did not turn well. This allowed Peter to slip sideways past the hull as Tony powered the craft away from the shore. He did not give up his one-handed stroke even as it looked like he might not make it around the hull in time.

He continued swimming as quickly as he could until he felt a foot brush against the sandy bottom. A few pulls more and he was firmly standing in chest-deep water. He turned around in time to see Bryce pulled face first into the water.

Val swam toward Bryce, trying to get to him before Tony pulled him out to deeper water. He was making a wake as the boat pulled him away from shore.

She reached out to grab him but couldn't hold on, and would only have made it harder for him to keep pressure off his arm had she been able to get a grip on him.

Just as he skimmed past her, a loud metallic noise came from the boat and the engine noise increased dramatically before suddenly stopping altogether. The boat stalled out and sank back into the water, allowing Bryce to come to a stop.

Val turned to see Peter standing nearly behind the boat, his body leaning back with arms extended overhead like the mid-point of a kettlebell swing. Hanging from his clenched fists was the end of the anchor chain. The middle of the chain was now wrapped tight around the propellers, disabling the engines.

"Nice work!" she yelled to Peter.

A splash behind them signaled Julio was joining the action. He swam toward them both as Val made it to Bryce and helped him stay afloat. Julio grabbed the dock line and sliced through it with his knife, freeing Bryce.

"Let's get him back ashore and try to get this out of his arm," said Val.

"You guys got this? I have a score to settle with Tony," said Peter.

"Yeah, go ahead. But take my knife. I don't know he if he has anymore ammunition left," said Julio.

Peter took the knife and began swimming toward the boat that was slowly drifting back toward them. Val and Julio assisted Bryce back toward the beach and ultimately onto dry sand. Elisa was there waiting for them.

"What happened? Is it over?" she asked, looking out at the disabled boat drifting back in.

"Not yet. Tony is still on the boat," said Julio. "Everything okay back at the villa?"

"Yes, Rebecca is guarding Emily with Noah's help. Hannah actually fell asleep on the couch."

Val smiled at the news and wiped a tear away. "Thank you Elisa, that's wonderful news. Bryce, I'm going to go help Peter."

"Me too," said Julio.

"I'll stay here with Bryce and see if I can yank this hook out of him," said Elisa, looking at her ER colleague with a look of genuine concern.

"What? No mocking insult?" asked Bryce.

Elisa shook her head as she stabilized the gaff and examined the wound. "Don't worry ER, it's coming. Just not right now."

Chapter Fifty-Four

Peter reached the broken swim deck of the boat and quickly pulled himself up onto it. He held the knife in front of him as he climbed the stairs leading to the cockpit. He found Tony inside, trying to get the engines restarted.

Peter pulled the door open and entered the cockpit as quietly as possible.

"Turn over, damn you!" screamed Tony, frantically hitting the button to turn the engine on.

Peter came up behind Tony and delivered a downward chop with his right hand, landing it directly on the broken clavicle.

Tony bent forward, howling in pain. He used his left hand to push himself back up and turned to see Peter standing there, left arm extended and holding a knife.

"You," said Tony. "I should have expected a cheap shot like that would come from you. I have a broken hand and collar bone and you have a knife. Is that what it takes for you to beat me?"

"You hit me while I was naked and tied to a bed. Would you consider that a cheap shot?"

"No, my hand hurt for days after that one. I'm used to hitting people while wearing boxing gloves."

"You realize it's over, right Tony? There is no next move for you. We disabled the boat, the storm is ending, and Emily is essentially in custody. It's over."

"Then get rid of that knife and fight me like a man. Or do you need a knife to beat a guy with two broken arms?"

Peter smiled and threw the knife out the door to the cockpit. He pulled his arms across his chest and turned a bit to his right, taking a fighter's stance.

"You doctors think you're so smart. That was a slick move, pulling the anchor chain into the prop like that. It killed the engines and now we're dead in the water." Tony reached behind himself to the port engine controls. He turned on the fuel pump and then held down the button to start the engine. It fired up and the familiar rumble resumed.

"But smart as you are, you're still idiots. See, you only tangled one prop. I just remembered the engines have a shut off feature if one of them seizes. It stops them both from being destroyed at once. There's no way you wrapped the chain around both propellers at the same time. It's too heavy. A rope maybe, but not a chain. One push of the throttle and we're out of here."

Peter leaped forward, his arm reaching for the lever as Tony's arm moved toward it.

Val heard an engine start up again and turned toward the boat. She saw Peter dive forward Tony and then the water churn behind the stern. *The boat's moving again!* She re-entered the water, searching desperately for the pole she had dropped earlier. The boat slowed to a stop just as quickly as it had started. She moved around, trying to feel the metal pole against her feet. There! Her foot struck the pole, which she retrieved from the bottom. She swam next to the hull and dove underwater.

She tried to lift the pole upright, but the water was too shallow to get it under the hull. She resurfaced and took another breath before going further out and trying again.

Peter reached Tony just after the throttle engaged fully. He slammed his shoulder into Tony's back, bending him over the steering wheel. He reached around to the throttle control and pulled it back into neutral, stopping the boat's forward movement.

Tony's right elbow struck backward and caught Peter on the side of his head, separating them enough for Tony to turn around in the confined space. Peter backed off and prepared for another assault, but stopped when he saw Tony holding a large bore gun.

"Ever see a flare gun? This will shoot right through you and cauterize the wound as it exits out your back. Now get the hell off my boat before I demonstrate."

Chapter Fifty-Five

Val swam back under the hull and pulled the pole nearly vertical, the sharp broken end making contact with the fiberglass bottom. As the boat lifted in a wave, she pushed back on the pole, standing it up straight. The boat sank down into the water as the wave passed, bringing with it fifty thousand pounds of displacement. As the boat lowered, the metal pole stayed in place and pierced the hull, sinking in two feet.

The next wave pulled the boat free, allowing Val to move the pole closer to shore. As another wave passed, she punched another hole in the hull, this time taking three feet of pole along with it. She kept repeating the process as the boat drifted closer to shore, coming up for air when needed and listening for a change in engine noise that would signal the propellers were again spinning.

"Fine, you win. I'll get off. There's zero chance you get out of here, Tony. The Coast Guard will have you before the day's over," said Peter. He backed up toward the cockpit door and turned to step through.

A sickening crunch sounded from the cabin below. Tony turned to see what caused the noise and heard a second splintering sound. He looked down the stairs and saw a metal pole sticking up through the cabin floor with water pouring in around it. "What? No!" he yelled.

Peter rushed forward and smashed into Tony from behind, his right arm striking downward as if stripping a football from a running back. He knocked the flare gun out of Tony's hand and pulled them both to the ground. Tony rolled onto his back and kicked Peter away before struggling to get back on his feet. He reached up with his left arm and pulled himself up, using the handrail at the top of the stairs.

Peter absorbed the kick that was really more of a push and landed in the plank position. He jumped to his feet in one acrobatic move and reached Tony just as he was standing up.

Peter planted his feet and put his entire weight and momentum into a right-handed roundhouse. Tony lifted his head in time to see the fist right before it shattered his nose. He fell backward down the stairs, legs splayed out, trying to find support for his body. Finding none, he landed flat on his back right above a small round hole in the boat's floor.

His eyes opened wide at the shock of landing as he did. His hands moved to a metal pole sticking through the left side of his chest.

"Oh my God," said Peter, rushing forward to top of the stairs. He jumped down to the cabin floor and knelt next to Tony, assessing the wound. The boat lifted on the next wave, ripping the pole out of Tony's chest and leaving a two-inch hole completely through him. Bloody froth gushed from the wound.

Tony looked at Peter and gasped, trying to breathe.

"Sorry dude, this is not a survivable injury. You're about to die, my man," said Peter.

Tony's lips moved, but he could barely make a noise. Peter leaned closer to hear better and try to read his lips.

"Tell everyone I'm sorry," he got out between gasps. Then his arms went limp and his head fell back against the cabin floor. Soon his arms were drifting side to side along with the water that continued to pour into the boat.

Peter stood and climbed out of the cabin. He pressed the button to kill the port engine before jumping into the water and swimming back to shore.

Val heard the splash and looked around the hull to see Peter exiting the water. She waited a moment and saw him talk to Bryce and Julio, then realized the struggle must be over. She swam back to shore and joined them.

"Is it over?" she asked.

"Yeah, it is. Tony fell down the stairs and got impaled by a metal pole that was sticking through the hull. Talk about unlucky."

Val gasped as a look of horror spread across her face. "He landed on that? I was just trying to disable the boat. I wasn't trying to kill him."

"You didn't kill him. His own insanity did," said Bryce. "We were just there to witness it."

"And I punched him in the face, knocking him down the stairs," said Peter. "That wound was gnarly. Gonna be hard to get that out of my mind."

"What about this one?" asked Bryce, pointing to his arm.

"Oh man, let's get back to the villa and get that out of you," said Tom. "Think we can use the string technique?"

Bryce laughed loudly. "I think this is a bit bigger than the string technique was designed for. I was thinking something more gentle."

The group took one last look at the boat as it continued to drift toward shore. In moments, its stern was hard aground and was slowly rotating with the waves as they pushed the bow closer to shore. The group turned and walked back up the beach onto the path toward the villa.

"We need a slo-mo video of us walking away from the destroyed boat and beach," said Bryce. "Can you imagine the hospital using that for a commercial?"

Chapter Fifty-Six

"Emily, why do you think you're alive?" asked Rebecca.

"What do you mean? Do you think they were going to kill me before they left?"

"No, I mean in a philosophical sense. Why are you here? Why are any of us here?"

"Who cares? We're not here for any reason, we just are. Until we aren't. Game over, move on to the next life."

"What a sad outlook on life, though I agree with you about the next life part. Our life on earth is not the end. If it were, we'd just snuff you out like a candle at the end of dinner. Who would think anything about you dying after a surgery on an island in a hurricane? But I believe we're here to do good. To help other people. These people you tried to harm have spent their entire adult lives trying to help other people."

"Whatever, they're just in it to get paid," said Emily.

"Sure, docs are reimbursed well for their actions. But my husband spent seven years after college learning to do what he does. His college roommate majored in business and had sold two companies by the time Tom graduated residency. My husband was just getting started in his career when his college friend retired and moved to Florida. It took us another seven years to pay off his medical school loans."

"So? What's your point?"

"My point is, doctors don't do it for the money. There are much easier ways to make a lot of money in life. They do it to help people. I hope that someday you'll come around and start thinking of others first. If everybody thought of how they could help someone else instead of themselves, think of how nice our society would be."

Emily didn't reply.

"That's Biblical you know. Many who are first will be last, and many who are last will be first. I'll continue to pray for you, Emily. Rebecca leaned forward and brushed the hair out of Emily's eyes, wiping away a few tears in the process. "You clearly need some Jesus in your life."

"I hear them coming!" said Noah, jumping up off the chair. He ran toward the front door and pulled it open as Bryce and the others returned.

"Dad! Are you okay?" he asked.

Bryce leaned over and embraced his son in a one-armed hug. "Yes buddy, I am. Well, I will be once they get this hook out of my arm."

"Where's Tony?" asked Emily.

"He's dead," said Val. "He tripped on the boat and died from the fall."

"You liar! You killed him!" she screamed, writhing against the restraints. Rebecca dropped her knife and tried to calm Emily down. Emily continued to struggle and rolled over on the table, running out of flat surface before completing the rotation and landing with a thud on the ground. She screamed again and flexed forward, trying to ease the strain on her wound.

"Careful, don't rip that incision open," said Elisa. "It's not held together all that well as it is."

Tom looked at the hook poking through Bryce's arm. "I think we need to just wrap the barb and back it out. That will not feel very good, my friend."

"I know. Let's just get it done. I'll try to be tough," said Bryce.

"Isn't there a toolbox around here somewhere? Maybe there are some pliers in it we can use to make the barb smaller first," said Julio.

"I think I saw one in the laundry room when I was getting the washing machine out," said Peter. He left the room and returned with a plastic toolbox. He opened it and removed a set of channel lock pliers.

"Someone steady the pole. I'll pinch down on the barb."

Tom and Julio held the hook stable as Peter pinched the barb as hard as he could, bending the tip down toward the shank. He stopped when it was nearly touching. He found a roll of electrical tape in the toolbox and wrapped it tightly over the barb, covering any potential areas that could catch Bryce's skin as they pulled the hook out.

"Ready?" asked Tom.

Bryce nodded but Val held her hands. "Wait a sec."

She moved in front of Bryce and wrapped her arms around him. He held her with his right arm and tucked his face into her neck. "Okay, do it," he said.

Tom rotated the handle while quickly pulling backward, reversing the original path the hook followed on the way in. It slid out of Bryce's arm with a pop as it exited the hole.

Everyone heard the wet sound of it breaking free until a deep groan from Bryce drowned it out.

"Okay, you're free. How's it feel?" asked Tom.

Bryce leaned back from Val and looked at his arm. He lifted it over his head, then flexed and extended the elbow, before turning his palm over a few times. "I think maybe it nicked my triceps, but I think it's okay. At least I can feel everything." He leaned on his left leg, wincing from the pain. "This leg though, it must have nailed my calf muscle."

Bryce found Hannah sleeping on the couch and sat down next to her, placing his hand on her leg. Noah came over and jumped in his lap.

The rest of the group found a chair to sit down and everyone sat silently for a few moments.

"Well, we still have five days left on the trip. What do you want to do next?" asked Bryce.

"Get the hell off this island and never vacation with you again," said Elisa. "And spoiler alert, I'm never trusting you ever again."

"Hey come on, I'm a good doctor. I just have terrible luck," he said, feigning a hurt expression.

"It's more than just bad luck ER, you have some sort of tractor beam that sucks bad things into your life and those around you. No, I'm never trusting you again. Not trusting you're okay. Not trusting you're safe. Julio and I will be checking on you and your family all the time now. If it's been a week since Val and I shared a drink and a joke at your expense, I expect you to call me out on it."

Bryce returned the smile Elisa was giving him and added a laugh. "I'm going to hold you to that." He tapped Noah on the leg and asked him to stand up. "Can you guys watch Noah for a minute, I want to have a moment alone with Val."

"Where are we going?" asked Valerie.

"Outside to enjoy a beautiful sunrise," said Bryce, taking her by the hand and leading her out the front door.

Chapter Fifty-Seven

"You really want to go on a walk? I just lost a lot of blood. You're shot in the leg and had a gaff in your arm. Can't we just rest for a bit?"

"Come on, just a quick walk. We'll go slow, I promise."

Val sighed deeply, but allowed him to lead her down the familiar path to the beach.

"I think you need to plan all of our vacations from here on out," he said. "I don't have good luck with them."

"You don't have very good luck with anything, mister."

"That's not true. Look who I married."

Val smiled and reached over to hook her left arm through his right. "Well, other than that, I mean."

They passed the last bend on the path, and then the beach came into view.

"Oh wow, look at that, Bryce. There is debris everywhere. Our pretty beach is ruined. I didn't really notice all the junk when we were fighting to save you."

"To be honest, I didn't want to come here for the beach. I wanted to check on something in the boat."

"Like what? Making sure Tony is still dead? From what Peter described, that's not really in question. I just want to lie down and take a nap."

"Hang on just a little longer. I've always wanted to see what one of these yachts looks like on the inside."

Val sighed and dropped to her knees in the sand.

"Are you okay?" asked Bryce, quickly dropping to the ground beside her.

"Yes, I'm fine. But I'm not getting on that boat again. Once was enough. You go, I'll just lay here for a bit."

Bryce helped her lie back on the sand and then continued toward the boat. It was hard aground now, pushed onto the sand by the waves and then abandoned there by the falling sea level. He stepped into the cockpit and took a look around. *Pretty fancy, maybe I need to get one of these.* He continued forward to the stairs, then descended into the cabin, careful not to step on Tony, whose lifeless body was floating in shallow water in the far corner, his blood already staining the fabric of the pillows and carpet.

I can't believe this is over and my family is safe. When we get home I'm going to take a leave of absence and hang out at home. The kids may even need counseling. Heck, Val and I may need counseling.

Bryce looked around the cabin, searching for what he wanted. The ornate room was trashed from the wave action of the storm. There was a row of empty bookshelves above a pile of books, scattered across the bed and floor. The two-inch wooden lip at the edge of the shelf was no match for the pitching and rolling of a yacht in a hurricane.

Bryce sorted through the books looking for one title in particular. He searched the bed and one side of the cabin floor without success. He moved to the other side of the bed but was blocked by a few pillows on the floor. He bent to move them out of the way and let out a shout of joy. "Yes! There it is." He carefully picked up the book from the floor and held it in front of him. *Nigel Calder's Cruising Handbook: A Compendium for Coastal and Offshore Sailors.* Bloody water dripped from the pages and the plastic cover.

He opened the cover and pulled back the plastic jacket. Taped on the inside of this was a piece of tan-colored paper with dozens of seemingly random characters divided into two lines. The longer line on the bottom was about twice as long as the top line.

Bryce quickly memorized the last few characters of each line and then put his fingers over them and took a picture of the card with his phone. He moved the photo to a secure folder on his phone and then tucked the card into his pocket before climbing out of the cabin.

He paused in the cockpit for a moment, taking in the view before him. The boat dock was destroyed and the small boat that remained was washed up high on the beach. Trees were down, leaves strewn about the beach, along with random debris from other islands that washed up. Laying in the middle of it all was Val, flat on her back, hands folded behind her head. Despite everything they'd been through, she looked peaceful and happy.

I love you Valerie Chapman. When we get home, I'm going to take a sabbatical and spend more time with you and the kids. No more crazy adventures. I'll be a coroner, a father, and a husband. For a year. Maybe do a few medical mission trips. I love practicing medicine, but I love you even more.

He took a deep breath and exhaled quickly. He then climbed down off the boat and rejoined Val.

"How did you think to poke a hole in the boat using that pole?"

"I didn't plan it that way. The pole was the only thing I found that seemed like it could be useful. Once I got it close to the boat and saw it bobbing up and down in the surf, the idea just came to me."

"You're amazing," said Bryce, holding a hand out to her.

Valerie shrugged her shoulders and smiled up at him. "I meant it when I said you were lucky to have married me. Now, can we get back to the house? I really want to lay down. I've never donated a unit of blood immediately after a hard swim. Being down four units and then saving your ass wiped me out."

She grabbed his hand and stood up from the sand.

"You brought me all the way down here just to get a book on sailing? I want nothing to do with boats at the moment. I think you can understand that."

"Absolutely. But this book can change our lives dramatically."

Val gave him a confused look, then it dawned on her. "Does it have the instructions to access Tony's crypto accounts?"

Bryce smiled. "I think it does, yes. We just need to get internet access to confirm. Let's get back to the house."

"I'm going to try the VHF radio. Maybe we can reach the local authorities and get some help," said Julio. He flipped on the handheld radio and walked out the front door.

"Pan-pan, pan-pan, pan-pan, this is the tourist group on Swan Cay. This is the tourist group on Swan Cay. Is anyone listening?"

Julio waited a minute and got no response. He repeated it once more and within seconds, a familiar voice crackled through the radio.

"Swan Cay, Swan Cay, Swan Cay, this is Edward, do you copy?"

"Roger that Edward, let's move to channel sixty-eight."

"Copy that. See you on sixty-eight."

Julio waited a moment before continuing. "Edward, you there?"

"Yes! Is this Bryce? How are you guys doing? Is everyone safe?" asked Edward, the concern evident even with the poor-quality audio transmission.

"Sort of. But that's a complicated question. We have a few injuries, but nothing overly serious. We have some uninvited guests however and will need the police. There has been a fatality," said Julio.

"What? A fatality? Who? What happened?"

"One of our uninvited guests. He was a wanted criminal who tried to kidnap Bryce. We have his girlfriend secured at our location, but she needs medical attention at a hospital. What are your recommendations?"

"Oh my, at least the rest of you are safe. I think the best option is to take a boat to Nassau. The authorities are handling rescues only right now, so it will likely take some time to attend to the deceased. They will want you to remain in the Bahamas until they have interviewed you."

"That's fine. We can talk to them in Nassau. Let us know if you're able to get us a boat out of here," said Julio.

"I will. Do you have power and water?"

"Yes, we do. You left us well supplied, Edward. Thank you."

"Okay, well, I am still worried. Stay on this channel and I will let you know when I have a boat lined up for you. I don't suppose the craft we left at the dock is seaworthy?"

"Uh, negative. It's working on becoming an artificial reef at the moment."

"I see. Well, I will be in touch. Be safe. Edward out."

"Thank you buddy, Swan Cay out."

Julio walked back into the villa and updated the rest of the party.

"So we just hang tight for now?" asked Bryce.

"Sounds like it. Why don't some of you get some sleep? I'm sure it's going to be hours before we know anything. Besides, the sea doesn't look like it will be much fun on an eighty-mile run to Nassau at the moment. I'll take first watch," said Julio. He started opening cabinets in the kitchen until he found what he was looking for. "Anyone else want coffee?"

"Coffee? No. Got any more mango daiquiri? I'm on vacation again," said Elisa.

Julio smiled at his wife. "I think you earned it. I'll even put a floater on it."

"Should I bolus and titrate?" she asked.

Bryce, Tom, and Peter all cheered her response. "Yes!" said Bryce. "We'll make an ER doc out of you yet, Elisa."

"We'll take two as well. But let's call them mimosas so it's okay to drink in the morning," said Jackie as she laid her head on Sal's thigh.

"It's not bad to drink in the morning if you worked all night," said Sal, his hand brushing through Jackie's hair.

Chapter Fifty-Eight

Several hours later the radio crackled back to life. "Swan Cay, Swan Cay, Swan Cay, this is Edward, do you copy?"

Julio picked up the radio and pressed the transmit button. "Yes, Edward, this is Swan Cay, what have you found?"

"I have a charter captain coming to pick your crew up. He should be there in thirty minutes. He can take your entire party to Nassau. The storm did not hit them very hard and they are fully operational. I have secured lodging for you at a five-star, all-inclusive resort for the last days of your trip."

"You didn't have to do that, but thank you. We could use some rest after last night. We will start packing up and head down to the beach to wait for the boat."

Julio started knocking on doors and waking people up to explain the situation. They quickly packed and prepared to leave the villa for the last time. Julio cut the bindings on Emily's ankles and the others helped her stand up.

"I need to pee," she said.

"Good. It means your kidneys are working. Now we'll see if your bladder does. You can pee in the water before you climb onto the boat," said Val. "Get moving."

Emily sighed and trudged out the front door, escorted by Julio.

Peter, Tom, Elisa, and Bryce gathered at the entrance and looked back at the dining room table. The washing machine with bloody tubing sat next to it.

"We made a hell of a team," said Bryce.

"Again," added Tom. He looked around at the room in shambles. "And a hell of a mess."

"I couldn't be prouder to count you all as friends and colleagues," said Peter.

"You guys can kiss my ass. I'm never returning a page to the ER ever again," said Elisa, eliciting a laugh from others.

"Oh, come on, it was not that bad," said Bryce. "You can write this case up and publish it. But if her wound gets infected, I'm adding it to the Morbidity and Mortality conference next week."

Bryce turned to his kids sitting on the couch. "Noah, Hannah, let's head down to the beach. We're going to take a ride to a different resort."

They stood and joined their parents on the walk down to the beach.

"See, this is nice. Right here. Right now," said Val. "Can we do more of this when we're at home? Less TV, less computer time, less phone time. I want more of this." She lifted her arms up, nearly picking them both off the ground.

"Yay, we do too!" said Noah.

When they got to the beach, a large boat with three outboard motors was floating close to shore waiting for them.

"Hey, that boat looks familiar," said Bryce.

"Yes, it does. Is that Captain Kyle?" said Val.

The captain waved from the boat before lowering a swim ladder and hopping over the side. He waded ashore and joined them on the beach. They met the captain last year when vacationing in Exuma. It was on that trip to Thunderball Grotto that Tony drowned and was ultimately saved by Bryce and Val.

"Bryce? Valerie? I didn't know you were going to be my passengers today. I'm not prepared for as much action as we had the last time I took you somewhere." He looked them over and saw the bloody bandage on Bryce's left leg with a matching one on his left arm. He saw Val's pale complexion and look of exhaustion. "But it looks like you already saw some pretty intense action."

Bryce shrugged. "What would a trip to the Bahamas be without death and danger?"

"It's usually not like that down here. The days of the pirates have long passed." Kyle pointed at Emily. "Is this the prisoner?"

"Yes sir. She needs to be delivered to the police in Nassau. There's a dead body on that boat too," said Julio.

"I heard. And that's the same guy from the Grotto earlier this year? What a crazy turn of events. Edward already spoke to the authorities about that. They asked that we secure the boat, so it doesn't drift out and become a navigational or environmental hazard," said Kyle. "They are busy with trying to rescue people now, they'll be by for him later."

"I'll go put the anchor back on," said Peter. "Maybe that will stop it from beaching too hard." He waded out into the water and swam around until he found it on the sandy bottom. The search was easier with daylight and improving water clarity. He carried it back to the exposed chain at the stern and re-attached it using the screw-pin shackle. He then rejoined the crew on the beach.

"Nice work, Peter. I would have helped you, but I didn't want to," said Tom.

"I don't blame you. Not a job for an old man," said Peter, slapping Tom on the back.

"Hey, I'm only seven years older than Bryce."

"It's a shame the dock is destroyed. No other option than to wade out to the boat," said Kyle.

"Nonsense," said Peter. "I'll carry anyone who doesn't want to get wet. Hannah, Noah, you two want to go first?"

"Yes!" they both said in unison.

Peter leaned down and spread his arms wide. "Come, jump up on Uncle Peter then."

"Uncle? Are you and my dad related?" asked Noah.

Peter picked them both up and held them above the water level. "I'd say we're family now. What do you think, Bryce?"

"Absolutely, my brother. Welcome to the family."

Peter turned and carried the kids to the boat, then made similar trips with the luggage. Rebecca and Emily also got carried to the boat, while Julio carried Elisa on his shoulders. Sal and Jackie slowly made their own way to the boat.

Captain Kyle followed and climbed onto the boat, starting the engines and letting them idle. He looked back on shore to see Val and Bryce still on the beach.

"Ready to get off this island?" asked Bryce.

"To be honest, I'm not sure. I haven't felt this alive in years. Maybe we need to move somewhere tropical." She paused, looking out at the water. "Or at least warmer than Indiana. I can start a watersports business catering to tourists."

"I was just elected coroner, though. It's a four-year term. Maybe we just need to vacation more?"

"How are we going to do that with your schedule in the ER?"

"I'm going to need some downtime to heal my leg and arm, so I'll be home for a few weeks." He put his hand in his pocket and pulled out the card containing the crypto wallet keys.

"Once we get to Nassau, I'm going to check out these accounts. We may have $100 million to play with. That would start a pretty awesome watersports company."

Val wrapped her arms around Bryce from behind. "Life has not been boring with you, mister. I'm lucky to have married you."

Bryce leaned back against her and closed his eyes, feeling her arms on his chest. "Aren't we both?"

Epilogue

"Can I refill your drinks?" asked the well-dressed server standing by the edge of the pool.

Tom looked down the line of empty glasses and replied for the group. "Yes, thank you. And we'll take a third round in about fifteen minutes."

"Bolus!" yelled Elisa from a raft as she floated next to Julio.

"And titrate," replied Peter, holding up the remnants of his drink in a toast.

"Where are the Chapmans? I haven't seen them since we arrived," said Jackie.

Just then, Hannah and Noah ran toward the pool and jumped into the shallow end. Val followed quickly, making sure Hannah was shallow enough to touch.

Bryce stopped the server as he was walking back to the bar and had a quick conversation before continuing to the pool. He took a seat in a shaded lounge chair and looked at his friends in the pool.

"Sorry, I had to handle some coroner's business. Turns out people still die even when I'm out of town. Do you guys remember the Hearst girl who struck and killed the police officer? You're going to be hearing that name a lot more in the next few weeks, I think." He looked around the majestic grounds of the resort. "But anyway, what do you guys think of the new resort?"

"Much less gunfire here, and the weather is pretty nice. So I'm going to say it's a step up from the last place," said Elisa.

Tom looked at his friend lounging on the chair. Bryce's arm and leg had fresh bandages that were applied at the hospital. They had followed the police to the hospital to give the doctors a report on what happened to Emily and what she needed done. They had offered Elisa a job, but she politely declined it.

Tom was standing next to Rebecca, who was lying on a floating mat. He looked at Bryce reclining in the shade. "Relaxation looks good on you, Bryce. You deserve it. No more stress for a while, okay? Doctor's orders."

"I appreciate that, but I still need to call Tony's dad and let him know what happened."

The waiter returned with two bottles of champagne and a tray full of glasses, along with an ice cold can of Diet Coke. He handed the first bottle to Bryce, who untwisted the wire cage and shot the cork up into the umbrella above his head.

"Hey, no more gunfire sounds for a while!" said Jackie, eliciting a laugh from Sal.

"Sorry, just one more." He opened the second bottle and handed them to the server, who filled the glasses and handed them out.

"What are we toasting?"

"To Tony and his crypto trading skills. I got into the accounts, and he turned a hundred million into a hundred and six million. That is worth celebrating," said Bryce, lifting his Diet Coke in the air.

"I'd rather toast something else, but if you're buying, I'll drink to whatever you want," said Peter. The group clinked glasses and downed their bubbly refreshment.

"I'll be right back. I want to get the call to Tony's dad out of the way. I need to tell him about the crypto and about Tony. Enjoy the second bottle on me," said Bryce. He stood up and walked to an empty corner of the pool deck, and pulled out his phone. He found the number for Tony's father and the call connected after two rings.

"Hello Bryce, this is Niles Profitt. What can I do for you?"

I'm still on his contact list, I see.

"Hi sir, I have some news I wanted to share with you. Some good, and some tragic. Which would you like to hear first?"

"Why don't you start with the good news?"

"Okay, I was able to recover the crypto account Tony was managing for you."

"The hundred million? Wow, nice work. How did you do that? And how can I get access to the funds?"

"I suggest you send a representative to accept the codes in person rather than sending them electronically. And it's not a hundred million, it has grown to nearly one hundred and six million dollars." Bryce's stomach turned over as he spoke the lie out loud. He had rehearsed this conversation dozens of times in his mind, but saying it out loud and for real was different. *I don't think twenty million is unfair compensation considering what my family has been through. Would you rather go through a very public civil lawsuit or just be happy with a five percent return on your investment?*

"That is good news. How did you happen to recover the accounts?"

Bryce pumped his fist into the air and raised his can toward Val. She smiled back and raised her champagne before downing it in one gulp. She then pulled her kids in for a big hug and spun them around in the water, eliciting happy screams from both. Bryce smiled at them and then turned around, allowing the smile to fade from his face.

"That is unfortunately where the tragic news comes in, sir. Are you sitting down?"

THE END

Mailing List Signup

I hope you enjoyed reading Vengeance! Please take a moment to sign up for my mailing list to stay up-to-date on my new releases. As a free gift, you will receive a copy of *The Muddled Mind: An Eclectic Collection of Short Stories*. Seventeen individual short stories I have written across several genres. I hope you see you on the list!

About The Author

Dr. Brian Hartman is a practicing Emergency Medicine Physician in Indianapolis, Indiana. He is married to his wife Cheryl, a dentist with whom he has two boys, Evan and Andrew. They enjoy traveling to tropical locations, including several of the settings of Redemption. Brian began the formal pursuit of writing as a creative escape from the stress of the COVID-19 pandemic.

Redemption is the first novel in his medical thriller series starring Dr. Bryce Chapman. Brian has written dozens of short stories and has several independent novels in production. He transfers his experience as a practicing physician to the characters and events of the books, letting the reader see inside the mind and emotions of the team caring for patients. The lives of doctors and nurses do not stop when they leave the hospital and his books explore the events and back stories that make our lives interesting.

Brian enjoys interacting with his readers via email and social media. Find him at his author website https://www.brianhartman.me/, email brianhartmanme@gmail.com, and Facebook https://facebook.com/brianhartmanme.

Also By Brian Hartman

Bryce Chapman Medical Thriller Series:

Redemption (Book One)
Deception (Book Two)
Vengeance (Book Three)
Hanging By A String (Book Four, pre-order)

Psychological Thrillers:

Lake Sinclair
It Happened In The Loft

Short Story Anthology:

The Muddled Mind

Printed in Great Britain
by Amazon

33191186R00175